GOOSE TRUMAN - THE HORSEMAN

THE HORSEMAN

DON A CAREY

THE HORSEMEN BOOK 1

GOOSE TRUMAN

DON A. CAREY

PROVIDENCE

GOOSE FELT the hot breath of air pass his right cheek before he heard the crack of the rifle.

"Shit."

This should have been nothing more than a simple scouting mission. Goose eased back into the trees where he had staked his horses. The cedar grove wouldn't provide any ballistic protection but hid him from view.

"Jake, Jessie. With me." He spoke low and gutturally, with a slight hand gesture to the two Tennessee Mountain curs. Jake was a larger brindle, good-natured dog. Jessie was a smaller fawn-colored female with the heart of a warrior and an intense devotion to Goose. She had once gotten her head swollen to the size of a basketball killing a hive of bees that had stung Goose. Not only did she kill the bees, but she also left them on the porch to show what she'd done.

With the dogs at his heel, Goose moved deeper into the woods to his horses, moving them a mile further into a hidden valley. It was a good spot covered by a thicket of cedar trees and sticker bushes blocking entrance to the clearing, and the roll of land would shield them from an errant shot. After checking to be sure he wasn't followed, Goose took the extra precaution of hobbling the horses, knowing he may be away most of the night scouting the double-wide where the shots came from. He hoped that by not returning fire and moving away quickly, he would allay suspicion, making the shooter suspect he'd merely seen a curious traveler who'd gotten the message and moved on.

The man at the double-wide needed time to relax and assume Goose had left. Back at his camp, as he unloaded the supply horse and unsaddled his walking horse Rocky, Goose pondered what he'd gotten himself into. That was the problem with being sober. A man would think too much. He didn't care about these people and would rather be at home with a drink. Those thoughts didn't last more than a second or two, however. The governor had asked, he had accepted, and that was it. His word was his bond. That was the end of it. Almost.

Since he'd come back from Lexington, he couldn't shake a burning hatred for people who preyed on others. That hate, and a reckless disregard for his own safety, made him a superb hunter for these types of men.

Goose had passed through different phases of grief over the last couple of years. Rage at what the world had become; despair over losing his wife and daughter; survivor's guilt over not being there to help them, or that it was them and not him.

After going to Lexington, finding out what happened, and visiting their graves, something broke inside of Goose. It ruined him inside, made him stay drunk, his body on autopilot with no reason for being. After taking revenge on the gang responsible for their deaths, Goose had been meandering north toward home when he encountered another fight. That was where he met the governor. This world was full of rot, and sending a few of those sons of bitches to Hell was the only thing that gave him a moment's respite from the grief. That and getting drunk.

Once the horses were hobbled and the camp hidden in a briar and cedar tree thicket most bad men wouldn't make the effort to search, Goose waited. Patience was a skill most men didn't have. Throughout history, the best fighters and hunters had it down pat. For many men, the waiting and sitting idle wore on the nerves. Goose had nothing else to do in the world but kill. After his rage had simmered down into a constant thrum of hate, he had time. It made the kill all the easier. If the wait unnerved a thief or murderer, then all the better. Sometimes, in similar circumstances, he would take a nap or read a book. Before the world had gone to hell, he'd enjoyed a good post-apocalyptic novel or historical fiction. Those weren't as fun anymore since he'd experienced it all firsthand. Now they were like some distorted version of the news that got most of the details wrong. Lately, he'd gone back to his roots enjoying westerns. His collection of Louis L'Amour, Elmer Kelton, and William Johnstone books were dog-eared and worn out.

With the crude fishing wire alarms set, keen ears of the horses, and thirty yards of cedars and thicket between him and the rest of the woods, Goose switched on his green light under a covered pine tree to read.

Sometime after two in the morning, enough time had passed and his bladder needed relief. Goose checked his gear and donned the turkey-hunting mask. He'd already changed out of his cowboy boots to jungle boots when he first got there. He had a pullover ghillie poncho in his pack but didn't plan to use it. It caught on the sticker bushes and barbwire fence so easily it could be more trouble than it was worth.

Goose chose a silenced CZ Scorpion AR 9 as his primary weapon and as always had his competition model Springfield XDM .45 on his hip. He also carried a V-42 Stiletto fighting knife that had belonged to his grandfather, who had been a member of the famed "Devil's Brigade."

He approached the double-wide trailer in what could only be described as a sprawling trailer park. The lots were as large as a normal home subdivision, not cramped up close like a normal trailer park. Goose paused. His biggest concern was for dogs. An alert dog might ruin this scouting mission. That was the reason he'd left Jake and Jessie behind at the camp. As his father used to claim, *"There is nothing better than a well-trained dog and nothing worse than one that isn't."*

He was in luck. The longer this new reality wore on, the scarcer dogs became for reasons he didn't like contemplating. Owning a dog had become a new sign of luxury and prosperity.

Goose scouted the trailer then settled in to wait. As the sun rose and activity picked up, he began to think he had the wrong place. Despite the slovenly appearance, this appeared to be the home of a family, although the relationships were hard to determine. He saw a woman and child sleeping in a bedroom at one end of the trailer and a man in a smaller bedroom at the other end. Perhaps he was a brother or uncle. The times had driven families back together for mutual protection and support.

Before the sun rose, Goose had found one clue that alarmed him. They had a third room filled with supplies. Alone, that might not have been a major concern. Many people stockpiled supplies when possible. However, when the governor urged him to check into this case, the only tip they'd had was about a gang raiding outlying homes and travelers of supplies and personal items. Most of the raids happened near I-71 between Louisville and Cincinnati. The tipster also said some of the stolen items could be purchased from the man who lived here.

Deciding he had enough information for now, he worked his way back to camp for a few hours' rest and to think this through. Clearly, if this man was a part of the attacks on the convoys, others had to be involved. Nothing about the scraggly man in skinny jeans screamed "leader."

Kelly awoke to a throbbing headache. She moved slowly, pulling her arm from under her son Brian, trying not to cause the bed springs to creak and wake him. The stress of not knowing, feeling out of control, and constantly bickering with Steve exhausted her, making her head pound.

His new friends had spent several hours here yesterday, unloading goods for Steve to sell. She had no idea why they didn't just sell it themselves. There weren't lawmen to chase them down these days. They could sell the stolen goods right in the open if they chose. She assumed they had several people around the country like Steve selling for them. They were a disreputable lot, riding in on Harleys following a truck, and they were accustomed to taking what they wanted.

Kelly almost felt sorry for Steve. He walked around like a banty rooster, thinking he was a member of a dangerous gang. He even acted tough and lorded it over people who came to buy the ill-gotten goods. Little did he know the gang made fun of him and pawed at her when his back was turned. In deference to their marriage and for both their safety, she didn't tell him of their advances. He hadn't realized yet what she'd accepted for a long time. Their marriage was all but over; she just had no place to go.

They had drifted apart years ago. The final straw had been when she discovered that his outwardly boastful and flirtatious ways were not just talk as he insisted, but that he'd been cheating. Looking back, she still couldn't say why she didn't leave the moment she discovered his indiscretions. Perhaps she tried to make it work considering she came from a broken family. She'd always wondered if her parents tried hard enough. Another part of her hoped she could make it last long enough to get Brian through school. Another factor was the state of the nation a couple years ago. With all the riots, shootings, food shortages, and power outages, it had been a terrible time for a single woman and a young boy to be alone. Kelly didn't like to think she needed any man and despised herself for the feeling of weakness it brought on. Yet there it was, all stirred together, adding up to nowhere to go. Her mother had been dead since she was young. Her father, who'd been older when she was born, died a few years before the country started spiraling down.

Thoughts of her father brought tears to her eyes. He'd been the kind of strong, ethical man she'd hoped to marry someday. She thought she had when she and Steve married. Perhaps her father had known, since he and Steve never clicked. Even though her father had always been very polite to him, Steve had been distant and aloof in return.

Steve was sleeping off the drugs and alcohol and wouldn't wake until after noon. That gave her the morning alone to prepare breakfast for Brian and see if Steve hit anything when he shot into the woods last night. He'd been high and drunk and claimed someone was sneaking up to steal their loot.

As Kelly scouted the copse of woods near their trailer, she couldn't shake the feeling she was being watched. She found some bullet strikes on the trees, but that meant nothing. Steve's new friends always shot at things when they got drunk. Kelly shook her head, turning back to the trailer. Brian wasn't awake yet, so she checked her "go bags" for the thousandth time. She had clothes, snacks, and a tarp in each bag, one to sleep on and one to sleep under. She also had a large, wicked knife that had once been her father's. As go bags went, it was pretty poor. That didn't matter. She had no place to go.

Any guilt she had of leaving Steve was gone. He had begun to hit her when he drank, and it was only a matter of time before one of his new friends took things too far. She held no illusions that Steve could or would even try to stop them.

Sometimes the gang brought around women they'd captured

in their raids. They were terrified, and their eyes had the hollow look of someone who'd died inside, but their bodies hadn't gotten the message yet. While Steve thought he'd been sly, Kelly thought Steve had taken advantage of more than one of those poor wretches. It was just one more way he kept trying to act tough so they would take him on a raid with them.

Goose had seen the pretty lady the night before moving around the trailer, cleaning up and doing chores. She intrigued him. She had blond hair with subtle red tints that showed when the light hit it right. Even from a distance, it was noticeable on her legs, arms, and chest near her neck that she had many tattoos. Part of Goose's old-fashioned upbringing made him think briefly that all that tattoos might mean she was a wild girl or with the gang working this area.

It only took a few seconds to discard that thought. She had her own tidy room where she slept with her son on the opposite end of the trailer. The boy was well dressed, had clean clothes, and his hair had been cut. In the morning, she moved with an alertness that showed no signs of a fog from drugs or alcohol use the night before. There was more to this woman's story.

It didn't matter, though. He had a single mission here, which was to watch the man selling stolen food and goods and learn. With patience and luck, the gang would come back, and he would track them to their lair.

When the tattooed woman went back in the trailer and things settled into a routine, Goose fell back to his camp further in the woods. The horses needed food and water, and Goose needed some shuteye.

· · ·

Later in the afternoon, Goose worked his way to a place where he could observe the trailer. This guy wasn't a major player. It didn't even look like he was in the gang. However, it was the only tip the governor had when he called Goose a few days ago.

Goose half dozed and half slept for a few hours, contemplating how he and the country had gotten to this point. Why was he hunting a scraggly man in a double-wide trailer? The country had settled in a new cadence in life. There was only a nominal amount of law inside the city centers. Much like the Old West, most small towns had a sheriff or marshal and a few deputies that kept order for the stores in town and a few blocks around. The larger cities had done much the same for their commerce districts, leaving the suburbs and downtown areas to their own devices. Sometimes that meant lawlessness and looting. Occasionally, a larger town split into a few smaller ones, hiring a marshal and deputies to provide security at the access points. More often than not, the city centers had fallen into a level of anarchy and gang rule that was too horrendous to contemplate. Sometimes it spilled out into the suburbs and country. Most people in those areas preferred not to think much on facing those hordes when they left the city center. Others hoped the herd would be much thinner by the time they did.

Like the Old West, when a crime was perpetrated within or near the city limits, it had once again become common practice to mount a posse and chase down the bad guys for as far as the posse dared, depending on the crime.

That left the expressways, roads, and large Amazon and Wal-Mart distribution centers to be protected by the state. The few state police and National Guardsmen at the governor's disposal simply didn't have the skills and manpower to deal with this level of violence and territory. Millions of people were hungry, angry, out of work, and becoming accustomed to violence.

Years of riots, protests, and damage had created a generation of people well versed in destruction but not so good at building and maintaining. By the time they realized they'd been manipulated into hating each other through the mass media and social platform moguls, it was too late. The America that had once been was no more.

That wasn't the end of it, though. The puppet masters who'd created this mess in an effort to have king-like power had miscalculated. They were a part of the secret cabals ascribing to an old United Nations Agenda 21 philosophy. In their arrogance, they never perceived it might get out of their control and go this far. Or perhaps they did, and this was what they wanted. It was possible they were all ensconced in some private enclave of mansions with power and all the comfort of home stockpiled for generations, while continuing to pull the strings of government and corporations.

None of that mattered to the average person anymore. As far as Goose could determine, the people were of little concern to those secret leaders. The destruction had gone further than intended, and now they were out of touch and of little help. The country was fragmented and knocked back to the Old West days.

Goose didn't seek out news or listen to gossip. Everything he cared about lay buried in Lexington. He'd left his civility and humanity back there as well. He was too strong a man to consider suicide. For being too late to save his girls, his remaining years would be a penance of tracking and hunting the breed of killers and rapists who threatened to take over this new world. He would persevere in this task, reveling in his burning hatred for the spoilers and killers until a lucky shot sent him to his reward to be reunited with Laura and Elizabeth.

Crossing paths with and saving the governor while he was out of his mind had given him a purpose in that rage. Not much of one, but it was all he had.

The governor was a good man, if a little rough with things he said at times. Goose had voted for him during his first term. The man had done a lot of good and had been reversing the tide of financial setbacks and corruption in the state. In the end, it wasn't enough. The corruption ran too deep, and the puppet masters were too strong. In a corrupt election, they'd been able to dispose of the governor and seat one of the most crooked leaders in the country. The new leader fit in well with a corruption taking over the country, rigging contracts, stripping citizens of their constitutional rights, and employing electronic tracking methods to combine with the massive databases at the government's disposal. Then he attacked churches and social gatherings.

Riots, arson, and murder had become commonplace in this new America and could not be controlled. Companies shut down, and the economy began to fail. The resulting national catastrophe made the Great Depression seem like child's play. Inflation crept across the nation, much worse than what Greece or Venezuela had experienced. A loaf of bread topped out at a hundred dollars before it became impossible to buy. Fuel costs soared to nearly a thousand dollars a gallon before settling back to around five hundred.

Then the second wave of the pandemic hit. The first wave had been exposed for what it was, a ploy by the secret cabal to regain control of a world that was becoming increasingly educated and independent. All they'd had to do was slightly enhance a particularly virulent version of the flu that was mostly non-lethal. The people they controlled, who in turn controlled the information flow, had done the rest. The virus itself killed a fraction of a single percent of people who contracted it. That was enough for the compliant news and social media outlets to tout the horrors of the disease. Obedient governments and healthcare organizations labeled every death they possible could a result of the virus. The result was terror on a worldwide level.

Somewhere, the puppet masters were laughing and toasting

each other. The riots, class war, and plagues they had engineered had spread fear, terror, and distrust. Fearful people were easier to control. As the Roman emperor Caligula said, *"I don't care if they respect me, so long as they fear me."* In return, the people offered up virtually all their freedoms and rights, begging the government to save them. They would give up their churches, their guns, their right to assemble, anything for just a little hope of being saved from the economic chaos and pandemic.

In the final act, a stroke of plot genius that would have done Shakespeare proud, their social engineering plan turned citizen against citizen. It was like Rome burning while Nero fiddled. It was not uncommon to see grandmothers and homemakers attack each other in a store for buying too much or not wearing a mask; college kids roamed in bands looking for people standing in groups of two or three to attack; and vigilante groups firebombed churches by the dozens for congregating and teaching dissension.

Not long before the second wave of the pandemic hit, people around the world began to awaken from the fear-induced dementia they'd been under for years. Much like a recovering drug addict, many were ashamed of the life they'd led and the fear that controlled them. It was too late to save the world, but they attempted to salvage what they could. The old rough-talking governor was sought out and persuaded to run for office again, winning in a landslide.

It was a hollow victory.

The federal government was virtually nonexistent by that time. The country was broke, and with no funds and no ability to field much in the way of armed forces or to enforce laws, people simply stopped going to work at the federal level.

State governments had a little more power but were short on resources. They were able to maintain a skeleton force of leadership, police, and National Guardsmen by bartering a place to live and food to eat for those personnel. The most they were able to do at that point was protect a small perimeter around the capital, guard major distribution points and trading posts, and provide security for convoys moving between major cities. All that remained to provide any support for the common man was at the local level with small town sheriffs providing an Old West style of police and courts within their town limits.

Governor Beady rolled up his sleeves and did the best he could to protect the distribution centers and keep the roads open and free of bandits. He was winning with the distribution centers but losing with the roads. They were pockmarked, full of weeds and crumbling bridges. They more resembled paths connecting one small town to another than the once impressive highway and interstate system. Whenever leaving the protection of one town for another, travelers banded together for the safety of a convoy. When possible, the governor tried to send troops with those convoys.

However, much like the Old West, sometimes the safety of numbers wasn't enough. Like the Apache raiding parties of the 1800s, settlers who lived outside the confines of a town, convoys, and occasionally even government troops could fall prey to a well-planned attack. The state forces were stretched so thin they could only escort the occasional convoy along the old expressways. They didn't have the manpower to chase down the various criminals.

That was where Goose came in.

When Goose was tracking down some thugs from Lexington, the trail led him to an attack on a convoy near Frankfort, Kentucky. Most of the defenders were down and bleeding out. The small group fighting a losing battle appeared well dressed and included women and children. A rage overtook Goose. He waded in, guns blazing, taking the goons from behind, breaking their attack. When the last of the attackers fled and Goose met the people he'd saved, he was surprised to find the governor, his wife, and their adopted children among them. Only two of the original guards sent to escort the governor and his family survived the ambush. Their attackers must have known who their prey was and either wanted revenge for some perceived slight or planned to get a big payday in ransom.

During the brief introductions, Goose kept looking around nervously. The last few weeks had taught him a great deal about human nature and the need to be always on high alert. "Sir, we need to get moving. I only surprised them. They'll be back."

"What about my men?" Governor Beady indicated the dead state police officers and Guardsmen near them.

"We must send someone back for them. Right now, the priority is getting you to safety."

The trip to the governor's mansion and protected area was not without incident. Twice more they were attacked. It didn't appear to be the same group. These attacks were less determined, but the last one forced them to take refuge in an old stone building and miss their opportunity to make it home before nightfall.

The attackers withdrew, and the defenders set a watch schedule. They had enough guns and weapons to stay safe. In the morning they made the quick trip to the protected zone. When all was settled, Goose broke out a bottle of top-shelf Kentucky bourbon he'd scavenged and shared it with the governor. Whether it was the bourbon or kindred spirits, they talked late into the night, becoming friends, and building a mutual respect.

Goose woke to Jessie licking his face. She had a sense about things and a closer bond to him than Jake. He also noted the cicadas buzzing in the background warning of a hot day. The horses stomped their hooves in the hidden grove of trees, not liking the heat and flies. He'd fallen deeper asleep than he'd planned, drooling from the corner of his mouth. The memories and dreams were still clear in his mind and unwelcome. Getting drunk or getting back to the mission would cure all that. He chose the mission, and after breaking out some food for the dogs and instructing them to stay in camp, he crept closer to a point where he could observe the trailer from a distance. If he didn't learn more soon, he would either need to find a camp further away from the trailer or go home and come back in a few days.

Goose had time. Nothing but time.

INTRODUCTIONS

SCOUTING the trailer had been a boring procession of watching people desperate for whatever they could get coming and going, bartering for the stolen supplies. Goose debated following one of the buyers away from the trailer to question him but decided the information he'd gain wasn't worth the exposure.

The notable moment of the day came when a man showed up in a working truck and backed up for supplies. It was an old, rusted, step side truck. In other times, someone might have restored it to a classic antique. Although a working vehicle wasn't so odd in today's world, the fuel to run it marked a person as rich. The man in the trailer loaded enough supplies to fill half the truck bed. That was another sign of the man's wealth. That piqued Goose's interest. What did the man have to trade that was worth fuel and a truckload of supplies?

He didn't have long to wait. The owner of the truck opened the passenger door, reaching in to roughly pull out a teenage girl, gagged and wrists bound, by her hair. Six months ago, Goose would have charged in guns blazing, not caring whether he lived or died as long as the bastard paid. Now, he was only slightly

more in control of himself. He'd become world weary. This sort of
thing happened so frequently his efforts to intervene were drops
in a bucket. He would save her, and exact retribution, but he
would take his time and get them all.

He resolved to follow the truck when it left to find out where
the man lived and if he had other women in captivity there. If the
man lived far, it would be hard to keep up on horseback, especially without being seen. Failing that, he needed a prisoner to
talk so he could deal with this new criminal as soon as possible.

No sooner had the girl been unloaded than two men on
Harleys rode up, foiling his plan. This place was getting busy. The
poor, dingy customers had stayed around when the truck drove
up. However, at the sight of the hogs, they fled.

One of the Harley riders began haranguing the skinny man
from the trailer and poking his chest. Goose noticed that when the
hogs rolled up, the tattooed lady took her son out the back of the
trailer to the woods. The other Harley rider grabbed the bound
woman by the hair, dragging her into the trailer.

That gave Goose pause. He wasn't here to save lives or get
involved, yet the longer he sat, the more he fumed. What was
going on wasn't right. Some of his old ethics began to surface, and
he quickly tamped them down. Whatever it was had been going
on for a while. The tattooed lady had known to get out immediately and make herself scarce. It was obvious the man in the
trailer was no more than a peon in their crime organization, with
little power and only useful for his ability to sell their ill-gotten
goods. It surprised Goose they trusted him to trade in human
flesh. A gang like that would use the pretty ones for sex, manual
labor, and other more nefarious purposes, which had come back
to prominence in this new version of America.

Goose leaned back against a tree in the scrub. He was tired
and feeling old. He ran a hand through four days' of scrubble on
his face. Or was it five? His hair was too long and a little greasy.

He probably stank but had stopped noticing. Jake and Jessie hadn't said a word. As he waited until things calmed some at the trailer and they let their guard down, his mind drifted to his former life interspersed with thoughts of men he'd killed. When a sharp image of his wife and daughter entered his mind, he jolted back to alertness. Goose reached for his pack and pulled out a flask. He didn't normally drink on a mission, but a little nip to chase the demons wouldn't hurt.

Then he heard the screams. A part of his mind thought the screams came from his daughter. While his head knew that wasn't true, emotionally, he couldn't stop himself. He sprang from his hiding place, face full of menace. He strode forward with purposeful strides that made haste without running, uncaring if he messed up the governor's mission. The people of his Le Cheval community would have to do without the tanker of fuel for his services. They didn't like him anyway.

He checked the Springfield competition .45, snug in the drop leg holster, the wicked-looking V-42 Elite Special Forces knife that had sat in a display box for so many years after his grandfather died. He left the silenced CZ Scorpion AR 9 at camp, deciding if he needed to fight today there would be no need for stealth and he wanted firepower. He moved in with the Winchester SX-AR held at the battle-ready position, thirty rounds in the magazine and more in his pack. It was a rare gun, and he was deadly with it at long range or short. The oversized .308 rounds left no doubt when they hit a man.

Onlookers would have seen him shake his head like a bear annoyed at flies as he approached the trailer. In reality, he kept seeing visions of his daughter. He desperately needed to clear the visions to save her. Or save the other girl. Sometimes he wasn't sure what was real or not.

When he got close and hadn't been spotted, he slowed, creeping forward in a half crouch, heel to toe, the Winchester held at low ready. The girl was screaming in one end of the trailer. In the middle, the owner and the other Harley rider were in what sounded like a one-sided fight. The front door was ajar. Goose knew better than to stand in front of a door when approaching a home, despite what all the actors used to do on the cop shows. Although the flimsy walls wouldn't provide any ballistic protection if a round came that way, it was safer to stand away from the door.

Moving quietly to his right on the old wooden porch in front of the trailer, Goose got a look inside. Through the crack in the door, he saw the big Harley dude standing over the weaselly trailer owner with a golf club, wailing away at his head and shoulders. Having seen a lot of blood and violence, Goose didn't flinch. The trailer owner had a thin beard and skinny jeans, as if trying to hold on to hipster days that were far behind him. Goose considered going in quiet with the fighting knife. He eased the door open a little more to get a view down the hallway. He couldn't get an angle to see much, but the grunting sounds told him where the other Harley guy was and exactly what he was doing.

Fuck it. This gig was blown and the Swiss cheese that was his mind kept seeing Lizzy back there with the Harley thug. His wits weren't totally gone; a part of his mind knew it wasn't his daughter back there, but it took a second to shake his head and clear his mind. This never happened when he was shooting or drinking. When he drank, he slipped completely into the past. When fighting, he was totally in the present, and it was time to fight. These bastards needed killing, problem solved.

Goose kicked in the flimsy door, put the SX-AR to his shoulder, and squeezed off a round, ready to fire another one for a double-tap. It wasn't necessary. The man's head had exploded all over his victim, raining blood and brains.

The loud percussion of the .308 in an enclosed space hadn't dissipated yet when the second man yelled, "What the fuck!"

charging like a wounded bull down the short hall of the trailer in nothing but a dingy t-shirt and leather vest, firing indiscriminately.

Goose didn't flinch, didn't care, and simply held the rifle to his shoulder, crosshairs of the sight trained on the corner of the wall where the man would appear any second. When he did, Goose squeezed off a round just a little off center. The man went down, a spray of blood pulsing from his chest. Goose was in no hurry. He knelt beside the man and grunted in his raspy voice, "How many in your gang?"

"Fuck you, man!"

Goose let out a sigh. This would not go well. "Jesus, dude, just answer my questions. Where is your camp?"

The man tried to spit on Goose. There wasn't enough force in him to do more than make it dribble down his chin. Goose reached for the drop sheath on his left leg made to hang below a winter coat and pulled the Special Forces knife that had spent so many years in retirement. Goose was left-handed but right eye dominant. That made him more comfortable shooting a handgun right-handed and welding a knife left-handed. He reversed the grip, deciding to use the pointed skull crusher on the end of the pommel. Without emotion or warning, Goose struck, crushing in the rapist's skull with the power of a man used to hard work on the farm and an unspent fury that would take a psychiatrist years to sort out.

He rocked back on his heels against the wall of the trailer and ran his hand down his face, exhaling deliberately. He moved slowly and showed no emotion during a fight. No one understood how confused he was on the inside, like an old guitar, some strings stretched too tight, and others broken or loose. Looking to his right, he saw the tattooed lady trying to peek into the trailer from behind a tree. Perhaps he could salvage something good in all this.

He stood and walked to the unsteady deck. "Come on in. I'm not going to hurt you." She didn't answer, darting deeper into the trees before looking back. "Wait," he called. "I promise I won't hurt you. I'm leaving soon anyways. I know this is your home. Your son can stay back if you're worried. We need to talk, though."

Stepping out from the tree, she asked, "How do you know I have a son?"

"Lady, I don't have time to play games. I've been watching your home. You shouldn't go in there. It's a mess."

The tattooed lady put her hand to her mouth, "Oh my god, Steve! What did you do?" She rushed past Goose into the trailer.

Her anguished wail cut deep into his soul. Leaning on the doorjamb to allow the woman some time with her husband, Goose was having one of those Swiss cheese moments again.

The tattooed lady's anguish raw as she shoved the dead biker off her husband, screaming, "Not this way!"

Goose was watching but didn't see her. He saw his wife Laura and didn't try shaking away the image this time. He knew it wasn't real; he just wanted to look at her a little longer.

Kelly was frantic. Steve's eyes were blinking rapidly, his mouth moving like a fish out of water, and blood was everywhere. Something grayish was mixed in the blood… it had to be Steve's brain. Torment and guilt mixed within her. She had filed for divorce before things started going bad, and she'd even gotten a place of her own far enough out of town to avoid the near constant riots and civil unrest. Then, amid the riots, the economy began to fail. Looking back, Kelly supposed it was inevitable. One bailout after another, followed by increased taxes and regulations to pay for it, and a generation of workers without the work ethics of their forebears had brought on the Second Great Depression. Someone else may well have explained the economics behind it all better. It didn't matter. When the price of gas rose to hundreds of dollars per gallon and a loaf of bread about the same, families and friends began moving back in together to pool resources.

Kelly's father had been older when she'd been born. Her mother died young from cancer. Her father raised her as a tomboy, hunting, shooting, and working on cars. He'd been a Marine and seen combat. Somehow, she'd fallen for Steve because he was a bad boy, into tattoos, alternative music, and dark clothes. Although Steve and her father hadn't got along well, her dad tried to be civil out of love for his daughter.

Originally, they'd found a shared passion, restoring old cars. However, that didn't last. Steve wouldn't hold a job and sometimes joined the protesters, which would have made her father roll over in his grave. Something evolved in Kelly, and while Steve was protesting and avoiding work, she regressed to her roots and the values her father had taught her. She began to see Steve for what he was.

That was before the fall, back when she had choices. People never realized how precious freedom to choose their destiny was until it was gone. She and Steve had been forced back together in a ragged motor home in an even more disreputable motorhome park in the country. She tried to make it work for the sake of their son. She couldn't. The chasm was too deep, the leap too far. She longed to be away from him and couldn't find a way. Now he lay there dying, the fish movements his mouth was making growing slower by the second. His eyes were now making long, slow blinks. She didn't know which one would be his last. She grabbed his shirt and wailed, "Not this way!"

Gradually she became aware of a stranger in the door, afraid he might kill, rape, or sell her and her son into slavery. She was also sure he'd listened to her words over Steve. She was too ashamed to admit what they meant. She didn't love Steve anymore. She'd wanted to be free of him for so long. Yet, *not this way.*

"Ma'am, I'm sorry to interrupt, but do you know these hombres?" the rough man asked, using his gun to point to the two dead Harley riders.

Kelly could do nothing but stare. It was all so surreal. Kneeling beside her husband who'd just been beaten to death, a part of her mind sensed the blood soaking into the knees of her blue jeans. When the killer asked if she knew his victims, all she could do was numbly shake her head.

"Damn, so there's no way to know if they'll be missed soon."

"They'll send someone to search for them tonight or tomorrow at the latest," Kelly responded. Her voice sounded like a stranger speaking. "By the way, it's Kelly."

"Pardon?"

"You said ma'am. My name is Kelly."

"Yes, ma'am. But I thought you didn't know them?"

"I was confused for a moment." Kelly stood, wiping her hands on her jeans to smear away some of the dust and blood. They were stained from the knees down with Steve's blood. "Anyway, I don't know them personally, just the gang they're a part of."

"What happens if they come back and find their men and your husband dead?"

"I suppose they'll force me to tell them what happened, then make me work for them."

"Work for them how?"

"I don't want to think about that. I don't intend to be here when they come."

"Where will you go?"

"I have no idea, but I can't be here. There isn't much here for me anyway."

"It looks like your husband was well stocked."

"Those weren't his things. Just stuff the gang wanted him to sell for a little kickback and food. As soon as they learn he's dead, they'll want their supplies back. Come hell or high water."

"Where are they based?"

"I don't know. They only took Steve there a few times. He never took me, said it wouldn't be safe. I suppose I should appreciate that. We've grown so far apart over the last few years sometimes I thought he'd just as soon sell me as any of the goods in that room. Letting that gang get their hands on me was just too much for even him, though."

Goose didn't know what to say. He let out a long breath. The tattooed lady—Kelly, he now knew—seemed in a daze, out of words and ideas. He touched her on the elbow to steer her to the door. "You should go get your son. What will your neighbors do about the gunshots?"

"Ha!" She let out a sharp laugh that changed her face and revealed a very pretty lady. "Nothing. This is the end of the road. The place people go to live when they are out of options and out of ideas. People come here to drink, do drugs, party, and fight. There are no nice families to come investigate. They'll wait 'till things die down then come see what they can scavenge. They'd have long since robbed Steve blind if they didn't have the gang to worry about."

"What will you do now? I can't stay here, and the gang will be back."

"Brian and I will have to go, although I have no idea were. I don't have any family. That's why I'm here at the end of the road with Steve."

Goose saw tears in her eyes as he stepped off the rickety deck in front deck of the trailer. He pursed his lips and left to get his horses, careful to avoid the rotten step in the deck he'd seen Kelly avoid. The horses were only about a fifteen-minute walk from the trailer.

Cursing, he worked his way through the briar thicket. The spotted horse nickered at his approach. The air was what the old timers used to call *thick* and getting thicker. That usually meant rain, and probably a storm. In the meantime, the humidity was so thick he could cut it with a knife, making his clothes cling to him with sweat. He didn't want to spend the night in the trailer waiting for the gang. He needed to fall back and come up with another plan. That meant a wet ride home. The spotted gelding was already saddled with the girth loose in case he needed to leave in a hurry. It only took a moment to remove the hobbles and tighten the girth. A few minutes later, Goose had the packhorse loaded up. He changed out of the floppy hat and combat boots into riding boots and a cowboy hat before leading the horses out of the thicket. Jessie and Jake followed obediently, sensing when it was time to play and when it was work time.

Once out of the bushes, he tied the lead rope for the pack-horse to the back of his saddle, moved to the left side of the spotted horse, put a toe in the stirrup, bounced twice, and swung into the saddle. Rocky hadn't always stood this well for mounting. Goose began having those old and new memories mixing again. He had visions of Rocky dancing sideways as he mounted and Laura laughing from the back of her horse, Copper, now tied behind Rocky as a packhorse. No one had ridden that horse since Laura had.

He stood tall in the stirrups to balance his hands on the pommel. The trailer stood in front of him a short distance away. His home was in the other direction, and a storm was brewing. He had no reason to stay, and help them and he needed to put miles behind him.

"Brian, we need to hurry." Kelly helped him pack his backpack. He was young and gangly but getting taller. He favored her dad.

"Why can't we stay here?" he said through a splotchy red face that had only paused crying a moment ago. A few feet away, his father lay covered in a sheet. Brian was a smart boy. He was aware his father was a weak man with flaws. Even so, he was still his dad. Kelly was at her wits' end. If the gang came back before she left, she'd end up working for them or worse. It would take hours to bury Steve and a storm was coming. She couldn't just leave him lying there, though. It wasn't civilized.

Just then, the rickety deck swayed and creaked under the weight of a man. She shoved Brian behind a chair and frantically scrambled for a gun, cursing herself for not being ready. She'd been so shocked by the traders, the Harley gang men, a shootout in her home, and losing her husband she hadn't been thinking clearly. She was out of time. A large man filled the door, blocking out the light. Kelly looked up from her knees.

It was the man from earlier, yet somehow he looked different in cowboy boots and a cowboy hat. Even though he had a modern gun, holstered low on his leg, he looked more like an Old West gunfighter. What she hadn't noticed before was the gold star pinned to his chest on a brown leather vest he hadn't been wearing before.

"W-What do you want?" she stammered.

"You said you have nowhere to go. Is that true?"

"It is."

"Gather up your packs. We need to be leaving soon to beat the storm."

"What about my husband?"

"Ma'am, this may sound callous, but he's beyond caring now. Regardless how much he changed over the years, I have to believe he'd want you two to be safe."

"But... I don't know what to do." She wrung her hands, glancing over at Brian.

"We can burn the trailer. It's the closest to cremation we'll get.

Gather any mementos you want. We need to get going."

To her credit, Kelly gathered herself and finished packing. Goose took note that she spent little time on mementos. She gathered clothes, food, a tent, sleeping blankets, and a handgun. She was no stranger to guns the way she racked it, checked the magazine, and loaded spare ammo.

Goose peeked in the storage room. There was a lot more than he could carry, but he gathered a few things. He was readjusting the packs on the horse when the woman stepped out on deck with her son. "Do you have bikes or something?" he asked.

"We did. Steve traded them."

"Well, you'll have to walk. Let's get going. Wait out by my horses." Minutes later, Goose emerged from the trailer, smoke already billowing behind him. By the time he'd mounted up, escorting the woman and her son out of the odd country trailer park, the trailer was fully engulfed.

"Where are we headed?" The woman almost sounded relieved. Grief was apparent in her face, but she'd compartmentalized it and sounded hopeful.

"I know a community that sometimes takes in people who work hard and have skills. You got any of those?"

"Not much that's useful in this new world. A few years ago, when jobs were plentiful and the world normal, I was in corporate America."

"So was I," Goose said in a low, gravelly voice mostly to himself, his mind once again remembering the days of nine-to-five work in an office building, dinners out on the town, and petty arguments. Before the world went to hell. Before…

"But I work hard."

It took Goose a moment to remember what they'd been talking about. "That's more than most can say," he replied when it came to him.

"So, what do I call you?"

"My friends call me Goose."

The boy snickered. Goose looked down and raised an eyebrow. The pair were struggling to keep up with his horses. Goose kicked the horse into a walking gait. He saw the woman's brows knit as he left them behind. He didn't like small talk.

The air was humid, the late afternoon sky darker than normal at this hour due to the dark clouds rolling in from the southeast. Occasionally lightning lit up the clouds to the east, spitting raindrops peppered his face, but not heavy enough to drench him yet. Goose heard the woman behind him urging the young boy forward. He was sure she was giving him evil looks and almost smiled. He preferred being the bad guy; it was easier.

Sometime later, the rain picked up. Goose broke out a poncho and kept up the pace, resting the horses periodically so the two didn't lose sight of him. As he pulled the poncho over his head, he glanced back. They were trudging on, woefully unprepared for this trip. They nearly caught him as he donned the poncho near the old Starview Nursery on Highway 146. Goose kicked the spotted horse forward. Considering the rain and their walk, it was a good thing this mission was so close to home, yet maybe not. The gangs had been getting more brazen. Last time he'd been to the nearby city of LaGrange, Sheriff Douglas had mentioned a few gang incursions into the small city. Those were the first attacks since the early days of the decline.

This wasn't the kind of apocalypse most had envisioned. The riots and social justice warriors had scared many people into prepping and preparing for the next civil war. In the meantime, the economy kept getting shakier. It didn't take long for the mobs to discover they could use a government in fear of them and businesses afraid to oppose the mobs to force their social changes and draconian controls on the rest of the country. Companies who had previously found success with shrewd corporate practices and building a great product tried to survive by kowtowing to the most extreme social movements. The officials in government, either in fear or pandering, got swept up in the national hysteria. Anyone who didn't share the extremist views was branded a racist, some type of phobic, or simply ignorant. Somehow, half the country convinced themselves they were being oppressed, abused, or killed at a much higher rate than their counterparts. It made little sense. It was as if Michael Jordan or Tom Brady tried to psych themselves up for a ball game by saying the other team didn't respect or fear them.

The final straw came when those groups found they were able to enrich themselves by pushing the weaker government officials into giving them benefits, money, and bailouts. While the country didn't die in those days, it passed a point of no return that many didn't realize until later. Looking back, they should have known they were heading down a path to their destruction, but that was how panic worked. When you were in the midst of it, you couldn't see the forest for the trees, and your judgement was impaired. When it happened at a mass level, it was contagious like a disease. That panic swept the nation and infected the world. Most people couldn't conceive of America failing, it had been so strong for so long. Many didn't care. They believed their own propaganda. Perhaps Michael Jordan and Tom Brady really believed the other team didn't respect them.

Suddenly, the quote Goose was searching for popped in his head, and he mentally snapped his fingers. Alexander Fraser Tytler said, "*A democracy cannot exist as a permanent form of government. It can only exist until the voters discover that they can vote themselves largesse from the public treasury.*"

A few minutes later, Goose turned the spotted horse onto Ballard School Road, the copper horse following dutifully behind. After going about fifty yards, they stopped to wait for the woman and her son. By this time, it was dark and raining hard, the wind blowing the rain at a forty-five-degree angle. It would probably be blowing sideways before it was all over. It was hard to see more than thirty to forty yards. Kelly and her son struggled. She slipped and fell. He helped her up. When they got close to Goose, he shouted over the storm, "We have another hour or two to walk, and a creek to cross."

The woman nodded, then glanced over at the packhorse. "Can Brian ride that other horse?" she asked, desperation in her voice. "I'll try to keep up or catch up later."

"Nobody rides that horse!" Goose said gruffly and turned his horse down the road. Images of his past life and teaching Laura to ride haunted his mind. Elizabeth, who'd learned to ride as a child with Goose's family, had helped pick out the horse for her mom. Laura had been new to riding, starting later in life.

It only took a few minutes to reach the horse trail off Ballard School Road. It appeared to be nothing more than a narrow animal trail between bushes. That was by design. Goose had transplanted some briars to either side of the trail a couple years ago when he began hunting men. He'd done similar things to other trails he used leading to or away from his home. Using one of the old community horse trails cut the distance home dramatically and avoided the patrols for the Le Cheval community. The men making the patrols had good intentions and tried hard. Even so, Goose got a perverse sense of pleasure at their anger each time he slipped in and out of the community without their knowledge.

The old trail was muddy. Goose stopped repeatedly to wait for the woman and her son. He glanced over at Laura's horse. There she was, plain as day, riding in the poncho she'd worn that day a few years ago at Big South Fork, when their group had been caught in the rain.

"Goose, you know I'm not really here. They're nice people. They can ride my horse."

"You might come back," he pleaded below his breath. "If she rides your horse then you won't come back. You'll really be gone."

The anguish in his voice was stark, tears running freely down his face mixing with the rainwater.

The ghost of Laura reached out to touch his arm and receded.

Goose rode on, stone cold sober and crying. He was a mess. There was a tree across the path. He took out a mostly sodden handkerchief to wipe his eyes and wait for the woman and her son. They had an hour to go and a stream to ford.

"Take a break!" he called to them, already angry with what he was about to do.

He tied the horses and rooted around in the packhorse's bags to find the green plastic tarp he'd packed and the waterproofed ground cover he used when he camped. It only took a few minutes to find another deadfall in the woods that was mostly dry underneath. Goose laid down the ground blanket and took a few trips to move the supplies from the trailer and much of his gear to the spot under the deadfall. He covered it with the tarp, staked it down, and covered it with a few logs. When that task was complete, he led both horses through the woods around the deadfall, back to the horse trail.

The woman and her son watched with interest but didn't say anything. In a short time, they'd learned he was a cantankerous man, better left alone. Like putting off a chore, Goose tightened the cinch on the copper-colored horse's saddle, then took out a pick and cleaned the gelding's hooves, resting his hand on the pommel, his head bowed in thought. Goose took a deep breath and turned to the woman. "Can you ride a horse?"

"Yes, sir. I mean, I haven't done it since I was younger, but I know how."

"What about you, boy?"

The boy seemed afraid, his Adam's apple working. "N-no...sir."

"Okay, your mom—"

"Kelly."

"What?"

"My name is Kelly."

"Just get on the horse...Kelly." This wasn't going how he wanted at all. He needed a drink. "Now you, boy. Put your foot in that stirrup and swing up behind your mom." When the boy struggled a few times, getting frustrated, Goose grabbed him by the waist and lifted him up behind his mother as easy as he might have a child's doll. "Hang on a minute while I adjust the stirrup for your mom's legs. They're longer than... well, it just needs to be longer." Goose grabbed her calf and pulled it out of his way rather than take time to explain. The last person to ride in this saddle was Laura, who was about 5'4".

Lost in thought, Goose saw Laura in his memory, riding Copper clearer than her shade had been a few minutes ago.

"Mister, are you all right?" Kelly asked hesitantly.

Goose shook himself out of the reverie that caused him to stare off into space for a moment and finished adjusting the stirrup. He had to let it out two notches. The tattooed woman — Kelly, he now knew — must be about 5'6" or 5'7". He repeated the work on the other side.

"Put your feet in these," he instructed. "Not too far, just so you can put your weight on the balls of your feet. Then stand up a bit out of the saddle. The point is to be able to use your legs for balance and like shock absorbers, so it's not always your butt banging into the saddle." Kelly stood up some in the saddle. Goose couldn't help noticing she had nice legs and a nice... *Dammit.* All that foolishness should be behind him now. He needed to get her to the community soon and go home for a drink.

"Is this right?" she asked.

"Yeah, except for the shoes. It's better if you have proper riding boots in case you fall so you can kick your feet free of the stirrups. But there's nothing to do about it now." Why had he said now? "Boy, put your arms around your mom's waist and hang on.

You…uh…Kelly, just follow me. That horse will follow mine wherever I go, so you don't have to do much but hang on."

"Thank you."

Goose nodded and walked to his horse but turned back after a couple steps. "And don't kick that horse. I don't care if he stops or lays down or anything. Don't kick him!" He hadn't meant to yell and sound so menacing.

The trail was narrow with a black four-board fence running along the left side and woods to the right. The path was muddy, going uphill, then back down to a small creek crossing and back uphill again. The small creek started running harder, which worried Goose. They had the larger Harrods Creek to cross, which was more like a small river. If it was up and running fast, they'd have to ride three or four hours through the woods to a bridge. Normally, they could reach Harrods Creek in thirty minutes or less. With this storm, that was plenty of time for the creek to get up and run fast.

At the last small creek they crossed before climbing the ridge that led down to Harrods Creek, the copper horse Kelly and her son rode surprised them by jumping the creek and stumbling to its knees when it landed. Goose turned his horse and watched. He almost smiled seeing the woman shift her balance in the stirrups when the horse stumbled, leaning back and taking the bounce in her thighs. She may not have ridden much, but she came by it naturally.

Goose turned back to the trail without a word. When they started down the muddy hill to the creek, he reined in to let Kelly's horse catch up. "When you go down the hill, put the weight of your body on the balls of your feet in the stirrup, push your feet forward, and lean back. You always lean back going downhill and forward going up. It helps the horse. Boy, you hang on to your mom."

The boy nodded silently, afraid of the big, mean man.

"Okay. Go on now." As he watched her head downhill, Goose mentally chastised himself. What was he doing helping this woman ride better? In an hour he'd drop her at the Le Cheval community and be shut of the whole thing.

She did do a good job riding, though. Her balanced was good, and she leaned back. Copper slipped a few times going down the muddy hill. Goose smiled to himself. He had always stumbled some but was surefooted, too, if that made sense. He'd been dependable on much tougher trails than this.

The creek was running hard, white caps showing and forty yards to cross. Goose considered going the long way around, then dismissed it. He needed a drink, and these two were getting to him. He wanted to be shut of them. "Ease him into the creek. Make a kissy sound when you want to go forward."

"It looks more like a river," Kelly said with a tremor in her voice.

"Can't be helped. Let the horse go a few steps then pause and let the water clear so you can plan next steps. You need to steer him around any large rocks. Horses don't have good depth perception. He'll be all right," Goose said loudly over the storm.

Kelly scowled. "He'll be all right? What about us?" she said under her breath, not caring if the grumpy man heard or not. She turned the horse into the creek and made the kissy sound. Five or six steps in, the water was running to the belly of the horse. She spied a larger rock in the water and guided the horse downstream of the rock. By that time, she was midway through the creek with the grumpy man riding a few yards behind her. The creek was up over her stirrups when suddenly the horse stepped in a hole. Kelly took the change in her thighs and rose out of the saddle a few inches. Behind her, Brian squeezed tight, his face in her back. Cold water rushed over the saddle and drenched her thighs. In a matter of seconds, the horse righted himself and took a few steps. Kelly allowed herself to breathe, her heart racing; she scanned the

water for a path forward and made the kissy sound, her heart
pounding in her chest with adrenaline driven by fear and accomplishment. She had stayed on the horse then looked back to see if
the man noticed or would offer a compliment. He merely
motioned her forward.

When the horse took three running steps up the other bank,
Kelly felt a sense of exhilaration. It wasn't quite cheating death,
but it was fun, and she was smiling, proud of herself. A part of her
felt guilty that she was able to smile only a few hours after her
husband's death.

The grumpy man exited the creek beside her, saw her smile,
and said, "You did good. Come on." He passed her riding
forward.

Twenty minutes later, they came out of the narrow muddy trail to
a paved road in the community. Goose liked this part. The self-
righteous leaders of the community had their own lawmen and
horse patrols, though none of them knew the trails and terrain
like he did. Goose had agreed to test those men to join his
"Rangers," as the governor had called them. So far he'd found no
one with the temperament he needed. Besides, he preferred
working alone.

The mounted patrols worked their way around the sprawling
community of small horse farms that had once been immaculate
and the envy of many. The four roads into the community were
blockaded. Even so, the killers and spoilers made their way into
the community to rape, pillage, and plunder from time to time.
They usually got away before the horse patrols caught up. Sometimes Goose would track down a particularly vicious miscreant.
He never brought them back for trial. That offended their sense
of propriety. Usually, he let the patrols do it. It was good practice
for them.

Because of those depredations, many in the community had moved to the new village center at the old sale center building. In reality, it was more majestic than a normal building. They had built it to have large conferences and sell multimillion-dollar horses back in the days before the horse industry had gone downhill. A rumor held that the Queen of England had once visited this place back when Goose was a kid. The palatial complex had only been kept up by a caretaker crew that stopped by once every few weeks for many years before the decline. The most important part of the structure nowadays was the arena on the lower level. It looked out through massive three-story windows to a reflection pool. It had private box seats and general stadium-style seating for spectators to watch and bid on multimillion-dollar horses.

Now the indoor arena had been converted to a marketplace with a primary thoroughfare down the middle and booths on both sides for vendors, the luxury boxes and offices converted to homes for the leading citizens. The community had their own sheriff who kept the peace and managed the horse patrols. A judge from the nearby town of LaGrange made the daylong ride out on horseback every second Tuesday to hear cases and dispense justice, for a fee of course.

LaGrange was a larger and much older city with the traditional brick courthouse and city square like many small towns in America. In keeping with the new norm in America, it too had a sheriff and a few deputies to keep the town safe, just like the newer Le Cheval community. This new norm resembled the small towns in the Old West in many ways. People lived close to town where the sheriff could keep the peace. Many towns also boasted a judge to hear cases and dispense justice, and a few a doctor, saloon, or baker. Much like the Old West, people who lived out in the country had to be of a hardy stock and protect themselves. Some did it as homesteaders would have many years ago, while others did it with a large farm and many riders to do the work and keep them safe.

In between the small towns, a kind of no-man's-land existed. The federal government existed in name only. Washington, D.C., was not safe and few preferred to travel away from their homes to vote on bills that meant nothing with no money to implement them. There wasn't enough money or supplies to equip an army, state police, or investigative agency. People merely subsisted while learning to transition to an old-fashioned sales and bartering system and self-reliance for their own security.

All of that boiled down to virtually ceding the roads and areas between communities to the bandits. That was where Goose came in. During their time together in the early days of the collapse, the governor had met a man bereft and ready to give up on life after losing his family. The governor had a problem to address, and Goose needed a mission.

When they got out of their predicament, he got Goose a satellite phone and occasionally tasked him with going after a bad guy or gang in his area that was extremely vicious. Goose was a sworn Kentucky Ranger, modeled after the old Texas Rangers. He'd been tasked with recruiting others but hadn't got to it yet. In return, the governor paid Goose and the Le Cheval community handsomely in goods they needed. They hated being indebted to Goose, and he liked that they hated it.

The last time a convoy escorted a fuel tanker from one of the convoys between Louisville and Cincinnati to Goose's place, Goose made sure the community got some fuel—after they filled his tanks, of course. The Le Cheval mayor had thanked the driver profusely, then turned to Goose through tight lips to thank him as well before leaving abruptly.

Goose wasn't sure how things had gone so south between him and the community. It could have been early on when he left a few dead bodies of marauders on the fence posts outside his farm as a message to any more who came by. It didn't help that that was in the early days before the blockades were up and the community police patrolling. Their indoor town was just getting set up in the old show facility across the street from Goose and they'd had words over the violence, drunken outbursts, and dead bodies. On a few occasions, when Goose was in his cups, he'd stumble into the show center to listen to live music on the weekends. He was particularly cantankerous when drunk. That was the way he liked it. He didn't owe them a thing and didn't have to worry about people stopping by for a favor or to talk.

The rain was pouring in a steady downpour as they rode past the reflecting pond to a covered area between the old show facility and a row of horse stalls near it.

"Stay," Goose commanded to Jessie and Jake, who obediently sat beside the horses. "You too," he said to Kelly before turning to walk inside, not bothering to look back as he entered the three-story building. Brushing past a guard, he entered the half-moon-shaped great room with stadium seating that used to host very wealthy people for parties and horse buying. As expected, Goose was confronted by the guard again, now assisted by two more.

"Ah, Mister… uh, Truman, we are closed. All the booths are covered and everyone's gone home."

"Dammit, boy, I didn't come here to shop. Where's Kim?"

"Mrs. Murrell said she wasn't to be disturbed. She said if anyone wanted her, she'd meet them in the morning when the market opened."

"I don't have time for this shit. I'm tired and I want to go home. She'll see me. So either you go get her or I'll go up there myself."

The young man was clearly terrified. He was working as a guard and hoping to make it on the mounted community police force someday. Those guys got to ride horses and wear badges, and everyone treated them with respect. But this was Goose Truman, and even though he lived across the street, he wasn't really part of the community. Most everyone was afraid of him. Those who weren't afraid didn't like him.

People talked about the time early on in the new world when three men had attacked Mr. Truman's home. Not only had he killed all three, but he hung their bodies from the black four-board fence across from the show center. At that time, people hadn't been living in the center full time, thinking they would be safe at home. When Kim had come to work and seen the bodies, she marched over to Goose demanding he take them down and bury them. He was drunk and said no. People kept gathering and his drunken rage mirrored her indignation as the two stood on the blacktop road separating his home from their new town. No matter how she harangued him or demanded others help remove the bodies, no one would defy Goose Truman. On top of all that, he wore a gold star from the governor as Kentucky's modern-day version of a Texas Ranger. In the end, she stormed off, and the bodies stayed.

A few weeks later, Goose had disappeared for a week. People thought he might be dead, yet no one ventured on his property. When he returned, he was followed by a fuel tanker. After going to Goose's home to top off his farm tanks, the tanker crossed to the show facility to fill their large storage tanks. If anything, that made the community leaders hate him more. While Kim didn't want to be indebted to anyone, especially Goose Truman, she was in no position to turn down fuel. The same thing had happened with other types of supplies several times over the last year. It always happened a few days after he came back from whatever mysterious mission he'd been on. Over time, Kim and Goose had learned to converse civilly, although just barely.

All that flashed through the young man's mind in a matter of seconds as he stood trembling in front of the gruff man known to the community as a half deranged, drunken killer.

As if sensing his dilemma, Goose said, "Well?"

The young man decided that Kim would be less mad at him disturbing her than if he allowed Goose Truman to go to her quarters. "I'll go get her." He hustled up the stairs to the luxury suites. Fifteen minutes later he returned, followed by a frumpy woman in a robe and a floppy hat over her hair.

"What's this all about?" shouted the blustery woman with long blond hair streaked with gray escaping from the floppy hat. She had a figure that might have been buxom or curvy a few years ago but had gone to seed.

"Mrs. Murrell, Mr. Truman here—"

"Get out of my way, boy." Goose pushed the guard aside. "Kim, I'm not here to start any more trouble. I've got a woman and a boy with no place to go."

"We don't have any room for 'em."

"Can't they sleep here in the arena? Surely there's got to be an empty room somewhere."

"Nobody who we don't know well or doesn't have a home in Le Cheval sleeps inside. We've had trouble both out at people's homes and some fracases inside the show facility. Most families are living here at night and working their farms by day, except for a few holdouts. Even if I could scare up a spot, I wouldn't for safety. We don't know her."

"It's a woman and a boy! They're no risk to anyone. I'll vouch for them. What about the stables? I've seen folks living there."

"Yeah, we have a few out there, and another time that might be an option. But all the stables worth staying in are full. The other ones have a foot of water in them from the storm. You might remember this place standing empty for years before the world crashed. They paid people to take care of the main building, but the stables went to hell."

Goose stared down at his feet, rubbed his thumb and fore-finger through the scrubble on his chin, and took on more of a pleading tone. "Don't you have any ideas, Kim? I'd appreciate it. I've brought a lot of goods to this town."

"That you have, and I suppose it's a good mark for ya, against all the bad. I never met you before all this, but since then, I don't mind saying you've been a drunken miscreant and a killer. This ain't about you, though. I truly don't have the room or the will to take on a couple of charity cases. If you're so sure of them, why don't you take them on? You should have plenty of room at your place."

Exhaling slowly to calm himself, Goose stared out the massive windows at the rain pouring into the reflecting pool. His home and small farm was less than a mile beyond. His tone changed to an almost whining sound. "Kim, that ain't no fit place for a woman and a boy. You just said yourself, I'm a disreputable drunk and a killer. I'm worse than that. I caper naked under the full moon and dance with the devil. People say I sneak out and kill children and eat them. There's no telling how bad I am."

Kim genuinely laughed for the first time since he'd known her. "Goose, you're a wicked man, a drunk, and probably not right in the head most times. But I know you've never killed children, innocent men, or molested a woman. Maybe you were a good man once, but you've gone to hell since. I never understood why the governor placed his trust in you. Maybe he sees something that I don't. In any event, they can't stay here. It's soaking wet in the stables, and I'm going to bed. They're your problem."

Goose stared after Kim as she gathered her robe in her right hand, put her left on the bannister, and shuffled up the stadium steps to the luxury boxes that had been converted to living quarters for many of the core families from Le Cheval who managed and ran the indoor town and market. The guard made himself scarce.

Goose didn't want to face the woman and her son. Turning to leave, he noted Kelly had dismounted and was standing in the doorway. Much to his chagrin, Jessie and Jake stood with her, her hand idly stroking Jake's head. "Come with me," he said gruffly as he walked briskly to the horses, forestalling questions.

"Where are we going?" Kelly asked.

"Just mount up," Goose commanded. The storm had let up some and faded to a soaking rain. Goose mounted with a practiced toe to the left stirrup and two bounces before swinging his right leg over. He was tired and needed a drink. He let the spotted horse move off a few steps and glanced back at Kelly. She mounted the copper horse well. The boy was having a problem. Goose walked his horse back to them. "Take your foot out of the left stirrup," he said to Kelly, not looking up. The rain was making her clothes cling to her body and had soaked her hair and face. "Boy, you're going to put your left foot in the stirrup and grab the pommel in front of your mom, then bounce twice and swing up behind your mom like earlier when I helped you up." It took three tries, and on the third his mom grabbed a handful of his shirt with her left hand and pulled him up. Once they were mounted, Goose merely nodded and turned his horse.

It was a brief ride down the access road away from the show facility to cross the road to the one leading to his property bordered by a black four-board fence. They halted at the large double iron gate to the property. Goose dismounted and unlocked the U-shaped bar locking the gates. He had barely pushed the gates back when the two dogs raced down the driveway.

Kelly tensed with worry that the horse might slip on the blacktop as the dogs came racing back up the driveway full of joy. They were wagging their tails, their entire bodies squirming like worms as they went to Goose, joyful at being home. He knelt on one knee, hugging the larger brindle dog first, pulling him in for a deep embrace. The dog lowered his head and held the top of it

against Goose's neck for several seconds before the smaller fawn-
colored female pushed her snout between the two and started
licking Goose's face. The spell was broken, both dogs frantically
happy to be home. Kelly had been raised to believe dogs had a
good sense for people. Everyone said Goose was a bad man. A
drunken, crazy killer. Yet the dogs obviously thought differently.

Goose stood and faced Kelly. "Take the horse through the
gate. I need to lock it." When she did, he locked the gate and
started walking his horse down the lane, and Kelly followed. It
only took a few minutes for the lane to go downhill and turn to
the left, facing a solid home that looked like a country chalet. It
stood just behind the hill enough to be hidden from the road
through the screening cedar trees that lined the fence.

Past the home, the drive led to a metal barn. He led his horse
in front of the barn and slid open two large doors, took his horse
inside and tied it, then walked out and grabbed the reins of Kelly's
horse, leading it into the barn and tying it as well.

"Get down," he grunted without even looking at her, pointing
to a couple of lawn chairs.

"How can we help?" Kelly offered.

"Just sit."

With well-practiced motions he stripped the gear, saddles, and
bridles from both horses, then the sodden blankets. He used a
squeegee scraper to pull the water out of their coats, then combed
each horse thoroughly and brushed them. He then lifted each of
their hooves to inspect and clean them before leading each horse
by the halter into stalls. Each stall also had openings to the
outside. Goose filled water buckets from a pump inside the barn
operated by lifting a handle. He also cut open a square hay bale,
tossing several flakes into each stall. Then he opened a yellow 55-
gallon garbage can on wheels and scooped out a bit of grain for
each horse.

That completed, he turned to Kelly and Brian, blinking as if

GOOSE TRUMAN - THE HORSEMAN

he'd forgotten they were there. "Come in here." He walked around the stack of square hay bales.

When Kelly caught up to him, she saw a hidden door just behind the hay bales. Goose opened it, revealing a large poker room with leather couches, a recliner, TV, exercise equipment, refrigerator, and two poker tables.

"Wow!" she exclaimed. She'd thought all the nice things people had grown accustomed to a few years ago were gone. An open door in the room's corner led to a bathroom and shower as well as a third room for storage and tack.

"You'll stay here for the night. Don't leave or wander around. There are a lot of ways to get hurt around here." He eyed her with the mean look she was getting used to. "Tomorrow we'll find you someplace more permanent."

The last words were a punch in the stomach to Kelly. She hadn't realized that in just a few minutes she'd begun to hope they might be allowed to stay here. It was perfect, and they were safe. Brian's expression displayed the same hope. Kelly could only nod back at the gruff man.

With that, Goose turned and left, the dogs at his heels. He needed a drink… or ten. The strange out-of-time memories were coming back again. This night would be a bad one. Perhaps it was because a woman was on the property again. It was like watching a jittery old home movie. Every time he looked around, he saw the place as it had once been, when Laura and Elizabeth had been here and he'd been a family man. As they'd ridden down the lane, he'd seen the sun out and Laura working her flower beds, despite the downpour that was reality. Laura had looked up at him from the flowerbed, smiled, and waved, welcoming him home. When he'd put the horses into the stalls, he'd seen Elizabeth, petite, yet powerful and full of energy, giving them treats.

RECALCITRANT

THE PAIN in his head resembled a throbbing metronome with waves of discomfort washing over him each time his heart pumped.

Consciousness began to return to Gus Truman in waves. He'd been called "Goose" for so long the name Gus sounded odd to him.

The late morning sun beat down on his face through the open window, making him afraid to open his eyes to the harsh glare. Sleep and sweat caked the corners of his eyes and mouth. He ignored the smell of stale sweat in his clothing and bedding.

Eventually he could avoid it no longer. He had to pee. He cracked one eye to accustom himself to the light. Any other person would have jumped in shock. Goose was too old, tired, and hungover to do much more than open a second eye at the gangly twelve-year-old towheaded boy staring back at him through the open window.

Goose hadn't slept in the house's upstairs since coming back from Lexington. That time in his life belonged to another person and another time. The house was solidly built, like a World War

II pillbox with a stucco exterior resembling a European mountain chalet. The half-basement where he slept opened to a rock-lined grotto and had once been Goose's home office and man cave. Now he had a twin bed beside the open window with just enough room for him and the dogs.

"Boy, what are you doing in my yard?" Goose barked. He was wearing last night's blue jeans and a button-up shirt, unbuttoned to reveal a chest with scars. He was an imposing, scary figure to most adults. To a twelve-year-old boy, he was terrifying.

"M-Mr. Goose, I was j-just looking," the boy stammered. To his credit, he didn't run or cry.

As his mind began to clear, details of the three-day mission he'd completed the night before began creeping back into Goose's mind. The damn alcohol was fogging his mind from memories both short term and long, which was exactly what he wanted most times. Life seemed so pointless lately without direction or a reason for being. Why some people lived, and others died.

"Boy, I told you and your mother to stay in the rooms in the barn."

The boy was trying his best to be strong. His eyes grew moist, and his Adam's apple moved as he swallowed. "Mom's asleep. She doesn't know I'm here. I just wanted to look around. Honest."

Goose thought he must be getting soft. "Go on back to your mom," he said. "Later I'll take you and your mom over to the show barn community. We'll talk to some other people and find a place for you two to stay long term."

As tough as the boy had been facing Goose, the prospect of moving again terrified him. "We can't stay here? You're making us leave?" His voice rose in pitch.

"This ain't no place for a boy and a woman. I don't like people, and I damn sure don't want company," Goose barked louder than he intended. "Now get back to your mom."

Despite his youth, the boy stood up straighter and steeled

himself. "She was up all last night crying. I don't want to wake her. I can help. I'm useful. I promise."

Before Goose could reply, the boy started picking up garbage in his arms. The boy paused at the empty and broken whiskey bottles and quart jars outside Gus's window. A part of Goose that was buried deep and had once been an upstanding member of society was embarrassed to see the detritus of his debauchery through the eyes of the child.

"Leave that!" He cuffed the boy on the back of the head. "If you're bound and determined to do something, you can stack firewood." Goose pointed to the grove of trees on the edge of the other side of the horse pasture. "Gather up as many of the logs as you can and stack 'em neat behind the barn. There should be uncut limbs too that are already cut for firewood size. Use the wheelbarrow over there if you need."

"What's firewood size?"

"Boy..." Goose blew out a breath of air in frustration. "Figure about the length of my arm from my fingertips to my elbow."

The boy got a quizzical look on his face, raised an eyebrow, and scrunched up his mouth. He looked at Goose twice as if to speak, then stopped himself. Finally, with some inner decision made, he screwed up his courage, walked up to Goose, and laid his pale, skinny left arm along Goose's dark, weathered, scar-laced right arm corded with muscle. Goose had to stop himself from flinching. No human had touched him since before Lexington. Then the boy added the palm of his right hand to touch the tips of his left hand, aligning his fingertips with Goose's. The boy pursed his lips, then looked around and found an old fence board and a nail. After laying his left arm and right hand together, he used the nail to scratch a line on the board with the correct length and smiled, satisfied with his work.

Avoiding eye contact with Goose, he put his board in the wheelbarrow and opened the gate to the pasture and grove of trees. Goose couldn't help smiling to himself when the boy closed the gate properly behind himself and went to work.

Then he caught himself smiling and frowned. He hadn't done that either in so long it didn't feel right. In any event, he had things to do. First thing was to go out to the barn and flip the switch on the Generac system to turn on the power. His home and barn had been completely off the grid before things had gone to hell. Goose didn't like the power running at night these days, knowing any light or sound would advertise what he had and make him a target. While the primary power bank was solar panels feeding a battery bank, the backup was a propane generator.

As the system came to life, Goose flipped on a few lights in the barn to test it. Then he heard a shriek echo from the deeper in the barn. Goose was instantly on alert, the Springfield .45 swiftly drawn, and he dashed to the back of the barn scanning for threats. As he rounded the haystack, the door to the man cave swung open. A disheveled woman shrieked again when she came face to face with Goose and the large .45. He jumped a bit at her sudden appearance.

She put one hand to her chest and with the other tried to smooth her hair. "I was sleeping, and the lights came on and startled me. I'm sorry. I haven't seen working electricity in a long time."

"I'd appreciate it if you keep that tidbit to yourself when you move on, ma'am. Also, there should be hot water in a few minutes if you want to take a shower. There's soap and towels under the sink."

"I have to find Brian." She looked worried. "He wasn't here when I woke."

"The boy's outside doing some chores."

"Okay," she said uncertainly. "I guess I'll get cleaned up and we'll leave whenever you want."

"That's fine. It may be a few hours. I've got some things to take care of myself."

"His name is Brian."

"What?"

"My son. You keep calling him boy. His name is Brian."

"I've never been good with names," Goose said, his gruff exterior returning. Without another word, he turned to leave, silently berating himself for being nice to them. He didn't owe her a shower, and he sure as hell didn't need people in his life prying into his business. This afternoon he'd find them a place and be shut of them.

He opened the stall door and slid in beside the big spotted horse. Even after all these years, the horse could be skittish when first approached. Someone had beat him as a young horse. They never forgot those memories. Goose produced a treat, rubbing the horse's nose and neck to calm him. Then Goose grabbed the halter. He always liked to lead him by hand from the stall or into a new pasture as opposed to letting him run free. The old timers had always told him it was important that the horse understand you were in charge and provide the route to food and green pastures. Then he opened the outer door for Copper and the older mare. Goose led them across the dry lot and opened the blue pipe gates to the near field, patted the horses on the necks, and released them to the field.

This part was always enjoyable for Goose. Almost without fail when he let a horse into a field they acted like puppies. Rocky and Copper galloped into the field and neighed for the older mare. They nosed around a bit before the two geldings found a good spot to lie down and roll on their backs like puppies. Even though Goose saw them getting mud on their coats he would need to clean later, it made him smile unashamedly.

A few moments later, they got up and began grazing. Goose

went to go check the well and the solar-powered motor pumping water to a larger holding tank.

With that done, his next chore was the house. He usually tried to clean up after a binge and make sure he hadn't broken something important. Later, he might watch an old movie or take a nap enjoying the A/C. After that he would find another place to take the woman and her son. He also had to plan the next steps in his mission to round up the gang attacking homes and convoys.

He hadn't even made it to the house when he spied the boy stacking wood at the pile. As he watched, the boy turned a larger cut log on end and picked up the axe. Goose was already moving toward him when the boy raised the axe overhead for a mighty swing. The axe landed awkwardly and glanced to the side, barely missing his foot and cutting off some toes. The boy scrutinized the log for a moment, then grasped the axe again for another wide, double-handed swing.

At the apex of the second swing, Goose grabbed the axe with his massive paw, yanked it out of the boy's hand, and roughly cuffed him with the other hand, knocking him off balance. "Boy, what do you think you're doing? I didn't tell you to split wood."

"I was just trying to help. I saw how the other logs had been split."

Goose could see he was trying hard to be strong and not cry.

"You almost cut off your dang fool foot!" Goose roared. "There ain't much of a doctor here in the community, and what's in LaGrange ain't much better. Doubt I could get you to the hospital in Louisville before you bleed out." Seeing the boy's spirits sink and his head drop dejectedly bothered Goose, though he didn't know why. "Let me get some of my other work done inside and get cleaned up. Then I'll come out and teach you how to swing an axe properly."

"Really!?" The boy looked up, his eyes gleaming in anticipation.

"Yeah, really," Goose said, trying to be gruff and not smile before reaching out to ruffle the boy's hair. He was startled by an angry scream before getting pummeled on the back and shoulders. Goose fell to his knee, rolled, and grabbed for his gun.

"Don't you dare touch my son! Take your filthy hands off him!" Kelly had raced across the rocky, muddy lot in her bare feet. She must have seen the first cuff and what looked like angry yelling from Goose, then what appeared to be another cuff and came running. Goose lowered his gun and held up his forearm to ward off her blows. The dogs were jumping and yapping, unsure who to bite, or if this was all play.

With a groan, Goose stood and turned to walk to the house. When he was halfway there, he bellowed, "Jake, Jessie, come!" They made a beeline to follow on his heels.

"Mom... he didn't hit me," said Brian. "Well, he did, but it wasn't hard. He was going to teach me how to swing an axe."

"I didn't know..." Kelly turned to follow Goose and apologize, until she heard the door slam and the lock engage.

Inside, Goose was berating himself. He'd begun to open up to those two. It was a slim opening to most people. For Goose it was a big deal. This was for the best. People died in this world, and he didn't need them in his life to worry about. He'd told the woman he would find them a home today. That could wait another day. He didn't feel like facing her and the boy right now, and it was too late to go back after the gang. Tonight, he would drink and listen to some old music.

He drank himself into a stupor in short order. The present faded. Goose had a lifetime of memories to live within. Good memories of the time before. Drinks after work, golf with friends, boating, and vacations to exotic places. Laura and Elizabeth were in all those memories. Laura had been his better half, all the things he wasn't. He'd grown complacent and forgot to fully appreciate her. Elizabeth was a beautiful pint-sized version of him. A tiny warrior willing to argue with him when others wouldn't. His heart burst with pride each time he thought of her. It never got old.

It was nice living with them in the past. He would happily spend eternity reliving the twenty-two years he had with his wife and daughter. It was the anger at his own body betraying him that caused him to rave. After a while, his body began to reject more alcohol and needed rest and food. Those things forced him back to his world of dread and killing loneliness. His only reason for being in this world was killing bad men. He would rather live in the drunken fantasy world of his memories with Laura and Elizabeth.

Goose woke, turning sideways on the twin bed, putting his feet to the cold floor, elbows on his knees, head in hands, willing the world to stop spinning. He saw both a bottle of Angels Envy Rye and a half-full bottle of Rare Breed on the floor. Apparently, the moonshine hadn't been enough; he'd raided his store of good stuff. As his mind cleared, remorse began to settle in. There were things broken and turned over, and he was late.

Then the second shock hit. The power was on and he panicked, worried he'd left it on during the night. That would paint a bullseye on his place. If that wasn't bad enough... mother of God! He smelled bacon!

He took a handgun from beside his bed and crept up the stairs. The floor was solid poured concrete covered in real bamboo wood. It didn't creak. He slipped down the hall to the corner coming into the great room facing the kitchen.

Kelly was there, her hair up in a messy bun, humming a tune to herself while making bacon and eggs. Brian sat at the sofa table, his back to Goose. And of all things Jake and Jessie were lying chins on their paws in the kitchen watching Kelly cook.

The dogs either heard or smelled Goose and jumped up running to him in that happy, squirming, kidney bean motion that dogs did. He set his gun aside and reached down to rub their heads and play with their jowls. That always made him happy.

"Traitors," he muttered under his breath. "Now scoot. I got things to do."

They scampered away to find their toys. Jessie and Jake could make their own fun. Goose had once read that boxers were referred to as the clowns of the canine world. These dogs may not be boxers, but they sure embodied that spirit.

"I'm glad you're up," Kelly said to Goose. "I was just about to ask Brian to wake you."

"What are you doing in here? How'd you get in?"

"The door was open. You must have left it that way during the night while you were…uh…indisposed and let the dogs out to do their business."

Goose merely grunted in response then glared at the two mountain curs. "Some guard dogs," he said, and they lowered their heads.

"As for what I'm doing, I felt terrible about what I did yesterday, and I never thanked you for saving us and bringing us here. I thought the least I could do was make you a homecooked meal. I don't have anything else to offer."

"Well, you can't stay here." Goose meant it to be stern, but it came out sounding peevish.

"I understand. You've told us, and I respect your wishes. For now, let's enjoy breakfast. I'm sorry I took advantage of your supplies. Eggs I understand, but how on Earth did you find bacon?"

Goose sat down at the sofa table beside Brian, and Kelly set a plate in front of him. "The Amish people," he said in between bites. "Did I leave the lights on all night?"

"No, I turned them on this morning after the sun came up. I

remembered what you said about lights at night, and I watched what you did."

"I said that?" Goose didn't remember telling her that.

"After breakfast, I'm sure you'll want to shower and clean up, then you can take us wherever you think is best and we'll be out of your hair."

"Mom, he said he would teach me…" Brian started before Kelly shushed him.

Goose shook his head. "I don't need a shower."

Kelly raised an eyebrow and stared at Goose for a few seconds. Goose returned a menacing expression. "Hmpff," Kelly said and turned to clean up.

While her back was turned, Goose lifted his arm to smell his pit and grimaced. He glanced over at Brian, who had an impish smile.

"I normally shower about this time anyway. I don't need a woman in here telling me what to do," Goose growled. He got up from the tall chair, heading to the main floor master bedroom no one slept in anymore. Towels and soap were laid out waiting, and the shower had instant hot water as well.

After he left to take a shower, Kelly eyed the overturned box of photos in the corner of the living room. When she'd let herself in earlier, it was clear from the loud snoring that Goose wouldn't be up soon. She had decided to straighten up a bit to thank him for the hospitality. The remains of a spilled drink, pillows on the floor, and two empty mason jars beside the pictures told the story. All of that was under a window overlooking the field beside a built-in bookcase with drawers, some of which stood open.

Kelly debated whether to clean up the drink. She didn't want him to think she was snooping, yet she hated to see nice things damaged out of neglect. In the end, she cleaned it, vowing to be honest if he noticed. Then her curiosity got the better of her and she sat on a pillow on the floor and began flipping through the pictures. Moments later, her face was red and swollen with tears. She wasn't sure if it was the images on those pictures or the reminder of a happier, easier time that was lost.

The man in the pictures was virtually unrecognizable from the man she'd met. If he weren't standing in this house for many of the pictures, she might not have believed it was him. He was a handsome, clean-shaven man in a suit in some pictures, golf clothes in others, and on a boat in yet more. Most of all, he was smiling in those pictures. Nothing looked more alien on the man she knew as Goose Truman than a smile. He'd been a larger, well-built man, but soft and a little pudgy. Not the rangy, broad-shouldered man of today.

What made her cry, though, were the pictures of his family. He'd had a beautiful wife and a daughter with a fierceness in her eyes that made Kelly smile. There were pictures of an extended family and others of a workplace party. She also gazed for several minutes at pictures of Goose with someone who appeared to be his mother. Although frail and older, she also had an indomitable spirit in her eyes.

Kelly wiped her eyes and began to place all the pictures back as she found them. It wasn't perfect, but she doubted Goose would remember exactly how he'd left them. Jessie and Jake watched her intently, probably because she'd found some doggy treats earlier and had given them each one and they hoped for more.

About the time she'd finished looking through the pictures, the tenor of the snoring downstairs changed. Goose would probably wake in a few minutes, even if only to answer the call of nature. Kelly went to wake Brian to come in for breakfast. He knuckled sleep from his eyes and yawned. She led him to the bathroom in the barn and instructed him to brush his teeth and wash his face and come inside the house. Idly she wondered if they should cut back on brushing their teeth to a couple of times a week. They only had one tube of toothpaste, after all, and no way to get more.

When Goose exited the shower, he stared at the visage in the mirror. The lines on his face ran deeper and his hair was longer. His scruffy facial hair had turned into a full hermit-style beard.

When did that happen? he mused, taking out his old beard trimmer to at least take it down to a five o'clock shadow. He craved a drink, which reminded him he needed more alcohol, which reminded him he hadn't seen his old family friend Mac lately.

Jim "Mac" McIntosh's family and his had been friends since Goose was a kid. They had a huge old family farm about ten miles away that had been split off to several family members over the years. The county road running through that area was called McIntosh Lane. Goose worried about them out there on their own and had invited Mac into the community on a few occasions, but Mac had a large extended family and knew the land very well.

Goose needed to get some moonshine from Mac and wanted check on him and his family. They might have an open room and need help on the farm that Kelly and Brian could do. Mac made some of the best Kentucky corn moonshine in the area. He flavored it like the old timers did, apple pie or strawberry moonshine mainly. His family farm grew plenty of corn, had apple orchards, and had gardens for strawberries. Finding cinnamon sticks for the apple pie moonshine was getting hard, however.

Crazy Joe was pissed. When he was pissed, most people made themselves scarce. Only his most trusted lieutenants dared stay close. They'd have preferred to make themselves scarce, too, but that would have only pissed off Crazy Joe more.

"Where the hell are Chad and Paul? They should have been back hours ago. I swear to Christ, if they stopped to get high or mess with some woman, I'll cut their damn innards out."

Crazy Joe made a point to stare down his lieutenants while he paced and ranted. When he wasn't yelling, the loudest sound in the room were the heels of his cowboy boots echoing on the old wooden floor. They weren't the kind of boots any real cowboy would wear. They had long pointy tips covered in silver with stars and doodads all over. Sometimes at night the sound of those boots pacing in the hall filled his men with dread that the footsteps might stop outside their door.

He never allowed any of his lieutenants to get too comfortable or too cocky. His mercurial moods and outbursts had earned him the nickname Crazy Joe. Although everyone thought he was a loose cannon, few knew how cold and calculating he truly was. Right now, he was brooding about what he deemed a decline in discipline. Deciding they needed a reminder of how precarious their positions were with him and what an angry boss could do, he snapped to no one in particular, "Get that damn driver in here!"

More than one man gave a prompt, "Yes, sir!" and scurried out of the room, eager to help direct his fury at someone else. While he paced, Crazy Joe studied the walls of the historic schoolhouse building in English, Kentucky, he'd chosen for his headquarters. For now, this had the room he needed and location off the beaten path. A posse wouldn't think to search here. This building and most of the homes in the small community were old enough to have wood stoves, wells or cisterns, and septic tanks. However, the most important reason to be here was the proximity to I-71.

The way things were now, state governments could do little

more than keep some semblance of order in the capital and the
outskirts of the big cities. They'd given sutlery contracts to the
large box warehouse stores like Sam's Club and Costco. Those
locations were well guarded with troops, barriers, and chain-link
fences. Many of the old-world luxuries could be had for those
who had money, although the value of things had changed
dramatically over the last couple of years. While a large flatscreen
TV could be had for twenty dollars, a bag of flour might cost four
to five hundred.

In between the box stores and major cities was a no-man's-
land. Convoys traveled the route a few times a week with a
contingent of guards. Sporadically, they would stop at a town or
truck stop to allow the locals to barter for or purchase goods,
avoiding the long trip to the distribution center. The last line of
civilization in the wilderness of no man's land was small town
America. While many towns had fallen or been burned to the
ground, others reverted to their roots with a sheriff and his
deputies protecting the town and neighbors helping each other,
whether with chores, gardening, or fighting off villains. The
outlaws soon learned it wasn't worth the gamble to practice their
trade inside these towns. Especially when there were so many
easy opportunities outside the towns.

Occasionally, one gang got daring and ventured into a city to
raid or steal. The most audacious among them tried treeing a
small town or attacking a convoy. The rumor mill said the
governor was trying to recruit a special type of men to chase
down the worst of the miscreants. He would call them Rangers,
operating off horseback most of the time, tracking the vilest trans-
gressors eluding local law enforcement. That took a tough, mean
man who wouldn't give up and wouldn't stop at boundaries until
he got his man. So far, Crazy Joe's men hadn't seen hide nor hair
of any kind of Ranger hunting them down. That was fine with

them. They were making a good living hitting convoys and outlying homes and farms.

"Where's that damn driver!" Crazy Joe bellowed, yanking open the door as they were coming in.

When the man screeched and peed himself a little, Crazy Joe curled his lip in disgust. They sure were scraping the bottom of the barrel.

"Stay out on the porch!" he ordered. "I don't want you stinking up my building."

"Y-yes, sir."

Crazy Joe clumped out to sit in a rocking chair on the old wooden porch. "Tie him to the hitching rail."

"Please don't kill me!" the driver wailed. "I didn't do nothing wrong."

"Stop your damned sniveling. I'd just as soon kill you for being a weak-assed embarrassment to my gang than anything you actually did. Now stand up and act like a man."

Hands tied to the newly installed hitching rail, the man stood and swallowed hard.

"Now, why didn't you go with Chad and Paul to get our stuff from that little rat Steve?"

"Paul told me not to. He said they'd let me know if I needed to go back. He wanted to try to get Steve's wife to come back here with him and I'd just be in the way," the driver poured out in a rush.

Crazy Joe leaned back in the ancient rocker and propped his boots up on the porch rail. Taking his silence for condemnation, the driver tried to add more to plead his case. Joe simply held up one finger, and everyone went silent. One of his lieutenants cuffed the bound man so hard on the back of the head he fell against the rail.

"That's right," Crazy Joe drawled. "You recommended this Steve to us. Aren't you two friends?"

"Well, not really friends. We just used to run together and deal some stuff before the world changed. I promise he's loyal to you. He's selling things for you, moving product, and wouldn't steal a dime."

"What's Paul want with his wife?"

"She's a real looker, boss," one lieutenant spoke up. "Tough too. Several of us would have brought her back a long time ago, but you said not to piss where we eat. You said if a man is working for you and doing a good job to let him be, just like he's protected by you."

"So I did…" Crazy Joe said slowly in a tone full of malice. "So why does Paul think he can defy me?"

"I don't know, boss." The underling was starting to get nervous. "If any of us had known, we'd have told you. I swear we didn't know."

"But *you* knew." Crazy Joe directed his beady, reptilian eyes at the man tied to the hitching rail.

"No! I swear. I had no idea!" the driver pleaded.

Crazy Joe leaned back in the chair. "Untie him," he said to his men. Crazy Joe pulled his bowie knife from the sheath on his thigh and admired the razor-sharp edge, wetting a patch on his forearm and shaving the hair with it. Then, shocking everyone, he tossed it on the ground at the prisoner's feet. "Pick it up."

"I uh…uh…uh," the driver stammered, clearly about to cry.

Crazy Joe rose swiftly, full of rage. "I told you once not to be pathetic. I have no use for a weakling! At least Paul stood up and tried to take something he wanted. I'll straighten him out. But *you*, you're a piss-poor excuse for a man. I got no use for weaklings. Can you be strong?"

"Yes! I swear!" he pleaded like a new convert at a Baptist revival.

"We'll see." Crazy Joe's lower voice was more threatening than the rage of a few seconds ago. "You've displeased me. Don't bother denying it. You disobeyed my order for you to go with Paul and Chad. I don't care who countermanded it." His voice rose again to rage. "Also, you didn't come tell me when you thought Paul was going to break one of my rules. That's three strikes, dammit! So now I got a dilemma. You're one of my made men. God knows why, but you are. That's why I gave you a knife so you can go out fighting. I asked you if you could be strong. Now's your chance to prove it."

"I don't want to fight you, boss. Anything! I'll do anything!"

"You've got a knife and I have three steps to walk down. When my foot touches the dirt, I'm going to kill you. Before that happens, you can use the knife on yourself or try to kill me, 'cause when my boots hit the dirt, you're dead."

"You want me to kill myself?" he almost cried.

"Either that or cut off your own damn ear like that artist Van Gogh did. That might prove your toughness and loyalty." Sometimes Crazy Joe didn't know where these thoughts came from, but when they did, it was like a close lightning strike. Everyone froze.

Crazy Joe sauntered to the steps, eyes on the prisoner, who was staring at his feet. He seemed to find some inner resolve and lifted his head, looking around at those watching him as if taking a mental inventory. At that moment, Crazy Joe expected the man to either charge him or raise the knife to his own ear.

Two more steps put Crazy Joe's boot on the first step. The piss-stained man raised the knife to his ear. As the knife bit in, he let out an unnatural sound, like a soul being dragged to Hell. Perhaps it wasn't that far from the truth. When he paused, Crazy Joe took another slow step down. The little man screamed a primal yell and sliced through his ear in one last cut, dropping it to the ground. Blood flowed freely.

Before anyone could react, a mangy cur who'd been living under one of the homes and eating scraps raced out, took the ear in his mouth, and scampered away.

"Well, gawd damn!" Crazy Joe said, both about the dog and the gumption his man had shown. "Didn't think you had it in you. We're all even now. Your slate's cleared. Give me my knife."

To the rest of his men Crazy Joe said, "We ride in ten minutes! We're going to find out what's going on at Steve's place." To the one-eared man he said, "Get yourself patched up and changed. You're driving and I'm riding with you. I'm in a hurry. I don't want to get caught in the storm that's coming."

VEXING

"Come with me, boy," Goose said, setting off toward the barn. Out of the corner of his eye, he noticed Kelly's pursed lips and a slight intake of breath as if she were about to say something, though she remained silent.

Goose headed to the barn, unsure what had upset her yesterday and made her so nice and reserved today. It wasn't lost on him that when he opened the door, Jessie and Jake hadn't run outside as they normally would have but stayed inside with her.

First thing he did was to go to the panel and switch off the power. The solar panels would continue to collect power and charge the batteries, but the switch to allow it to flow to the house was dead except for the separate circuit to the refrigerator and deep freezer, which would run every other hour while the rest of the power was off.

Then Goose opened the feed bin to portion out a half of scoop in the stall for each of the horses. While the yellow plastic garbage can was new, the scoop was an old pewter one that had been in his family for decades.

A pre-pubescent voice interrupted his reverie. "Can I help?"

"Hang on, boy. I'll have something for you in a bit. Right now, watch what I do and learn. Stay behind me, but not too close, so you don't get in the way."

Brian looked back at Goose, a tuft of hair standing up from the crown of his head, and responded seriously as if taking a solemn oath. "Yes, sir."

Goose nodded, not looking the boy in the eye. This was how boys were meant to learn from the older men in their lives. Where had society gone so awry, when the simple act of a boy trying to find a role model was such an exception? Realizing he was beginning to take a shine to this boy encouraged Goose to get moving. He needed to be rid of him and his mother soon.

"Come on, we got work to do."

After putting a spot of feed in buckets hanging in each stall, Goose grabbed one of the plastic feed tubs and walked through a stall to open the outer door. He banged the side of the tub, shouting, "Hya, hya, hya!" in a loud drill sergeant voice that carried. He followed up with, "Rocky! Copper! Toni!" and soon the horses came trotting into the dry lot. Copper was first, headstrong and a glutton for food. Rocky was second; he loved the treats but had been abused when young and was always wary. Toni followed last. She had been a great horse, trained for voice commands, but was older now and had fallen in the pecking order and was prone to get picked on by the other horses.

Goose opened all three outer stall doors. Copper trotted in and Goose closed the door. Toni soon followed suit to the next stall, leaving Rocky in the dry lot looking wary. Goose held the treats and spoke soothingly to the spotted horse while moving to him with his head down in a non-aggressive posture. Soon the big horse took the treat and Goose took hold of his halter and began rubbing his head, neck, and ears. Rocky leaned his head down against Goose's chest and exhaled, as if to say, "*I'm sorry I didn't come to you right away. Sometimes I can't help myself when old memories come back."*

After all three horses were in their stalls, Goose said, "Boy, go get your mom. She should see this too."

"Okay!" Brian took off at a run.

"Boy!" Goose barked, bringing the boy to an instant halt. "Don't run! It scares the horses."

"Yes, sir." He looked chastened but not broken.

Goose led Toni through the barn to the wash rack and clipped the crosstie chains to her halter. When the boy and his mother arrived, Goose said, turning around, "Mom, there is a glider there if you want to take a seat. Boy, come with me."

Jessie and Jake followed Kelly to the glider and sat at either side of her. It annoyed Goose to some degree that she could so casually scratch their heads and that they had accepted her so readily.

The boy took two running steps before slowing to a walk. Goose nodded as he patted Toni's neck and rubbed behind her ears, unhitching her from the crossties to lead her around the gravel lot. "Watch what I do. Hold the halter with your right hand down at the bottom like this. Watch your feet so she doesn't step on them. If a horse ever gets antsy, keep her chin down and tucked in while you put your hip into her shoulder like you're checking a basketball player to take her off balance. Then just turn her in a couple circles 'till she calms down." Then looking at Brian, he added, "You might have to wait a few years to do that when you get taller, but remember not to fight them, just get their head tucked down and turn them in circles 'till they calm down."

"Will she fight you?" he asked in awe.

"Nah, not Toni. She's a sweetheart now. She was headstrong when she was younger. She was born the same year as my daughter. My mother and stepfather owned her then."

The young boy nodded seriously. Kelly noted the information

he shared as well. Goose lost himself in memories for a moment, seeing Laura and Elizabeth here in the barn laughing and talking in that way mothers and daughters do. He latched Toni in the crossties and walked to the room behind the hay bales. Opening the door, he stood in confusion for a moment. Laura and Elizabeth had set this room up as their craft room. Yet now, all the sewing machines and other paraphernalia were shoved against a wall. Had someone robbed them?

Closing the door, he turned to go check the house and saw Toni halfway latched to the wash rack. There was a young towheaded boy standing beside Toni and a beautiful woman rising from Laura's glider peering in the barn with concern. They didn't say a thing, only watched Goose, beginning to learn his moods.

Goose's heart rate increased. Laura would be pissed, wanting to know why this woman was here, even though he'd done nothing wrong. Then the colors got crisper, his vision cleared, the memories faded, and his heart sank. The change in his posture was evident to Kelly and Brian. He dipped his head and hooked the other side of Toni's halter, busying himself brushing her before saddling the old girl. They seemed to understand he needed his space. It only took a few minutes to do the same for Rocky and Copper.

"Bring your bags," he commanded in a tone that didn't allow for debate. He used saddlebag panier packs and cords to tie everything behind the saddles, then stood back for a moment staring at the horses, his memories once again threatening to overwhelm him.

Goose fought to clear his vision. These horses belonged to Laura and Elizabeth. No one was supposed to ride them. Yet here they were, saddled and ready to go. Had some deep part of his mind known it was time to move on and these were good people? He shook his head when a faint voice in his mind said, *"It's okay."* While it might have been the ravings of a broken mind, Goose knew better. It was her, whispering sweetly in his ear as she did sometimes. He was seeing her shape less often. That drove him to drink more than seeing it had, soon after he found out they had died. That Laura had come to him so clearly the night of the rainstorm when he brought these two home with him had been a comfort and perhaps a sign, yet so jarring when she'd left.

He led Toni out of the barn to a mounting block and helped the boy into the saddle, then adjusted the stirrups to the boy's legs, letting them out a notch or two; the boy had gangly legs, and both Laura and Elizabeth had been short.

"Now, boy, don't get your foot too deep in the stirrup like this." Goose pushed the boy's foot all the way in to the heel. "Only far enough that you can stand on the balls of your feet to take the pressure off your butt if you need to. If you were going to ride more, you should have cowboy boots so your feet can slide in and out easier, but I 'spose you're good for now."

Too nervous to speak, Brian only nodded. He had never ridden before other than behind his mom a couple of nights ago. His real dad would have never trusted him to ride a horse.

"This is how you hold your reins." Goose showed him how to take them over his middle two fingers with a thumb on top. "Try to keep your hands even with the front of the saddle. Don't let the reins get too loose or you'll lose control. Too tight and you'll hurt the horse's mouth. Pull the right rein to go right, left for left, and pull both back to stop. If you have to stop, say *whoa* loud enough for the horse to hear you. If you want to make the horse go faster, make a kissy sound. You got all that?"

"Yes," the boy squeaked.

"One more thing. When we go up a hill, lean forward. When we go downhill, lean back. If she skips or stumbles and you feel like you're losing your balance, put more weight on the balls of your feet. Okay?"

"Yes, sir."

Turning to get Copper, Goose saw Kelly watching him quizzically. "Did you get all that?"

"Yes," she answered softly.

In a moment, he had Copper by the mounting block and Kelly
in the saddle. For a second he felt a rush of embarrassment
looking at Kelly's leg as he adjusted the stirrup. "Do you need me
to go through all the instructions with you like I did for your
son?"

"No, I think I have it."

"Okay, let's go. We're burning daylight."

They rode up the long driveway, only stopping for Goose to
shut and lock the heavy iron double gates. Even that threatened
to let his mind slip into that other place again. Laura had picked
out the design for the gates with the large fleur-de-lis in the
middle.

Jessie and Jake had followed them excitedly up the drive,
bouncing and hoping to go on this trip. As if sensing Goose's
mood Jessie pawed his thigh and licked his fingertips to get his
attention while he was locking the gate. He knelt to rub her snout,
and Jake bulldozed his way in for his share of the attention.
Standing with a groan to old aches and pains, Goose spoke to the
dogs. "You two stay here and guard things."

As if they understood English as well as any human, their
postures slumped, and they sat on the driveway just behind the
gate. Goose mounted and led his three-horse procession to the left
on Le Cheval Parkway.

Most of the route to Mac's place would keep them inside the
Le Cheval community. The community covered nearly a hundred
square miles and would take half a day to cross. Le Cheval only
had four ways in and out, all blockaded and guarded. Still, the
community was too large to keep all the two-legged varmints out.
It was early on while Goose was in Lexington and after several
raids that many of the homeowners had moved to the huge show

facility and transformed it into a kind of indoor town and market.

For protection, the community had a group of young guns on horseback that did their best to patrol and keep crime down. Like most people, they mostly steered clear of Goose. The governor had asked him to recruit more men for his Rangers, but the kids in the community patrol were young, naïve, and wet behind the ears.

When and if he chose to recruit someone to this elite band of crime fighters, they would have to be every bit as mean and ruthless as him yet be able to cling to a moral high ground whether people recognized it or not. That was a rare mixture.

The horses were shod thanks to a blacksmith at the community. Goose wasn't good at it and didn't like it but carried clippers, a file, and hammer in his pack just in case. When the horses drifted onto the road from the grassy shoulder from time to time, the clip-clop gait of a walking horse provided a relaxing and peaceful metronome sound, allowing Goose's mind to drift...

"Gus, I need to speak to you in my office."

"Sure, what's up?" Gus walked into the glass office on the fifteenth floor of the office tower in downtown Louisville overlooking the river.

"There will be a meeting at the end of the day announcing layoffs. I need you to keep this under your hat until then. I called you in to tell you that you won't be included, but don't tell anyone. However, the few people kept on will work from home indefinitely."

Things had been rough since the economic crisis hit. It hadn't been something that came on like the crash of the early 1900s. It had resulted from years of social unrest, bad economic policies, and voters who elected people to give them everything for free and tell them nice things, not do good for the country. The concept of working hard and sacrificing comfort now for something better in the future had died in America. On top of all that, some of the international bad actors, emboldened by the internal strife, had upped their efforts to take out bridges, dams, and power plants. They weren't terribly successful, but it was one more straw on the back of the camel. A once great nation and world power was crumbling from within just as Rome had centuries before.

Gus had been one of the smart ones. Early on he recognized the signs of decay and rot in the country and moved an hour's drive outside the city. It was a dream home for him, Laura, and Elizabeth. A beautiful modern home on a small horse farm with all the conveniences. The fact that it had thick walls, an alternative power source, and no close neighbors was an added benefit that Gus valued when others hadn't yet. All he had to do was add the heavy iron gate and a well with a solar-powered pump.

"So, when do you want me to start working from home?"

"Monday is fine. You'll need to get your stuff together and make sure your remote connectivity is sufficient."

"Sure, boss. Is there any way I can get out of this meeting? Sounds like it's going to be brutal."

"I was told not to tell anyone. If you're not there, it will be obvious. Why don't you stay in the back so you can slip out as soon as possible?"

"Sure."

"By the way, how is your family?"

"Laura is great, putting in a lot of hours at the hospital. At least that's a job that may be safe if the economy continues to crumble. Because she is in administration, they are making plans for her to work from home too. Elizabeth is great. She just got accepted into law school at the University of Kentucky, so she's super stoked."

"That must be hard on you."

"Yeah, it's always hard letting them leave the nest, especially in these times. I worry about her a lot. I haven't said much to Laura and don't want to rain on Elizabeth's excitement, but I have a bad feeling about all this."

"Maybe you're letting all the prepper conspiracy theories get to you. I understand the campuses have ample protection. We just can't pull an entire generation of kids out of school. It wouldn't be fair to the kids, and we would lose a whole generation of people."

Gus lowered his head and ran both hands through his hair, mostly to give him time to gather his thoughts. Sometimes he regretted sharing his prepper side. Even though more and more people had begun to see the need these days, millions of Americans thought prepping was silly and that somehow, someway the government would get everything sorted out and continue to take care of them. It colored a lot of the conversations and made people look at him in a different light.

It hadn't taken long for the economy to go from bad to worse. Gus and Laura still had their jobs, but the money they earned purchased less and less each week. The social justice riots were continuing, but at least there was a bright side. The federal government kept issuing stimulus packages and free money, which pacified the protesters to some degree. The checks had a secondary effect of making money worth less each week. However, they also included loan modifications and payment forgiveness programs, which allowed most people to stay in their homes and not make payments.

Eventually most of the banks went bankrupt. The government didn't have the resources to repossess the homes and no one to sell them to if they did. Millions of Americans all over the country were effectively squatters. A water or electric payment might cost most people several months' wages, in the few locations where the service was still running. Without the funds to perform the costly perpetual maintenance, the utility infrastructure was slowly crumbling from within. With the cost of a gallon of gas or loaf of bread at close to sixty dollars and rising, it made most jobs not worth the effort of getting there.

Early on, Gus had taken a calculated risk. He took out a loan against his 401k retirement program to pay off his bills and stock up on supplies and backup equipment for the solar panels and water pump. Had he been convinced things would go this bad, he would have cashed out his savings completely and paid off the house and bought even more. In the end, it didn't matter. The banks that owned his loans closed, were looted, and burned down. The roads and bridges were crumbling, and working power plants and utilities were a distant memory or a fanciful rumor somewhere else.

Then, as fast as the riots had sprung up, creating a frenzy of panic and violence, it all just stopped. At some point along the way, the protesters realized hardly anyone had working electricity, meaning no internet or television to view their antics. They were hungry too. All the free government money wasn't buying them anything, and there was no one left to oppose them or care about the destruction they inflicted anymore. The people had fled the major cities in droves. Most police forces and a good portion of the military had simply gone home to take care of their families. The rioters were burning buildings with no opposition or audience. It took them a while, but in due course they discovered the futility of their actions and went home to beg, borrow, and steal in order to eat.

As a famous author once predicted, *"When the people can't take from their neighbors via taxation or politically driven fees, and they can't borrow against credit or their grandchildren's future to fund social programs today, and they're forced to live within their means, and by the fruit of their own labors for that day or week, that's when they all become conservatives."*

That pivotal point in American history passed in a blur for Gus. Early on, the cities and universities had been relatively safe. Elizabeth desperately wanted to complete her degree. She couldn't contemplate living in a world where education wouldn't matter. Truthfully, Gus and Laura couldn't bear thinking of her needing to endure a world like that, either.

Laura had gone to stay with Elizabeth for a few weeks while Gus continued to work and protect their home and supplies. The girls fortified themselves in the high-rise apartment near campus. The few classes that required in-person attendance sent a bus with an armed escort to pick up students. Everything should have been fine. But it wasn't.

By the time Gus got word of the escalating riots and burning in Lexington and a full capitulation of the city government and police, it was too late. Roads were blocked, bridges were down, and there were mobs and gunfights. Gus frantically tried to get there in his truck. He detoured around downed power poles and bridges several times in the first ten miles until being forced to walk if he wanted to continue forward. Raging against the lost time, he turned back to get the horses.

Days later, Gus entered the city leading Copper and Toni behind the spotted horse, desperately hoping to lead his girls home astride their own horses. It was late in the day when he tied the horses in a patch of trees beside the dumpster and entered the mostly burned-out building. Gus took the stairs two at a time and found the eighth-floor condo bullet riddled and smoke damaged. Someone had put up a fight. He nodded in satisfaction, knowing how tough his little girl was. In a growing rage, he searched the building from top to bottom. He discovered a few elderly women hiding and eking out a subsistence.

Gus terrified them. In truth, that was probably the day Gus

ceased to exist, and he reverted to his old childhood nickname. *Gus* had been a white-collar worker, part-time prepper, and a husband and father. *Goose* was nothing but plumb mad through and not quite right in the head. He calmed himself enough that one woman pointed him to two graves out in front of the building. She said that she and a couple of others had buried the adult woman and college girl from the eighth floor themselves.

Something inside Goose broke at that instant. He collapsed and sobbed like a child on the mound of dirt beside a burned-out condo building.

Time lost meaning as he lay there. He couldn't leave his girls buried here outside a condo in Lexington. Another part of him couldn't handle exhuming their bodies. As he raved, his memories became disjoined between remembering them as they'd been, envisioning how the final fight had gone, and their bullet-riddled bodies. He preferred to think they'd died in the gunfight and were not taken alive.

At one point, he resolved to excavate them to take home to the farm and began digging. One of the older women touched his arm and said kindly, "They're not really there anymore."

Goose pulled his arm away and dropped the board he'd been digging with and fell to the ground, bereft.

The roar of a couple dozen Harleys could be heard for a mile before they got to the country trailer park community. A single vehicle running on gas marked someone as wealthy these days. Two dozen Harleys marked the gang as rich to the level of the pre-collapse cartel gangs. The gang had come south on I-71 to the Pendleton exit for the short ride to the spread-out country trailer park.

When they roared into the trailer park, no one was in sight.

Some had hidden in their trailers, though most ran to the woods nearby. A pink child's bike lay on its side, the wheel spinning as if abandoned only seconds before. The bikers parked in front of Steve and Kelly's burned-out trailer.

Crazy Joe stepped out in front of the others fuming, his posture tight as a piano wire. "Slick!" he yelled.

"Yeah, boss," Slick replied, moving past the others, trying not to show panic.

"Am I at the right trailer?"

"Yes."

"All my shit burned up in that trailer?"

Slick shrugged in a desultory fashion. "I reckon so, if it was in there. More likely someone stole it and burned the trailer after."

"Where's Paul and Chad?"

"Beats me, boss. I s'pose they might have stolen it and run off. That doesn't make sense, though. They were our brothers and loved the power of being in the gang."

Crazy Joe side-eyed Slick for a moment. Sometimes the man was too smug. He was loyal, though, and did good work. "Van, get me a chair!" he yelled. When no one moved, Crazy Joe let out a loud laugh. That was when he was at his most dangerous. "I mean you, one ear! I'm going to call you Van from now on, for Van Gogh. That good with you?"

"Yeah, boss. Perfect." He rushed up to Crazy Joe.

There was a pause as if the one-eared man was waiting for another command.

"The chair," Crazy Joe prompted, and the one-eared man rushed off to scavenge one from a nearby trailer. "I want witnesses, and don't keep me waiting!" Crazy Joe bellowed to the group.

CONSEQUENCES

It must have been hours later when something brought Goose to his senses. He was out of tears. They'd been replaced with an icy rage filling the place in his heart where love once dwelt.

Pushing himself to a kneeling position, he noticed the sky was darker and people were watching from the street. One man pointed to his horses tied among the trees nearby. Gus sat back on his rear end, arms around his knees. Why fight it? The world had gone to Hell. He'd lost all that mattered to him. There was no prize for fighting and surviving, nothing but pain and loneliness. It might be better to just let them kill him and take his belongings. His blood would sink into the dirt here with his family.

Yet that wasn't how he was wired.

He rose to his feet with a primal scream, half anguish, and half rage. The shout wasn't at the bad guys so much as at himself. Why couldn't he just give in?

One of the men was reaching for the big spotted horse, breaking the final strand of restraint in Gus. "Get away from my horse!" he bellowed, getting to his feet.

The man was unkempt and raggedy looking but had an air of

confidence. "What are you gonna do, crybaby?" His friends howled with laughter from a hundred yards away.

The two men advanced on each other shouting insults as men might have in a road rage incident a year earlier.

"This is our building; this entire area is ours." The raggedy man swept his arm around. "Anyone that can't accept that gets buried." He pointed to the graves.

Gus quickened his pace and in a single swift motion pulled the stiletto fighting knife. The man was in mid-rant when Gus drove the knife through the base of the man's throat up into his brain, killing both the outlaw and Gus the business and family man all in one fell swoop. There was a look of surprise on the dead man's face as Goose shoved him backward by the forehead.

It didn't take his buddies long to unlimber their guns and start peppering Goose with shots. Goose grabbed his Winchester FX-AR, running crouched from cover to cover to present less of a target and draw the fire away from his horses. He was in a killing rage. A few moments before he was a grieving father and husband, and now he had a direction for his rage. When he let the big .308 talk, it drowned out the 9mm and higher pitched .223 rounds the heathens were using. Goose hit one in the chest, knocking him backward, and another in the thigh, leaving him down with blood spurting high enough to indicate Goose had hit something critical.

The others beat a hasty retreat. In another situation, it would have been comical to see men who fancied themselves tough killers who controlled a portion of the city get on their bicycles and peddle away. Goose didn't hesitate. He slung his rifle and grabbed a dirt bike lying next to the man he'd just killed and peddled after them as fast as his legs could work. A few times they turned to loose a random shot at Goose. He didn't bother to return fire. The distance was too long for more than a lucky shot, and shooting off a moving bicycle made that lucky shot even more difficult.

The bicycle chase lasted for blocks, passing through alleys and side streets, speeding up when rounding corners. Goose stuck with them. While they were tiring, he was running on rage and pure adrenaline. Finally, they dropped their bikes in the front yard of a brick two-story home built-in the fifties, with a covered front porch that ran the width of the home. Goose was only seconds behind, pulling and firing the Springfield .45 as he dropped the bike. He caught the last man as he mounted the porch with a shot between the shoulder blades, throwing him forward like a bully shoving a little kid in the back. His momentum made his face slap the doorjamb before his body disappeared through. His feet twitched twice and went still.

Shots rang out from the house. It sounded like five or ten people firing at Goose. He took cover behind a huge old oak. It wouldn't be hard for them to send someone out to circle behind him. It was almost full dark, though, and Goose was willing to bet he'd see them before they saw him. He had nothing to lose and no intention of staying behind the tree. When the shots died off for a few seconds and the defenders began yelling insults, Goose took a chance to move from the tree to a rusted old muscle car on cinderblocks in the driveway.

He expected gunshots to follow, but nothing happened. That gave him an idea. There had to be a side or back door. These guys weren't professionals. Goose was confident that if they guarded the back entry, it would only be by a single person whose attention would be on the front. He heard the bangers inside the house bickering. They were foolish enough to use candles or camping lanterns to see their way around the house. Luckily, not enough light to damage Goose's night vision. His rage had changed from a white-hot thing that clouded his vision to a cold, hard thing like a frozen snowball in the pit of his stomach. These guys needed to die. Before they did, he wanted to know what they meant when one of them said, *"This is our building. This entire area is ours. Anyone that can't accept that gets buried."*

Goose moved from the old car to the side of the house. No shots followed. He crept around the corner of the house to an old wooden screen door at the top of three concrete steps. The wooden door behind the screen door stood open. The shadow of a man stood in the screen door appearing like nothing more than a large void behind the door slightly darker than his surroundings. Goose might not have noticed if not for the cherry ember that alternately got brighter when he took a drag that gave him away.

While Goose paused to decide his next move, the arguing at the front of the house got louder. Heavy steps retreated from the back door, indicating the man was gone. Goose unslung and rested the .308 against the house and checked his spare mags for the .45. He had a smaller Walther CCP as his backup gun in an Australian chest rig. The confines of the house would be too tight for the long gun. The screen door screeched as he entered, but no one seemed to notice. He was in the kitchen and could just make out the men in the front room. The house stank of old food, weed, and unwashed men. Goose bumped something and a dish fell. There was barely a second's pause of surprise before they went for their guns. Goose was ready and opened up with the .45, dropping two of the killers in the first salvo. The fiery breath of lead passed his ear, a ghostly whisper of death dodged for the moment. His senses dulled, and everything slowed down like an old film noir silent movie running in slow motion. In that moment, Goose didn't care. Death would be a release, as long as he slid into Hell on the blood of his enemies.

Although outnumbered, that attitude gave him an advantage. They expected him to take cover and return fire. He changed magazines and ran through the door to the great room, .45 blazing. In seconds, they were all down, some crying for the mothers. That was good. He had questions for them.

Without warning, Goose was driven to his knees with a punch to the ribs. He lost his breath and pitched forward, losing the .45. Two women came running down the hallway screaming like banshees. One held a handgun, blazing away, hitting her own guys as much as anything else. Her partner held a large butcher knife over her head, ready to drive it into Goose's chest. He rolled over, pulling his backup gun, a Walther 9mm CCP, from his chest rig, firing as fast as he could pull the trigger, hitting first one, then the other woman center mass. The one with the knife fell on top of Goose, her knife sticking in the floor beside his head, her lifeblood spilling on to his chest.

He shoved her off, retrieved his .45, and checked on the would-be killers. One was alive, screaming that he couldn't feel his legs. Goose knelt beside him, putting the point of the stiletto below the man's eye. "Brother, you don't know me, but I'm mad clean through. I have a few questions, then I'm burning this house down. The way you answer determines whether I pull your carcass out before I set it on fire or not. Do you understand?"

"Yeah, man. Anything."

"People very dear to me lived in that high-rise condo building a few blocks away. One of your guys said it was your building, that you guys control the entire area, and that anyone who couldn't accept that would get buried. What exactly does that mean?"

"Nothing, man, we're just trying to survive here. This is all just a mix-up."

Goose pressed the stiletto forward, puncturing the man's eyeball with little emotion. The thug shrieked an unearthly howl. Goose got up and scavenged the dead men for ammo calibers he needed. He also added several bottles of top-shelf Kentucky bourbon to his pack. He felt the need for a good drunk like he hadn't done in many years.

Soon the man's screeches turned into sobs. Goose once again knelt beside the gangster with his knife poised below the remaining eye. "I don't think I made myself clear the last time we spoke. My wife and daughter were in that building."

"I… I didn't…" he began, an anguished cry overriding the sobbing.

"Do you think you can be more helpful this time?"

He nodded through sobs that didn't stop, his ruined eye bleeding down his cheek.

"Now tell me everything about that high-rise condo building."

"I don't know anyth—"

Goose added pressure to the knife.

"Wait! I meant I don't know much. I'm telling you everything. It was mostly old people that lived there. The guys thought they'd have lots of drugs. It's in our territory, so we figured they owed us. I wasn't part of it, but they said it was all good 'till some women in one of the higher floors put up a fight. They took out three of our men before we killed them. I swear it wasn't me. I wouldn't have done it. One of them was real pretty. I even heard the old ladies buried them all proper like, said words over 'em and everything. We didn't stop them or mess with the graves or nothing, man. I swear."

"Uh huh." Goose's voice was flat and distant. That was the first time Laura came to him. She was a younger version of herself. He saw her lips moving, but he didn't listen because he didn't think she was real at first. Seconds later, he dismissed her image, his rage rekindling to a white-hot stage after seeing his wife. He glared down and sliced the one-eyed man's throat. Seeing surprise and betrayal on the dead man's face, he said, "Sorry, I lied."

Goose got up, found some cheap vodka, and broke the bottle

in the living room. After that he took a Zippo lighter off the dead man and set the home on fire. Stepping outside, he retrieved the bike and pedaled toward the condo building, already hitting the first bottle of bourbon, the house fully engulfed behind him.

"Mr. Goose. Mr. Goose."

Shaking himself from his reverie, Goose barked, "What?"

"Where do we go from here? We've been stopped at this crossroad for ten minutes."

Goose looked up, noticing the woman sitting atop Copper as if for the first time. She was very attractive with long legs and curves in all the right places. The kind of shape that would cause young men to act silly and old men to weep in remembrance of better days. Tattoos crept out of her shirt both at the cleavage and forearm, yet she didn't seem like a hipster. A boy of about twelve sat on Toni behind her.

Toni! What was he doing riding Toni?! That horse belonged to his daughter Elizabeth. Then it all came rushing back. His shoulders stooped, the weight of reality settling in.

"Left," he said. "This is Highway 42." Goose clucked his tongue, urging the spotted horse forward, and the others followed.

The sounds of mayhem came floating over to Crazy Joe. His people were rounding up nearby residents, despite their attempts to hide. He smiled. The weather was becoming hot and muggy, though it was late enough in the day that a breeze flowed through, taking out some of the closeness.

The first witnesses brought forward were an elderly couple from near the front of the trailer park. The man was bruised and

bleeding, the woman crying. She reminded him of his grand-
mother. While some might have thought that sentiment would
stay his hand, they would have been wrong. Sentiment and
emotions made Crazy Joe feel pathetic. He hated weakness. It
made him angry.

"Stop crying, woman!" he roared. Turning to her husband, he
said, "Did you know these people?" He hooked a thumb over his
shoulder to the burned-out trailer.

The older man looked defiant, as if he might argue. He saw
the amusement on Crazy Joe's face and something in him broke.
"Not hardly. The man was a scumbag. His wife and son seemed
all right, though."

Crazy Joe raised an eyebrow and turned to one of his lieutenants. "A wife and son? Why wasn't I told of this?"

"Boss, we didn't think it mattered. The wife was the looker we
mentioned, and we didn't think the son mattered. We weren't
trying to hide nothing, I swear."

Under his breath Crazy Joe muttered, "Idiots." Then he
turned back to the old man. "What happened here?"

"I can't be sure," the old man replied. Something had broken in
him, and there was no use keeping any secrets. Resigned to his
fate, he explained, "We're kind of used to hiding when we hear the
motorcycles. That's what happened the day before yesterday. Most
people go hide in the woods. We're too old for that nonsense. We
lock the doors, draw the shades, and hide in the bedroom."

"Don't you worry someone will come kick in your door?"

"That's possible, but the yard is full of weeds and we're poor,
so there wouldn't be much in it for them if they did."

"What happened after the motorcycles got here?"

"I can't say for sure. There were a lot of gunshots. An hour or
two later we saw flames rising in the air from the trailer."

"You didn't get curious and go look?"

"No, sir. It was about dusk, and a thunderstorm was rolling in. Besides, we didn't know who was still there."

Crazy Joe made a dismissive gesture with his hand, and the relief on the older couple's faces was stark. Then in an afterthought he said, "Wait. What about all the stuff this guy had?" Crazy Joe pointed to the trailer. "It would have taken a couple of truckloads to move it or the men on motorcycles a dozen trips or more."

The old man appeared confused. "The bikes are mixed in with the rubble of the trailer there." He pointed. "We didn't see no other trucks or nothing."

Crazy Joe looked where the old man indicated, spotting a piece of a Harley frame sticking out from the smoldering ruins of the trailer that had slumped over on top of the bikes. "No vehicles..." he mused to himself.

"Well..." the old man started to say then hesitated.

"Spit it out, old man," Crazy Joe snapped.

"It was getting dark, and the rain was picking up. My wife thinks she saw something."

"Talk, old man!"

"She thinks she saw an old-fashioned lawman on horseback leading two other horses."

"A lawman? How could she possibly know that?"

"He was dressed like a cowboy with a long slicker. When lightning struck, she swears she saw a gold star pinned to his chest. She reads old cowboy books."

Crazy Joe shifted to stare at the old woman as a hawk might a mouse.

Either in discomfort or to prove she hadn't lost her mind, the old woman added, "A woman and a boy were walking behind him."

That got Crazy Joe's attention. He waved them off, then said to his men, "Question the rest. Find out if anyone else knows anything."

Crazy Joe leaned back, deep in thought. The questioning didn't go easy on many of the residents. He didn't care. This wasn't a turf war or another gang; it was something else altogether.

One of his lieutenants interrupted his musings. "Boss, Van thinks he has something for you. He has a teenage boy."

Crazy Joe gave a sardonic smile. That little man was trying like hell to get back in his good graces. "What've you got, Van?"

"Found this little bastard hiding in the woods. He ran like hell, but I caught him." The other bikers laughed. "He was friends with the boy who lived here. He didn't see it all, but he saw some of it."

"See, gentlemen? This is what I'm talking about. With the right amount of motivation, Mister Van Gogh has turned into a right useful member of the team. Something y'all might keep in mind when you're working for me. Better yet, something *I'll* keep in mind." Van's chest pumped out with pride. Crazy Joe turned to the teenager. "Boy, is this true? You saw what happened here?"

The young man looked like a caged animal, scared witless and searching for a way out. He stammered but made no sense.

"Boy!" Crazy Joe yelled in a drill sergeant's voice. It had the effect he wanted. All eyes were on the leader, and it became quiet enough to hear the breeze blow across the trailers. There was a flapping sound of laundry on a clothesline and a few snaps and pops from hot spots in the burned-out trailer. "Go slow and start from the beginning. Don't worry about making me mad or saying nothing bad about my men. I reckon they're dead now and I'm already pissed off at them."

The boy gulped, steeled himself, and said, "The men on motorcycles came the day before yesterday, and me and Brian hid to watch."

"Watch what?"

"Well…stuff…" The boy glanced over at his parents.

"Look at me, boy! I can promise you, pissing me off will hurt a lot worse than anything your mom or dad might do." His mother keened in fear.

"The other boys said that sometimes they make the girls take off their shirts and stuff. I didn't mean to do nothing wrong, I promise!"

Crazy Joe side-eyed one of his men, who got nervous and said, "Boss, they know they're not supposed to mess with any of the girls here. Sometimes Steve takes one in on trade. Everyone knows they're supposed to come back to our place for you to meet first. That's the rule!"

"We'll talk about this later." He turned back to the boy. "Okay. Go on. What happened next?"

"Brian's mom came and got him and took him deeper in the woods to hide. She always did that when the motorcycles came. I think they had a girl in there, 'cause I heard her screaming after Brian and his mom left. I couldn't see nuthin', though. Pretty soon, this guy comes out of the woods dressed like an army guy. I thought I was hid really good, but he just looked over at me and put his finger to his lips to be quiet. I don't know what happened after that, but right after there was a lot of noise in the trailer, then he went in and there was a lot of shooting.

"After that, Brian and his mom came back. Brian stayed in the woods, but I was too afraid to move. His mom went in the trailer and started crying so loud I could hear it. The man left. When he came back, he was dressed like a cowboy with a hat and boots and all. He had three horses."

"Was he wearing a badge?"

"Yeah, a gold star. Just like a cowboy."

"Then what happened?"

"They loaded up the horses with things from the trailer and left."

"What about Brian and his mom?"

"I was afraid to say anything to them. It started raining anyways and I had to get home, but they followed behind him. He rode off on horseback, and they walked behind him."

"They didn't ride, and they weren't tied?"

The boy shrugged, raising his shoulders in a gesture that was universal among preteens.

"Van, give him some kind of prize for his help. The rest of you men spread out. I want to get word to all our contacts. Find out who this cowboy is. We meet tomorrow at noon back at the old schoolhouse. I expect some answers by then!"

COMRADES

THIRTY MINUTES LATER, they turned off the highway to a side road. The street sign still stood, reading McIntosh Lane. A hundred years ago, the entire area had been one big farm owned by the patriarch of the McIntosh family. Today they owned more than half of that original spread, but it was divided up among a dozen descendants. Goose headed to Mac's place, a small ranch-style home about an hour's ride down the lane on the right.

The barriers on McIntosh Lane were mostly to stop cars and trucks. They didn't guard them and didn't really have to. The McIntoshes were very clannish and had a virtual army of nieces, nephews, cousins, friends, and other relatives roaming the area. They hunted, farmed, made moonshine, and were generally a tough bunch to tangle with. You couldn't just fight one, and everyone around these parts knew it. If one of them hadn't seen Goose and the others start down their lane, they would before long and spread the word.

The SAT phone in his pommel bag beeped again. It had been doing that for the last couple of days. It was someone from the governor's office, if not him personally. No one else he knew had a working phone. They wanted to find out if he'd died or gotten back on the trail of the gang terrorizing the area. He'd call them in the morning, when he was back after them. The rage and vengeance he'd felt when he first started out had faded. Now it was a job, one that needed doing, and he was damn good at it.

The woman riding behind him made a clucking sound like he had earlier, urging her horse up close to Goose. "I hear music," she said with a perplexed expression.

"That'd be Mac. He was in a well-known bluegrass band before. Most of the guys in his band live close. They get together and play from time to time."

"I thought you said he was a farmer."

"He is. And a damn good moonshiner too." Goose's chuckle sounding more like rocks rubbing together.

Kelly looked at him quizzically for a moment before allowing her horse to drift back beside her son.

A few minutes later, they came up to Mac's home. There were several horses tied up to the small barn beside the house. Goose got Kelly's attention and pointed to an old-fashioned horse and buggy belonging to the McIntosh family matriarch. Beyond the buggy were a couple of trucks that Goose recognized. One belonged to his old riding buddy Larry Curry, who lived forty-five minutes away by truck or a long day's ride by horse.

Finding an open spot at the other side of the barn, he dismounted and untied a lead line from behind the saddle and tied it from the halter under the bridle to the barn, long enough to give some slack, but not so much that the horse could get his hooves tangled in it. Turning to the woman and boy, he realized they didn't know what to do. He repeated the process for them while they were still mounted. The boy squirmed off Toni in a second, smiling a toothy grin with a few tuffs of hair going in different directions, proud of himself. His mom struggled and almost fell before Goose put his hand on her back to steady her. A shock ran through him like an ice-cold bucket of water to the face. Other than fighting and killing, he hadn't touched a single person in two years, much less a pretty woman. He snatched his hand away like he'd touched a hot stove and averted his gaze. Apparently sensing his feelings, Kelly gave him space.

"Gus!" Larry boomed as a group of men rounded the barn. "We didn't think you'd come!"

The confusion on Goose's face must have given him away to Mac. "You didn't come for the pig roast?"

"Well, I…"

"Don't worry about it. You're here now," Larry boomed, giving him a hug. That was the second time someone had touched him lately. It was making him claustrophobic.

Kelly was surprised to see a different side of Goose. Everyone at Le Cheval was afraid of him as the big, mean killer who hung bodies on his fence, but these people appeared to love him like family.

In the short time she'd been around him, she knew him as a mean man, a killer, and a drunk who was most probably at least partially insane. Yet at this moment, he was deferential to the lanky older farmer who was a little gray around the edges. Many of the other guests, including children and matronly women, made their way over to offer him a hug, condolences, or well wishes. It was apparent they had a lot of love for the man who was so damaged.

"And who are these folks you brought with you?" Larry said in a welcoming way. In truth, Larry never met a stranger.

"This is uh…uh…" Goose turned to her somewhat apologetically.

"My name is Kelly Connor, and this is my son Brian. Mr. Goose rescued us when he was fighting a gang of outlaws. My husband was killed in the fighting," Kelly made sure to mention in an attempt at avoiding any assumption of impropriety.

Mac clearly caught on. "Goose, uh… we uh…it's not that we don't want… what I mean to say is we just don't have much space. We had some more family straggle in."

"Don't worry about it, Mac. We're just nosing around. I need to pick up some more of that good apple pie moonshine anyway," Goose said, sounding more like his usual gruff self.

Larry stepped in to avoid any awkward silence. "It's a pleasure to meet you, Mrs. Kelly. I'm Larry Curry. I have a place over toward Simpsonville. That old reprobate there is Bruce Ellis, and that's Roger Travis." He pointed to a tough, grizzled man beside Bruce. "And the mountain of a man behind him is Paul David Heightchew. Everyone just calls him PD. Normally Tony Sanford would be with us, but he volunteered to stay back at my place looking after the cattle along with Roger's friend Lance."

Before Kelly had time to do more than nod, Mac said, "We need to get back to the party. It's PD's turn to rotate the pig, and I'm supposed to be playing again in a minute."

As they walked around the barn, Larry stepped up alongside Kelly. "Well, little lady. I'll introduce you to my wife and she can show you around and you can meet the other women."

Goose caught up and asked, "Larry, did you drive over here? That must have cost you hundreds in gas."

"Yeah, but this is worth it, and I hoped you might turn up. Besides, I'm flush. They're paying top dollar for cattle. One of the government-protected trading posts is at the Sam's Club about a forty-five-minute drive from me. I've made a deal to get the protected convoys to stop at the Simpsonville exit on the expressway near my place once a month. Sometimes we trade for goods, sugar, or whatever. Other times they fill my farm tanks with fuel. That means they get beef and corn for hungry people and I get what I need to run my tractor and raise that beef, corn, and other stuff. Gus, you're looking at a rich man," Larry joked.

"Probably the only one left in this whole part of the country,"

Goose said mostly to himself. "What made you think I'd be here? I didn't even know I'd be here or that there was a party going on."

"Mac said he sent someone to drop a note at your house. I trust in the Lord's providence, and you should too. Besides, you're here, ain't you?"

"That Lord stuff was Laura's thing," Goose muttered.

"It used to be yours too," Larry slipped in before steering Kelly off toward a group of women. They didn't notice Brian standing a few feet behind Goose watching everything he did, trying to emulate his posture and movements.

Goose watched her go, then followed Mac and the others.

Roger Travis fell in alongside Goose. "How you been, boy?" he said in a gravelly voice that was hard to understand.

"Fair to middlin'," Goose replied in an attempt at levity.

"Hmppf." Roger looked at him from a face that could have belonged to a boxer, Harley rider, or a bank robber from the Old West. Few people knew he had a soft heart on the inside.

PD had already grabbed a couple of quart jars of apple pie moonshine from Mac's stock. They would settle up later. The farms in Mac's family grew plenty of corn for the moonshine and had a couple of orchards for the apples floating in the alcohol. It was the cinnamon sticks flavoring the drink that surprised Goose. Mac must have had quite a supply laid back.

PD was a mountain of a man with a jovial smile who had played sports at the collegiate level and could really put down the drink when the mood struck him. Goose was only mildly surprised when PD handed him a jar and asked how he was doing. Why did they keep looking at him like that?

Mac had plenty of lawn chairs and a stage built beside the roasting pit. They'd set up horseshoe pits too. The clang of iron on iron when a shoe connected with the stake brought back memories. Goose found a shady spot under a tree and sat on the ground.

Mac got on stage with the rest of the band and began tuning his instrument. He could pretty much play anything. Goose liked to see him with the banjo most, but he was tuning his old guitar, the odd sounds amplified through speakers powered by a generator set behind the barn to muffle the noise.

Mac stepped up to the microphone, and the crowd, who were mostly his family and neighbors, quieted. "Folks, we got a special guest here today. Most of y'all know KT." He motioned to Goose. Not many people were aware that Goose's parents had called him KT, for Kid Truman, as a nickname until his classmates gave him the Goose moniker a few years later. Hearing that old nickname brought up memories he'd rather leave buried deep. He took a long draw from the mason jar and held it up to Mac in salute.

"In honor of KT, we're gonna play one of his favorites," Mac said. "It's a song we did real well with a while back. We even got invited to play it in Ireland back when people could afford to fly in a plane. This is 'Old Dogs Never Die.'"

Goose leaned back against the tree, taking it all in. Many times, they'd gone places like Big South Fork, Tennessee, to ride, camp, and talk. Several of the guys were in a church group together and for them the rides were a religious retreat. All the men prayed before each meal and shared fellowship.

One song turned into two, three, then ten or more. Dusk settled in. The pig was done. The kids had enjoyed turning the spit; now the adults were slicing off chunks, served with the side dishes so many had brought to the potluck. Kelly was laughing and talking with the women, apologizing for not bringing a side. She started to say she would bring extra next time, then stopped, realizing there probably wouldn't be a next time.

Brian stayed close to Goose but didn't make a nuisance of himself. The men around him were his old riding buddies. Years fell away and Goose was back to who he'd once been. He laughed, talked, and told stories. He was getting drunk and appreciated the warm, happy, buzzed feelings and the inability to pull up certain memories. Somehow, this was a different type of drunk. It was happy and full of comradery, unlike the self-loathing, angry drinking he had done so much the last year or two.

The music, comradery, and drink loosened his tongue. Goose had been a talker once, and it came back naturally. Talking amongst his friends, he described how he'd met the governor, agreed to be a Ranger, and how the governor wanted him to recruit other men to help, admitting he had no plans to do it. This was his task. Capturing or killing took something out of a man down deep that he couldn't explain and wouldn't ask a friend to do or trust a stranger with.

Everything became blurry after that. He vaguely remembered Mac taking him in the house to a couple of pallets in the basement. Many of the visitors slept upstairs or in the barn.

"Boss, we didn't find out much. Nobody knows much about that cowboy."

"I should send you back out there. I doubt you did much more than ride around, get high, and hump women. Any of you got anything better than this?"

Another lieutenant stepped forward. "It ain't much, boss, but I found a few people who seen him. One said they had some neighbors who got their home broke into and the men killed. The attackers used the women hard, then killed them. 'Bout the time them ol' boys were loading up a cart with things they stole, a man dressed like a cowboy with a gold star on his shirt come riding in on a black and white horse, guns blazing. He shot two of them right off their feet and injured the third. He got off his saddle, kicked the injured man in the knee, and put a boot to his throat whilst asking a few questions, then shot him in the head. He told the neighbors the men had been doing that all over this part of the country. He told them he was sorry he didn't get there sooner, but he only got word from the governor's office the day before the men were headed their way. The cowboy told them they might as well take the guns and supplies and that he was authorized to pay them to bury the dead."

"Are you sure he said he was from the governor's office?" Crazy Joe rose from his throne-like chair and stepped closer to his lieutenant.

The lieutenant hesitated for a brief moment, losing some of his cocksure attitude, then swallowed hard. "Yes, sir. I'm sure that's what they said. I can go get them and bring them here to tell you."

Crazy Joe waved his hand for silence and began pacing. A heavy pause hung in the air like the moment before thunderclaps, lightning strikes, and a downpour comes. Caught in a conundrum and unsure what to do, he stalled for time.

"Anybody else have anything?"

The one-eared man who was rapidly turning into a trusted lieutenant spoke up. "Boss, it ain't much, but I got a crazy old man outside who claims to have seen him several times up at the four-way stop in Pendleton."

"What are you waiting for? Bring him in!"

"Boss, I ain't arguing. I'll bring him in, but I left him outside 'cause he's crazier than a junebug and stinks to high heaven."

Crazy Joe laughed. This was the pause he needed to consider how bad this was and if the governor really was involved. Van was turning out to be pretty damn good. Maybe he'd been too soft on the others.

Van led the way. Crazy Joe hadn't made it within six feet of the old man before the stench hit him like a wall of bricks and he stopped where he stood. The old man had a tangled mess of red and gray hair, his beard hanging halfway down his face. His crystal blue eyes darted around like an animal in a cage.

"This is Darryl," said Van. "He lives near the four-way stop in Pendleton."

"Where exactly is 'near?'"

"He just said the old skeeter hole."

From a distance, Crazy Joe turned his attention to Darryl. "Old man, I've been around this area off and on for at least twenty years. I never heard of no skeeter hole."

"It's right there, ya idjit. It's the old drive-in movie theater."

"Get him out here before I shoot him," Crazy Joe ordered. "He's addled and can't help us."

"That's the problem with you youngsters! Y'all think everything begins and ends with you. Skeeter hole's been closed for most of your life. It's right there behind where the liquor store used to be. The old concession stand by the pond that plagued all the moviegoers with skeeters is still there, just covered in weeds. Makes a right nice place to lay down. Then I'm only a short walk from the truck stop when the convoys stop."

Van leaned in. "I know the liquor store he's talking about, but all my life there's been nothing but an overgrown field behind it."

"All right, old man, tell me 'bout this cowboy you say you seen."

"The Ranger. That's what the convoys call him."

"What are the convoys doing stopping here? They aren't supposed to stop until they get to the Costco by the hospital closer to Louisville."

Darryl shrugged. "I think he calls them."

"That's bullshit. No one can redirect the route of a government convoy."

The old man shrugged. "Maybe the governor can."

Crazy Joe began pacing again, then stopped after a moment.

"Jorge, this is your area. How is I-71 between Pendleton and Louisville?"

"Much like the rest. Potholes and weeds growing up. Two years of freezing and thawing and no maintenance hasn't been kind to it."

"There wasn't much maintenance for ten years before. Are there any bridges or overpasses down in that stretch forcing convoys to get off the interstate and back on?"

"No, but just past the Crestwood exit there's been a rockslide on the incline. It looks like some previous convoy moved some rocks, but it's still one lane and a slow go uphill."

"Hmmm. Maybe…"

"Boss, no one's ever hit a government convoy. They got the Army and automatic weapons." The gang glanced around at each other nervously.

"No one's ever hit a convoy *yet*. The troops aren't regular Army. They're only National Guard. Yes, they have automatic weapons, and I want them. They're lazy and so sure they'll never be attacked their guard is down. That Ranger and those convoys are getting too cocky in our territory."

"It could work," Jorge drawled. "If we put people in the rocks aiming down at the road from both sides, we would have them in a helluva crossfire. We could roll some big rocks in front of them last second so they would have to stop. If we find a way to block them in from behind too, they might surrender. We could take the people, trucks, *and* supplies."

"Perfect!" Beaming, Crazy Joe slapped him on the back. "Put a man watching that truck stop. Find out when a convoy is coming through. I want the rest of you scouring the farms near the Crestwood exit for any bulldozers or tractors you can get running. Take our truck, a few spare batteries, and some fuel. I want at least four working dozers or tractors. Two for up top to push boulders into the road in front of the convoy and two to block them in from behind."

"Boss, I gotta say it's perfect. Even if they fight back, they can't hold out for long. No one will come to their aid. I'm sure they'll surrender."

Facts dawned on Kirk, one of the newer lieutenants. "Boss, what are we going to do with a bunch of Army guys as prisoners?" Several of the others edged away from him as he spoke, wanting to avoid Crazy Joe's wrath.

With a steely eyed gaze, Crazy Joe said, "We don't take prisoners. Normally."

The rough men of the gang cheered until Crazy Joe raised his arms and laughed. "Although, if I find me a cute little number, I just might keep her for myself! That and a few worker bees to clean up after you slobs."

SPIRITS

MORNING CAME TOO SOON, with rays of sunlight striking Goose in the face from the small window high on the basement wall. He glanced over to see the boy and his mom sleeping on another pallet nearby. A part of him registered that he no longer got as hungover as he once had. It was just a general crusty feeling like most people experienced when they got sleep in the corner of their eyes, only Goose felt it all over and seeping into his bones. He needed a shower.

Not liking goodbyes and anticipating the apologetic expression when Mac would try to stretch things thin to make a place for Kelly and Brian, Goose decided to leave early. All this normalness was awakening feelings of things he'd lost. He began slipping into a dark killing mood, and that was a good time to get back on the trail of the bad guys. He turned to wake the woman and paused with an intake of breath.

Laura was lying there as plain as day. Not the faded version he'd been talking to lately, this was *really* her, Elizabeth right beside her. Elizabeth appeared younger, but it was her. They weren't buried beside a building in Lexington. They'd been here at Mac's place the whole time waiting for him to come get them! Not able to bear waking them, he fell to his knees weeping unashamedly. They were alive and here! Nothing else mattered.

Something in Goose's movements awakened the girl. Her eyes fluttered for a second, staring at Goose in confusion. The mean, drunken killer was kneeling in front of her crying. In a way, that was scarier than the gruff, easily angered man she'd first met. As awareness crept in, his eyes changed from hopeful, happy, and full of tears, to sad and hollow. It hurt Kelly's heart to see such pain. She reached out to touch his arm.

Goose's world had just come crashing down harder than it had in a long time. When the woman's eyes opened, they were a shade of green with flecks of copper, not the piercing blue that had belonged to Laura. He reached down with a gnarled, work-calloused hand and held her forearm for a split second longer than he needed before gently removing it from his arm. "We need to get moving. I want to be on the road in ten minutes."

Kelly had always been told she had an "old soul." This was one of those times when it came in handy. She nodded to Goose and turned to gently wake her son. "Come on, honey. We need to go. Be quiet so we don't wake the others."

To the boy's credit, he mumbled, "Okay," and started getting his things together. They didn't have much anyway.

Minutes later, Goose led Kelly and Brian up the narrow steps and out the back door. Mac came out of the barn and angled over to meet them as Goose headed to the smaller outbuilding. Mac had created stalls in the old building with old metal gates for the party. Not wanting Kelly or Brian to overhear the conversation, Goose asked her, "Kelly, do you think you and Brian could water the horses and brush them down a bit while I talk to Mac? I saw some buckets and an old curry comb near the stalls."

Kelly's eyes narrowed and her mouth got tight. Who was this man who could actually be polite and suddenly remembered hers and Brian's names when he wanted something done? Had he been toying with them the whole time? Thoughts swirled in her head, and she got angrier. She was no charity case! She had a lot to offer!

"Fine," she said through pursed lips. She needed this man for now, but she needed to be away from him too.

Goose cocked an eyebrow at her response. Having been married before, he knew he was in trouble; he just wasn't sure why. "There are buckets in the shed and an old iron hand pump over there." He pointed. "You don't need to fill them all the way."

Kelly nodded firmly and took Brian by the arm to get to work and away from Goose.

"Mom, you're hurting my arm." Brian twisted his arm out of her grip. "Why are you mad?"

"I'm sorry, honey, I didn't mean to."

Goose headed over to intercept Mac halfway between the larger barn and outbuilding where Kelly and Brian stood watering the horses. Uncharacteristically, Mac got straight to the point. "Goose, I been thinking. We got extra space downstairs and—"

Goose held up a hand. "Mac, don't worry about it. I mostly came for some of that famous apple pie moonshine. I just brought these two along to look around. The timing was lucky, I reckon, seeing that you were having a pig roast."

"We sent you a note. Everyone worries about you. They always ask after you."

Goose shook his head and waved a hand to cut off that train of thought. "T'aint nothing ta worry about. I'll be fine or I won't. It's nothing worth frettin' about." Although he had gotten used to speaking differently in his old job when traveling for meetings or giving board presentations, he tended to slip into a more country way of talking with his old friends. "You know me, I get indisposed from time to time. Your note's probably waitin' for me at the Le Cheval community. They'd be too afraid to bring it to me on their own."

"That don't seem right. Everyone loves you, Goose."

"Maybe before. I didn't know how good I had it. I'm different now. Anyway, I've got to get headed back. I've been dawdling too long. I promised the governor I'd chase down some men raiding homes and convoys. They've killed good people and made the roads unsafe. Well, more unsafe than normal."

"I heard about that. These days, vermin like that creep up as fast as you knock 'em down. Why do you gotta be the one to go after 'em, though? You wasn't even a lawman or nothing before everything went south."

"Hell, I don't know, Mac." Goose took off his hat, running his hand through his hair. He gazed over at the sun just breaking on the horizon, already burning the mist away and drying up the dew. "Just, well..." Goose hesitated. Mac gave him time. He wanted to hear what Goose had to say and suspected Goose needed to tell it. "...Laura and Elizabeth were in Lexington without me when things boiled over. My head was in the wrong place. I stayed home to work."

"You couldn't have known that week would get bad. Things had been simmering for years. It could have gone on for a week or a decade. Elizabeth wanted that degree so much, and I don't blame her."

"Maybe, but I wasn't there when they needed me. I tried like hell to bring my girls home when the crisis went from simmer to full-blown chaos. It was anarchy out there."

"I remember."

"Well, it was bad. Back then you couldn't hardly get gas for any price. The riots and anarchy were going full-fledged. It was chaotic. I don't want to go all into it. Then I ran into some of the guys responsible for what happened to Laura and Elizabeth."

Mac's face turned white, and he let out a low, long whistle.

Goose nodded. "I was in a rage and killing mad. Well, you know how that turned out. I'm here and they ain't. Thing is, I didn't feel any guilt. They were killers and rapists and would have kept doing it if I didn't stop 'em. Wasn't like the old days where we let 'em kill and rape and give 'em a two-year time out, then call 'em rehabilitated and let 'em do it again. Those men would have kept killing and raping and tearing up people's lives until someone stopped 'em. Because I did, a few more people get to live longer. It seemed right somehow. I couldn't save my girls, but perhaps I saved someone else's."

"Makes sense to me."

"Later I was kind of just driftin'… and drinking. I didn't have no place in mind to go, didn't care whether I lived or died. Around Frankfort I come up on the tail end of a big fight. There were dead men on both sides. At first, I planned to ride away, but for some reason I didn't. It was easy to tell who the bad guys were. I think both groups started with ten to fifteen men, and by the time I got there, it was about four to two. I lost my temper and waded in. When it was over, the four bad guys were down and one guy on the defender's side. Turns out it was Governor Beatty."

"I voted for him, even though he was a bit too cantankerous to be in politics back in those days."

"He's a good guy. He's got a good heart and a sense for what's right. So, you're damn right he didn't fit in with the politicians then. I got him home, though, to the protection of his National Guard unit. First time I sobered up in weeks. I s'pose he figured I needed something. One night he and I had a long talk about how the towns are kind of reverting to the Old West and establishing sheriffs and courts and safe areas inside the town limits. He said the state level police and bureau of investigations are so over-whelmed they can't do much. Frankly, most of their people have quit and they're having trouble paying the ones who didn't. Then we got to talking about history and the Old West and somehow the Texas Rangers come up. He said he needed some old-fash-ioned manhunters like the Rangers to chase down some of the worst, no matter where they go. We'd been drinking in the gover-nor's mansion, and I thought it was a lark, so I agreed.

"The next day he arranged a ceremony, and he pinned a badge on me, which wasn't a big deal 'till they loaded my packhorse with supplies, handed me some SAT phones and a bag of badges. He told me to recruit deputies and he'd be in touch."

"So what'd you do?

"Went home and stayed drunk for a few weeks."

Mac waited. He knew Goose well enough to be sure there was more.

"A few weeks later, that phone started going off. I had no idea what it was at first. Then I tried to ignore it, but Laura told me to answer it, so I did."

Mac's face scrunched in confusion.

"It was the governor, and the more he spoke, the more curious I got. He told me about some bad stuff going on that wasn't too far from me and shouldn't be happening with no response whatso-ever. It didn't seem real. I had to know, and I guess he figured I would. I saddled up and took a few days riding down toward Taylorsville. People 'round there were suspicious at first. When I showed 'em the gold star, they calmed down and helped."

"How'd they know it wasn't some dime store piece of junk?"

"Hell, I don't know. I reckon they just needed to believe in something. I said I was chasing bad guys and looked the part, and no one else was helping them. They told me that the billowing smoke of a burned-out home gave testimony each time another home was struck and another family terrorized. Even though the farms and homes over there are pretty well spread out the smoke was thick enough to be seen for miles. There'd been four or five men who would hit a house at night and kill the menfolk, then spend a few days abusing the women, eating the food, and drinking the booze. When they finished their foul deeds, they'd kill the women, burn the home, and ride off. When people saw the smoke, they'd go investigate, but it was always too late."

"Damn." Mac had a pained look on his face as many good men did when something bad was out of their control. "So what'd you do?"

"People there think I did some high-falutin' detective work, and I said nothing to dispose them of that thought. Mostly I rode to the burned-out homes, snooping around for some kind of pattern. Then I kind of sank into some of my bad habits. I ended up nosing out some of the places where they trade whiskey and the services of a woman. No matter what everyone thinks, every town has those places. You know I wasn't after women."

"I know, Goose. You don't have to tell me."

"Anyway, I don't know how long I'd been there, but I'm sure I stank to high heaven and had been on some kind of bender. I guess I fit right in with those scumbags. I had taken off my badge out of shame. One night, I was at a table in a corner with my head down and I see these hombres are trading women's jewelry for booze and turns in the cribs. They were bragging 'bout what they'd done and laughing. Some of the others laughed with 'em. Other people kind of looked uncomfortable. I was trying to decide how to handle it. There were five of 'em and I was hung over, making my hands a little shaky. Then one starts bragging on how sweet the teenage girl they raped and killed had been. I kind of lost it. Laura tried yelling at me to back down, and Elizabeth was quiet like she's been, but it didn't matter. I blasted the one bragging about the teenage girl, then showed 'em the badge and told 'em they were all under arrest. Hell, I didn't know what I'd a done with 'em if they hadn't paused when I told them to surrender."

"Goose, you sure it was Laura telling you not to fight them?" Mac asked softly.

"Yeah. She never did like violence and used to say I lost my temper too easy. Anyways, I figure they thought they had me outnumbered and started clawing for iron, so I did too. Thing is, they tried shooting while diving for cover. I was mad plumb through and just walked at 'em. It couldn't have lasted over twenty seconds. There they were, all bleeding out in the makeshift bar, a place that used to be a gas station. I looked over and the barkeep had a shotgun pointed at me in hands so shaky he could have shot his own foot just as soon as me. I had to do some smooth talking and show him the star and the paper from the governor. Once he learned I wasn't there to shut him down, he got right helpful. Even got some people to write down statements to what the marauders had said before they died. Some people down the road where the more respectable people lived started talking about a reward, and I got the hell out of there and went home."

"Was that the only case you did?"

"No, I've done several. They sent me to Carrollton once to chase down some guys robbing and shooting people on their way out of town that the sheriff couldn't catch. They got up a posse a few times, but they lost 'em in the hills. People in the posse didn't want to be away from their own homes that long and gave up too easy."

"I can see that."

"All I did was follow the trail and nose around, getting closer all the time. They committed more crimes while I was in the area. I'm not proud of that, but each time they did, I got a little closer. I'll tell you and I told no one else, but I didn't feel like risking my hide again. So I shot 'em from a ways off. My intention was only to injure them, but when I got down there, they were hurt pretty bad. I didn't patch 'em up. I let 'em lay and headed back and told the sheriff where his criminals and the loot were and rode off. I can tell you he was pretty pissed." Goose finished with a gallows laugh. "I couldn't give a shit what he thought. This ol' world done went and got hard as nails. I've seen it firsthand. That was three more bad guys dead and I'm still riding astride my saddle, not across it. That's good enough for me."

"Reckon so. What about this lady here with the tattoos and boy? How'd you come on her?"

"That's a tough one. She was married to some no 'count jerk who was fencing goods for the gang I'm after now. Things went bad and he didn't make it. I think they were on the outs anyway. She's a good woman, and that boy will make a fine man, if he gets to grow up."

"Yeah," Mac sighed heavily, "there's always that these days."

"Ahh hell, Mac, I didn't mean that toward you. Just that life's hard all over and ain't nuthin' guaranteed. Hell, I may not make it through the next week. This new profession I got myself in ain't exactly the healthiest, and this gang's a tough nut to crack."

"That bad, eh?"

"Well, it ain't good. I reckon I'm just going to keep tracking and whittlin' down for a while to get 'em to a size I can handle. I don't aim to play fair."

"Why would the governor send you after a gang like that by yourself? That ain't right!" Mac's voice and temper rose.

"Now calm down, Mac, this one's on me. He gave me badges and told me to swear in more deputies and train 'em up like the old Texas Rangers. I'm finding my own way, though. I got nothing to lose. Everyone I'm aware of who might be a deputy has family or commitments. It wouldn't be right."

"Damn it, Goose! What ain't right is throwing your life away 'cause you're pigheaded."

Goose laughed. "That's almost word for word what Laura says."

"Goose, you keep mentioning Laura. I mean, well... I guess I thought..." Mac shrugged.

Goose got a sheepish look in his eyes and gave a self-deprecating laugh. "I'm sorry, Mac. You're right. She and Elizabeth are buried in Lexington. I know that most times, as much as it hurts to say it. Also, I know I may be crazy as a junebug, but I swear she talks to me plain as day. Sometimes I forget she's dead. When it comes back to me, that's when I need her. Sometimes when I'm lonely and need more of the shine, she comes to keep me company." Goose pointed to the case of full mason jars Mac had just brought from the still. "When she comes, I see her as plain as I see you now. It's a comfort no matter whether I'm crazy or not. She's such a part of my life that I sometimes talk to her."

"I'm sorry, Goose, that's got to be hard."

Goose looked down and kicked a pebble in a desultory fashion, reminding Mac of a schoolkid who'd been caught with his hand in a cookie jar and expected a reprimand. "Elizabeth is there too," he said in a much lower voice. "But she doesn't say anything. She's always kind of back in the shadows and she looks sad."

Mac set the case of mason jars down and gave his old friend a hug. Mac was older than Goose, younger than Goose's parents, and a good friend. "Goose, why don't you let me get my horse? I'll go with you. Two old boys like us can wrap this up in no time."

Goose's visage changed in an instant, like a summer heat storm that opens up without warning. Mac got a glimpse of the hard edges that Goose's foes had come to fear over the last year. "Mac, I won't let you do that. I'd tie you to a tree with nothing but a dull pocketknife and take your horse. You've got a big extended family that needs you and people to love you. I've got too much death on my conscience as it is. Yours would tip me over the bend. Be honest with yourself. You're getting older, got a bad knee, and you're not cold enough to shoot a man down the way it has to be done these days. If you're not mean as hell and ruthless, you'll end up dead."

"Ah hell. You're right, but I can't watch you ride off with some kind of death wish. Why don't you deputize some of the cowboys and take 'em with you? They've been working with the sheriff over in Shelbyville to keep the town safe. They're all steady men and good with a gun."

"Yeah. They're only cowboys though 'cause they own a few cows and like to dress up and ride horses. That's what we used to call ourselves when we took trail rides together. Every one of them's got a family, and I can't be worrying about that. Besides, being around people from before makes me think about stuff. Thinking about stuff makes me need a drink. This is hard enough without all that too."

Goose leaned down to pick up the case of mason jars at their feet. "What do I owe you for this?"

"Nothing, just keep yourself safe and bring the jars back. They're scarce."

"I gotta pay you. This shine is worth a lot these days."

"You're a friend. I can't charge you."

"Tell you what. Y'all got a truck with fuel bladders for the farm, don't you?"

"Yeah."

"If I'm able, I'll send a runner over here in a few weeks with a date. You get that thing up to the old truck stop in Pendleton and I'll get you topped off with fuel."

"Whoa, Goose," Mac protested, "that's way too much for a little shine."

"You just said we're friends and this ain't about money. Well, so is this. It's a perk the governor sends me for getting shot at. If you don't take it, the Le Cheval community sure as hell will."

Mac stuck out a hand, they shook, and that was the end of it.

As the three-horse procession headed out of McIntosh Lane nosing around the lonely concrete barriers, Goose took the lead. Kelly and her son lagged behind. She was mad, and he'd be dammed if he knew why. He definitely needed to get shut of this woman.

The boy kicked Toni up and managed to stay in the saddle, all elbows and knees, at a bone-jarring trot. "Mr. Goose, where do we go now?" The question was innocent but fully loaded. Goose heard Kelly cluck her horse up a little closer to hear his response.

"Right now, we'll go home." He wasn't sure why he said *home* and not *my house*. It was already out by the time he caught himself, though. "We'll figure out something for you and your mom later. I've got some work to do that I've put off too long."

"You mean chasing down the men who killed my dad?"

"They've done a lot of bad to a whole lot of people who are just trying to get by."

"Mr. Goose, when you catch up to them, just kill them. I don't ever want to think about them getting out of jail. Then I'll go wherever you send us."

"Don't worry, boy. Jail's too good for that scum, and you won't ever have to worry about seeing them again."

Goose glanced over, and the boy gave a solemn nod that was too mature for his years. "Don't borrow trouble worrying about where you're going. It'll all work out. Besides, I promised you I'd teach you to swing an axe, didn't I?

A grin split the boy's face from ear to ear. Goose figured he might have gone too far. He glanced back at a bemused expression on Kelly's face and *knew* he'd gone too far.

He needed a drink.

Crazy Joe's scout came roaring in so fast he almost wrecked his hog. "The convoy's only thirty minutes behind me! They didn't unload in Pendleton! They didn't even stop at the truck stop. They just pulled over to eat and take a piss."

"Van Gogh! Get my lieutenants over here now! You got two minutes."

Minutes later, the men stood on the shoulder of I-71, at the Crestwood exit looking up the incline where the expressway ran uphill between two rock walls.

"Are we ready?" Crazy Joe asked with less bluster than he'd had a couple minutes ago.

A stocky lieutenant named Drew stepped forward. "We've got the equipment up and running. I was just coming to talk to you. With a slight change in plans, I think we can seal them in tighter. We won't be done in thirty minutes, but if we get enough big rocks in the road in front and behind them, the dozer men can keep shoving rocks while the rest move in and start taking down the National Guard troops."

"Give me the high points fast."

"Just past this incline between the rock walls is a slight dip and then another incline between two rock walls. Just past the second incline is the rest area. I've split the six pieces of excavating equipment we found among those two rock walls overlooking the inclines. I had the men start loosening the dirt and rocks. If you approve, we can start pushing stuff into the road now. It will be close getting enough in the road to keep them from getting through. If they get cautious, though, or stop to investigate, it will give us more time. We'll keep shoving rocks and debris off the cliff. Before they know what's going on, we'll have them trapped in the dip between two rock wall choke points both front and rear."

Crazy Joe motioned to another lieutenant who stood a little over six feet with red hair in a ponytail and a wispy beard. "Take a few of your men and help with those dozers. Make those men fear for their lives. I want every rock they can get in front of that rest area in thirty minutes. Also, I want a mountain of stuff ready to push into the chokepoint behind the convoy on my signal." Crazy Joe whistled for attention. "The rest of you, I want you, you, and you," he pointed to three men, "to take your guys and spread them between the rest area in front and both rock walls. Stay on your walkie talkies and wait for my signal. Move!"

The men wasted no time hustling to their bikes and moving up the expressway.

Crazy Joe turned to stare back down the hill at the Crestwood exit on I-71. As with many places on the interstate, the bridges and overpasses were crumbling and falling into disrepair. This one was no different. Most travelers and convoys used the off and on ramps to bypass the bridges, just to be safe. Looking back up the expressway, there was an obvious dusty, winding path around potholes and burned-out cars, leading down the off ramp and back up the on ramp to this location. The men not digging, their bikes, trucks, and other debris would be a dead giveaway. It was too late to clean up the detritus of their stay, but everything else needed to be hidden fast. He turned to his remaining lieutenants. "Get the rest of the men into hiding on either side of the road ready to attack. Keep a few back to close the rear. I'll personally shoot any man that gets seen before we close the trap."

He paused to eyeball them and let it sink in. He got nods in return.

"Van Gogh, you're in charge of plugging the pass after the convoy goes through. Get it done or fill it with bodies."

The brutal message he'd given the little man more than a week ago had sunk in, and he was rapidly rising in Crazy Joe's esteem and trust.

"Yeah, boss," Van Gogh said in a surly tone that revealed confidence in his growing status in the gang and how he liked the new power.

"I'm going up on the cliff to watch and give orders. Keep your radios close. No one attacks 'till I say so."

INVIDIOUS

THEY RODE MOSTLY in silence to the end of McIntosh Lane, turned left on Highway 42, and made their way to the back entrance to Le Cheval. Shortly after, they came to the concrete road barriers guarding a cut in the road, which often stood unattended. The community wasn't too close to major population centers, and the young group of roaming horsemen who acted as community constabularies were stretched thin. This time two men guarded the barricade. Two more had started riding away when Goose, Kelly, and Brian came over the rise approaching the barrier.

"Halt! One of you can approach on foot. The others stay back with the horses."

"Kelly," said Goose, "you and Brian stay back here with the horses. I'll go talk to them."

"Oh, it's Kelly and Brian now, is it?" Kelly huffed. "Why do you only remember our names when you want something?"

"Woman…" Goose blew out breath in a long sigh, shook his head, and nudged the big black and white horse toward the barrier.

"We said dismount and approach!" the young man at the barrier said in a nervous, high-pitched voice.

"Boy! I'm only going to tell you once, you put that damn gun down. You point it at me and I'll damn sure kill you," Goose said with a burst of misplaced frustration he took out on the young guard.

"Toby, put the gun down. That's Goose Truman," said one of the mounted guards who'd been riding away but who came back when he saw the potential altercation.

"Oh my God!" Toby hurriedly lowered his AR-15, bumping it on the concrete barrier and dropping it to the ground with a clatter. His partner rushed to retrieve it.

Goose ignored the two young men at the barrier and moved his horse alongside the mounted cop. The patrolman's partner hung back a ways to provide cover. "Kevin?" The second mounted patrolman sounded concerned.

"What's this all about?" Goose swept his arm toward the barricade. Kevin's horse danced sideways at Goose's arm swing. "Boy, you better work on that horse. If you ever do get into a fracas, you can't have him throwing you in the middle of something."

Kevin got control of his horse, pursed his lips, and said, "Judge Berger came in last night for court day and the market weekend. He told us to up our guards because some gang has been raiding convoys and outlying communities all up and down I-71."

"Been two weeks already has it?" Goose said in a different tone, his previous bluster already forgotten. "I might just have to swing by and see the old man."

"I thought you two are the same age?"

"Yeah, boy, but we're both getting older."

"Hmmph," Kelly snorted. She had quietly eased Copper up to

listen. "I think he just likes to act old and grumpy," she said to Kevin. "So, what's this you say about a market weekend?"

Kevin glanced at Goose and raised an eyebrow.

"I didn't get time to tell her about the community yet," Goose said gruffly. "And it's not like I get a warm welcome when I do stop by."

"That's because you're mean and frequently drunk." Kevin turned to Kelly, interrupting any possible response by Goose. "Well, ma'am, considering how things have changed, it's about the best market in the whole area once every two weeks. I think you saw the show barn facility. Well, right in the middle is a huge arena where the old millionaire horse buyers used to party. Most people in the community keep a room in the facility or something erected around it to live in part-time. It's kind of like the old southern tradition of a town home and country home. When things are dangerous in the country or people have business to conduct, they come stay at the show barn townhomes."

"That sounds sensible," Kelly replied. "And fun."

"It is!" Kevin inched his horse closer to Kelly, earning a glare from Goose that he ignored. "We have a few permanent booths in the arena for normal trade. However, every second weekend a dozen or more booths pop up. The judge comes in from LaGrange to hear cases or deal with any criminals we have. There is music and a dance on Saturday night." The way Kevin said it made it sound like an invitation.

Kelly slid her eyes sideways to Goose, noticing the tight lines on his face. "Why, thank you, Kevin. I would love to see it! Mr. Truman has graciously decided to let me and Brian stay at his home a few more days. He also has some work to do that may take him away. I would have never gone to a party by myself, but with you there, I wouldn't feel all alone."

A wide smile split Kevin's face. "Yes, ma'am. I'll sure be there all right."

"Let's get a move on," Goose said gruffly. "I need to talk to the judge. Then I have some killing to do. I'm in that kind of mood." He glared at Kevin. "We'll see you later."

Kevin smiled at Goose, not flinching from the glare. "That's okay, sir. I'm headed that way. Bill and I can ride along and help provide security."

Goose exploded. "Boy, the day I need you to—"

Ignoring him, Kelly urged her horse forward, and Kevin fell in alongside her, animatedly talking about all manner of things. Brian gave Goose a funny look and followed his mother. Goose let the spotted horse fall to the rear and reached into his saddlebags for a quart of Mac's prized apple pie.

Kelly looked back at Goose as he took a swallow of the moonshine, and their eyes met for a second over the lip of the jar. Kelly had a sad expression and gave an almost imperceptible shake of her head before turning back to her riding partner. "Kevin, how long does the judge stay at Le Cheval?"

"Usually he spends the night and goes home Sunday. We send a couple of riders with him for most of the trip back."

Kelly glanced at Goose again. He'd already become a little unsteady in the saddle and had begun to sing. "Kevin, Mr. Truman may not be able to meet with the judge this afternoon. Would you be so kind as to tell him that Mr. Truman would like to speak with him before he leaves tomorrow?"

Kevin cast a glance at Goose, who had a quart jar of apple pie turned up, finishing it, and nodded. "I understand. I'll tell him. Or you could at the party tonight."

Kelly reached over and touched Kevin's arm. "I may not make tonight's party. Would it be asking too much to have a raincheck for the next one... if I'm still living in the area?"

Kevin's face fell. "Surely you're not leaving? You just got here."

"Mr. Truman has been helping me find a new place to live. I'm not sure where that will be yet or what the future may hold."

"There are so many great places here in Le Cheval! You will meet people tonight at the party and have your choice. Many of the homes are empty, and the council has been discussing how to allow homesteaders who are properly vetted and contributors to the community to settle in some of them."

Kelly once again looked back at Goose and absentmindedly replied, "Perhaps."

Laura leaned forward and rested her chin on Goose's shoulder from behind. As he swayed unevenly in the saddle, she murmured, *"You started early today."*

"Mhmm," he mumbled, eyes closed, afraid to break the spell. He felt her breath on his neck, her arms around his waist as she rode behind him as she used to do.

"She likes you."

"What!" Goose yelled louder than he intended, earning an over the shoulder glance from the group ahead. He expected Laura to vanish with his outburst. She didn't.

"It's okay. You need someone to help take care of you. You're doing a terrible job on your own."

"I don't want anyone else! You're all I need, even like this!"

"Darling, I can't stay. Surely you know that. Even now, it's harder for me."

"What do you mean harder for you?" Panic crept into his voice.

"Let's not worry about that now."

"What about Elizabeth? She doesn't even speak. She never comes close to me and barely looks at me. Is she mad at me for not protecting you two?"

"Elizabeth is... different..." Laura then tried to change the subject. *"Perhaps you could let Kelly and her son stay on a longer term to*

help with chores around the house. That would be okay. They might stay in Elizabeth's room or my old office."

"No!" Goose shouted again, earning another glance from Kelly and Kevin. "At least not in your office or Elizabeth's room," he said in a lower voice.

"Perhaps in the secret poker room in the barn," Laura whispered thoughtfully. "For now."

Before Goose could reply, her arms disappeared from his waist, her chin vanished from his neck, and nothing remained except the scent of Laura's favorite perfume. Goose couldn't stifle a guttural sound like an animal in pain.

"What's with him?" Kevin said to Kelly, unable to hide the derision in his voice.

Kelly wanted to defend Goose and explain about his dead wife and daughter, ultimately deciding not to. It felt like a betrayal. She'd begun to feel protective over the big, angry man behind her. Kevin's tone of derision angered her. "He has some ghosts to deal with, but in this day and age don't we all?" she said primly before urging her horse forward.

It was a close thing getting the equipment and men in position. It was only seconds between when the last man got in position and the convoy came over the rise a mile away, headed south on I-71. The dozers at the first cut had stopped moving and wouldn't start up again until the convoy had passed. The dozers closer to the rest area had to keep working to seal the gap. With luck, the noise wouldn't be heard until the convoy had passed the first cut and could be blocked in. This would be their biggest, most audacious prize, if it worked.

Crazy Joe stood on a ridge behind a mound of debris ready to be pushed into the expressway below. From this vantage, the expressway looked wide. He raised the walkie talkie and called to Terry, the skinny lieutenant with the red ponytail. Terry bore the scars on his face from the penance Crazy Joe had dealt out for some misdeed related to the fiasco at the trailer the night after Van Gogh lost his ear. Chad hadn't survived the punishment. "How's that work coming?"

"It ain't done, boss, but we got a lot of stuff in the road. Enough to slow them."

"It better stop them cold," Crazy Joe threatened. "Van Gogh."

"Yeah, boss?"

"Get the trucks and tanks manned and ready to fill the gap behind the convoy in case we can't get enough rocks in the road. And, Van, no one squeamish. They have to pull the trucks right in among the rocks while they're falling."

"I'll drive the first one myself, boss. I'll shoot any man who doesn't follow."

"By damn, man, I think you're getting the hang of this!"

Less than five minutes later, the convoy came downhill to the Crestwood exit bypassing the damaged overpass, preceded by a Hummer acting as a scout. They stopped long enough at the bottom of the exit ramp that Crazy Joe nearly called for a strike then and there. He didn't realize he'd been holding his breath until they started up the inclined on-ramp to I-71 and he exhaled in a *whoosh*.

Crazy Joe keyed the mic. "Terry, you ready?"

"They might be able to shove through the smaller rocks if they try. Ten more minutes and we'll have it blocked."

"You got two. When they get to you, have your men pin 'em down with fire and take out the lead trucks first. Keep the dozers pushing through the fight."

"On it, boss."

Seconds later the convoy crested the hill south of Crestwood on I-71 and the taillights disappeared.

Crazy Joe keyed the mic again. "Drew, you're on now. I want this pass closed on both ends. No one gets out."

"Yes, sir!"

"Van Gogh, get your trucks in place about a hundred yards below the pass. If I see anything coming back this way, I want your men plugging any hole in the rocks they might get through."

"They won't get out."

Before Crazy Joe released the push-to-talk button, gunfire echoed across the ridge and through the radio. "Terry, sit rep."

"Pass is blocked. We took out the Hummer leading the column. One of the trucks tried to push through. He got hung up and we shoved a load of rock on top of him. We're buttoned up tight here. It's like shooting fish in a barrel. You got a few breaking off and turning around."

"Outstanding! Cease fire when they lay down their arms. I want to talk to some of them."

Terry ran his hand down his face after lowering the walkie talkie. Even some of the more hardened criminals cringed at what Crazy Joe's *talks* turned into. *Better them than me*, he thought.

"Drew, how's it coming? We got stragglers heading your way now!" Crazy Joe yelled into the mic.

"It's gonna be close, boss. We got a strip on the edge of the fast lane and shoulder where everything's bounding away. They could get through there."

"Van Gogh, that's you."

"On it, boss." Driving an old deuce and half that had seen its better days thirty years prior, Van Gogh directed two men to get in the bed and shoot on the oncoming vehicles. He took an old t-shirt that had been left in the truck and shoved it in his mouth so his face was puffed up like he'd just had dental surgery. Then he gunned the engine of the old truck. It started up the incline with a slow lurch and picked up speed. His vision limited to a wall of debris and the gap Drew had mentioned, he didn't know what

was coming from the other direction. What he did know was that whatever was going to happen would likely involve a huge collision. The t-shirt was the best mouth guard he could think of.

On top of the ridge, Crazy Joe watched Van Gogh's deuce and a half speeding up the incline, the other trucks falling behind. Above Van Gogh, five trucks from the convoy, led by an old military five-ton, raced down the incline, trying to break through the narrow gap in the rocks. It would be a close call to beat them to the gap. Crazy Joe was too mesmerized to lift the walkie talkie.

Van Gogh beat the five-ton by seconds, but the five-ton was bigger and newer. They crashed with a sound so loud it drowned out the gunfire. The tail end of the deuce lifted to almost a forty-five-degree angle before coming to rest in a pile of junk and broken truck parts. The momentum of the bigger truck pushed the deuce back into the gap, just in time for Drew's dozers to dump more rocks on it, blocking the pass for good.

With the pass blocked, the fight went out of most of the convoy defenders except for a few small pockets here and there putting up a strong resistance.

"Ease up on the firing. Just focus on the ones that are fighting hard. Somebody get me something to sit on," Crazy Joe commanded.

The defenders were pinned down and blocked in, ridges on both sides and a wall of rock front and rear. They might have had radios or SAT phones and the ability to call Louisville or Frankfort for help, but everyone on both sides knew help wouldn't be coming anytime soon. Crazy Joe's people could wipe them out in minutes if they chose.

"Cease fire!" Then Crazy Joe stood up and yelled down at the defenders, "Can y'all hear me?"

"We hear you! What do you want?" The voice belonged to a woman trying to sound tough, but she was too mad or scared to pull it off.

"I want to talk to your commander, not no damn woman!" Somehow, the sneer in Crazy Joe's tone carried down into the valley.

"You're speaking to Major Sarah Redman of the Kentucky National Guard. I'm in charge of this convoy, and you've committed more crimes than I can count as well as treason. The best you can do is give yourself up and hope for a liberal jury."

Crazy Joe's laugh echoed on the canyon walls. "Now that's where you're wrong, little missy. There ain't no laws left outside of what some judge and a sheriff can enforce in small towns. The only reason they get that luxury is because I haven't decided to ride in and take their towns yet. Out here, well, this belongs to whoever is strongest, and as you can see, that's me. As for treason, I ain't seen no sign of the federal government in two years. Your state government ain't got no power 'cept in Frankfort and a few trading posts near the big cities. Hell, you can't even protect your own convoys. You *might* have got a call in to Louisville or Frankfort and they *might* send backup, but even if they had trucks and men on standby, they won't make it here until tonight at the earliest. My bet is tomorrow. If I send my men in, you'll all be dead in twenty minutes and we'll cart off whatever we want."

There was a long pause. Clearly the major was contemplating their situation. That was what Crazy Joe wanted.

Several long minutes later, she yelled up at the canyon wall, "What do you want?"

"Now see, that wasn't so hard, was it? What I want is for y'all to drop your weapons and walk your way back to the way you came in. We'll open it up for you. 'Course we'll take the supplies and any working trucks."

"What about my people?"

"We'll go somewhere and talk. When I'm done, I'll let you all go. Sure, you're going to tell me things you'd rather not, but in the end you're alive." After another pause, Crazy Joe got impatient.

"Major!" he barked, the friendly demeanor gone. "You don't have a choice. It's nine fifty by my watch. At ten, if I don't see a bunch of unarmed people lined up at the bottom of this cut, I'm sending in my people with a take-no-prisoners order. I'm done talking!"

Eight minutes later, the major had her people unarmed and trudging down the incline to the rock barrier. Twenty-three of the forty who had entered the cut less than thirty minutes prior were able to walk out.

"Drew, hook a dozer to the deuce Van Gogh drove and pull it out from under that rock pile. Have someone bury him proper. He was starting to turn into something. T-Bone, I want men all over that hole Drew makes with guns on those people. They come out one at a time and they go in zip ties ASAP. I want them secured and loaded in twenty minutes. Then get every mechanic we've got checking out their trucks. Get all we can save turned around and back on the road headed north. After that, we need to get gone lickity split, just in case a relief column is on its way."

Terry came on the radio. *"Boss, we're moving into the pass over the rocks up front. I don't want no one shooting us."*

"You heard 'em," Crazy Joe growled.

"You want us lined up north on 71 or should we take the back way?" Terry questioned. Everyone got quiet. That strayed dangerously close to disagreeing with Crazy Joe.

Although not heard, the sigh of relief was palpable when Crazy Joe replied. "Good point. The people at LaGrange may not control the expressway, but they do the town beside it. They're sure to notice these trucks coming back through. We'll head south on 329 from the Crestwood exit and take the back roads. People are going to notice a convoy no matter what we do, but the news will be less reliable this way than driving right by LaGrange."

No sooner had Crazy Joe finished speaking than a crash of rocks and screech of metal drowned out anything else he might have said. The dozer engine revved again, black smoke poured from the pipes, and the twisted deuce was pulled free. Drew drug it to the side of the road and then got to work shoving rocks and dirt, making the hole large enough for vehicles to get through. A few men used crowbars to pry open the twisted metal of the driver's side door, and Van Gogh's body slithered to the ground bonelessly.

"Shit!" one man exclaimed loud enough to make them all pause and look.

Covered in blood and limping, Van Gogh used the side of the truck to stand. It wasn't clear where his mouth was behind all the blood except from the bubbles when he said, "What happened?"

Crazy Joe let out a howling laugh that filled the canyon and reminded people where he got his nickname. "Get that man a drink and a doctor, and after that a woman!"

Terry called in from the canyon while T-Bone was securing the prisoners with zip ties. *"Boss, it's a mess in here. It's gonna be a least an hour getting all these trucks and supplies turned around and redistributed if you want to save it all."*

"Yeah, we want it all. Get a scout up past the rest area watching toward Louisville and another on the ridge near the Buckner exit, watching toward LaGrange. I'll question the prisoners while we're waiting. Bring them down to the office building by the off ramp."

Crazy Joe sneered. "So, you're in charge?" He leaned back in an office chair, his grease-covered boots on the corner of the desk. They had brought in the prisoner to stand in front of him. Crazy Joe's men stayed outside the door. She wasn't imposing but stood about five foot five, with dark auburn hair, green eyes, and legs that made her uniform look great and probably a gown and high heels even better.

"My name is Major Sarah Redman." The rage in her voice was barely contained.

"Major, you're a part-time soldier and in over your head here. What kind of work did you used to do in the old world before —"

"I hardly think that's any of your business," the major cut in. "As a matter of fact, you are under arrest. Looting and killing is a capital offense under martial law. If you don't release us immediately, you will be captured, tried, and shot. You —"

Crazy Joe uncoiled like a striking snake, his momentum slamming the chair back against the wall, his fist striking Sarah squarely across the jaw before she could even raise her hands in defense. Her knees buckled, and she began to lose consciousness. Crazy Joe grabbed the front of her uniform and slapped her face repeatedly. The men outside the small room glanced at each other and shrugged. Crazy Joe had a reputation.

Inside the office, Crazy Joe whipped out a large bowie knife and began slicing at the major's clothes. He was in a killing mad frenzy and didn't care if he got skin or clothing. He notched her ear as he often did with women as a kind of brand. Sarah tried feebly to protest, but her head swam in a fog and her arms moved with a lethargic motion as if she was drunk. Punch drunk.

Sarah was in a haze of pain. Part of her mind knew what was going on, but it seemed so distant, as if it was happening to someone else. She felt herself being bent over the desk and was powerless to stop it. She could only endure what was happening and hope he didn't kill her. When Crazy Joe took her from behind in a savage, unnatural way, her head exploded in pain. She let out a shriek that turned into an unearthly howl of misery.

"Goddamn," one of the men outside the room remarked. "She must have really pissed him off. That sound gives me the shivers, like a cat walked over my grave."

The other man shrugged. "He's the boss."

Shortly thereafter, Crazy Joe came walking out of the office, buckling his belt. "You all got ten minutes with her. Then I want her out there in shoes and pants and no shirt. I don't want her cleaned up. The others need to know who's in charge and how we treat people who don't get that."

"Yes, sir," they both mumbled.

When Crazy Joe was out of earshot, the first man glanced into the room. "Ken! Damn, look in here. She's all curled on the floor in a fetal position. Her shirt's cut to shreds and her pants are around her ankles. She might be dead."

"She ain't dead. He rarely kills them right away. Ruins the enjoyment for him if they don't know what he did and have to live with it. You want her?"

"Hell no. You can't even see the skin for all the blood!"

"Suit yourself. Go help get the other prisoners loaded up. I'll have her out in a few minutes. The rest of the guys will be working over the other prisoners to make sure they know their place. They just don't do it quite as thorough as the boss does."

Ken turned his back, not wanting to see the major lifted to the desk. When he stepped out into the parking lot, the scene wasn't much better. It was a Roman orgy of pain, abuse, and blood in broad daylight.

He didn't notice a man on horseback with binoculars on the ridge overlooking the scene.

TRAGIC

By the time Bart Ellis made it to LaGrange, it was nearly dusk, and his horse was lathered in sweat and lagging. He ran the horse alongside Highway 146 to avoid I-71 and notice of the gang. There were a few anxious moments as he galloped the horse across the overpass at the Buckner exit. He was sure the gang's lookouts saw him, but they didn't shoot.

Bart came into town from the west, passing LaGrange Elementary School and several hundred-year-old Victorian homes at the heart of the old part of town. Before everything went to hell, a group of the newer residents had planned to demolish the two-hundred-year-old courthouse in favor of a slick new one and a shopping district down the hill, closer to the expressway. In the new reality, the smaller, older part of town at the top of the hill was the safest place to live, work, and shop. It was more defensible, and Sherriff Douglas and his three deputies could keep the old town safe while occasionally patrolling down as far as the expressway.

Bart swung off the horse in a rush and tied it to the new hitching rails the town had erected around the courthouse. He ran

into the building fast enough to make people pause and watch.
"Where's the sheriff?" he gasped to the first person he came
across.

The shocked young woman merely pointed to a door on the
right behind her.

Sherriff Douglas stood with his foot on a chair talking to a
couple of deputies. "Sheriff! They hit the convoy! They're torturing, raping, and killing the people and stealing everything!" Bart
poured out in a rush.

Sherriff Douglas stood up straight. He was a large man.
"Where did this occur? When did it happen? Quickly, man!"

"Crestwood! They blew rocks into the road, trapped the
convoy, and made them surrender! It was horrible!" Bart
collapsed into a chair, sobbing. "You wouldn't believe all they
did."

The sheriff motioned a deputy to close the door from people
trying to listen in from the hallway. He too found a seat, put both
hands to his temples, and then ran them through his hair, sighing.
"How long did it take you to get here, sir?"

"My name's Bart Ellis," he said in a deflated tone. "It
happened several hours ago, between Crestwood and the rest area
on I-71."

"We watched the convoy go by this morning from the overpass," Sheriff Douglas said as much to Bart as his deputies.
"Later, we heard a lot of chatter on the shortwave radio. We
couldn't be sure, but it didn't sound good."

Bart looked up pleadingly. "So what do we do now? Can we
put together a posse or something? Can we call the state
police?"

The sheriff straightened in his chair, removed his hat, and set
it on a table nearby that had magazines from before the world
changed. "How many men do you say were in the gang?"

Bart was edgy, but the adrenaline from the long ride began to fade and realization started creeping in. "I can't be sure. Thirty or forty."

Staring at the floor, Sherriff Douglas exhaled heavily and ran his hand through his hair again. The two deputies exchanged glances. They were clearly outraged about what had happened only a few miles away. The trail of the killers was still warm, yet they suspected the sheriff was about to tell Bart they could not respond. "Mr. Ellis," the sheriff said with barely controlled frustration, "you're looking at the entire LaGrange police department. Sure, we have some auxiliary volunteers to do patrols or act as lookouts, but —"

"What about a posse?" Bart cut in. "We could —"

"Mr. Ellis," the sheriff said sharply, holding up a hand to get control of the conversation, "a posse is a possibility. However, consider what you're asking. Me and my deputies would go. We could possibly gather another ten to twenty men. That would leave this town undefended, with no police protection. We have women, children, and a school here. This is an island of order in a sea of chaos. What would happen to these people, to our families, if we don't come back?

"I don't know…" Bart said in a barely audible voice.

"You said there might be forty hardened criminals in the gang. For all I know, there might be twenty more close by, and don't forget they took out an armored convoy with soldiers. What could I do against them?" The anguish in the sheriff's voice was evident. "There isn't much law left in the country except for small town sheriffs and good citizens. The National Guard is doing their best to protect the convoys of food from warehouses and the few factories and farms still producing. The state police disbanded after their pay stopped, and many of them stayed home to take care of their families or join their hometown sheriff's departments. Sometimes we get wind of a rumor that the Army or Navy is coming in to help, but the news is so mixed it's like a fairytale. Some say they disbanded, others say they're restricted to a base, and even others say they're at the border fighting off invading armies. Who knows? We haven't seen any real Army people in years. Fort Knox is only a couple hours away in the old days. Now it's a more like a week or two by horse, riding careful and dangerous. It's just not worth it."

Bart leaned forward, his head hanging down to hide his face, crying unashamedly. "You didn't see what they did. The rapes, the blood... I'll see the torture in my dreams for the rest of my life. There are still cut-up bodies in the parking lot."

"I have a way to contact the governor in Frankfurt via the shortwave. I'm told he is trying to run down the worst of these brigands." Bart looked up with hope, like a child on Christmas. Sheriff Douglas held up his hand. "Don't get excited. The governor ain't in much better shape than we are, guarding down-town Frankfort and trying to arrange protection for the convoys. There is gossip that he wants to recreate the old Texas Rangers here in Kentucky. Although, from what I understand, he may have only one or two signed up so far. One of those men is in this area, but if it's the man I'm thinking of, he ain't much more than a mean drunk. He's no match for forty hardened killers."

"What's the world come to?" Bart moaned. "People get raped, tortured, and killed right down the road, and we can't do a thing. How long can we keep our humanity in a world like this?"

"I don't have a good answer for you, Mr. Ellis. I just ain't got the power to do much beyond this city. Within this place, we got law and order, schools, churches, doctors, and a judge, and that's something to be proud of. Things have gotten so much simpler and smaller, I guess. The things we used to see on the news in Eastern Europe or Africa now happen in the next town, and we are as impotent as if it was happening in Africa. That's a hard pill to swallow."

Bart sighed, giving a slight nod of his head in understanding.

"I suppose we can take up a collection or ask for volunteers to go bury them, though even that's a risk."

No one was immune to the changes that had overtaken the world in the last couple of years. Sometimes it took a moment like this to drive it home.

The sheriff and his deputies gave Mr. Ellis a moment to compose himself, promising to get some people together to go bury the dead. He asked for directions to a place to get a strong drink on Main Street and slipped out, shoulders slumped, looking defeated. After Bart made his way down Main Street to a bar and sandwich shop, Deputy Samuels found a room to vent his anger and frustration. Flashbacks of mutilated women and soldiers and headless bodies from his time overseas as a Marine flooded his thoughts as he'd listened to Bart Ellis speak. People down the hall and as far out as the courtyard heard him destroying the file room. When he exited the room somewhat more composed, not a piece of furniture remained intact. Sheriff Douglas locked himself in his office with a bottle of Scotch he'd been saving and hung out a "Do Not Disturb" sign.

Seeing Kevin flirt with Kelly stirred something in Goose. Something he hadn't felt since he'd been pursuing Laura, so many years ago. Laura had been so pretty, and Goose wasn't the only man hoping to date her. That part of his life was dead and buried, though, and these feelings made no sense. By the time he got back to the farm, he was drunk as a skunk, alternating between singing and bouts of melancholy silence.

Kevin offered to help unsaddle the horses in order to talk to Kelly more. Kelly was friendly but didn't give Kevin an opening. It was obvious he wanted to ask what'd he done wrong, but Kelly expertly steered the conversation away to safer subjects. She only allowed him to stay long enough to help get Goose into the room in the basement where he drank, raved, and slept when he wasn't chasing or killing some of the worst people to survive the last few years in the U.S.

As if sensing he was getting the brush off, Kevin changed topics. "I've never been on this farm." He gave a low whistle, gawking at everything. "Even though it's right across the street, none of us have. People tell boogeyman stories about this place. Kids use it to scare each other. I reckon that's normal when you know he once hung dead bodies from the fence and has come to the community market drunk a few times, raving and shooting his gun in the air right outside the building. We all know he's a stone-cold killer and wants to die. People talk about him being crazy or touched by evil. You know how when people get to talking, the stories get bigger and bigger."

"Maybe you're right," Kelly said with a world-weary tone that had seen too much in the last few years. "Although it's a rather grim assessment. He is a man like any other."

Kevin shrugged. "Not like any other."

Kelly made a point to send Brian to their room in the barn in front of Kevin to allay the rumor mill at the Le Cheval community. Kevin's comments about how the people at the community viewed Goose angered her. She wanted time to process those thoughts. Kevin misunderstood her silence and made another attempt to ask if there was anything else he could do.

"Thank you for escorting us home tonight, Kevin. I'm too tired to go to the party tonight. Will you remember to ask the judge to wait for Goose tomorrow?"

"Sure, but Kelly, I—"

"Thank you, Kevin. Would you be so kind as to shut the gate on your way out?"

· · ·

A few moments later, Kelly checked from the barn to make sure Kevin had left, then ducked her head into the room she and Brian shared. "Brian, I'm going to go check on Mr. Truman. I may be awhile. I'm going to clean up a bit in there. Will you be okay?"

"Sure, Mom."

Kelly checked that the solar cells and electric panel were shut down since dusk was fast approaching. She entered Goose's home from a heavy door near the barn that squeaked. Goose wouldn't have heard anyways. He was in the living room, jamming to an odd mix of music from an old iPhone and Bluetooth speaker. Goose was swaying, and the dogs bounced around him excitedly. He had a huge smile on his face and appeared years younger. Kelly felt like an intruder on a private moment and started to sneak back out when Goose saw her.

"Come on in!" he boomed.

"It's okay, I'm sorry to interrupt. I just wanted to make sure everything was okay in here and perhaps clean up some."

"Come on in. Have a drink," he said, speaking with the boisterous tone of a drunk, spilling some moonshine as he extended the jar to her.

It was the needy, boyish look in his face that convinced her. "All right, just one. What are we drinking?"

"Anything you like, milady." Goose tried to bow and stumbled instead. "Bourbon, shine, or wine?"

"A glass of wine would be nice."

He disappeared into the pantry to search the wine cooler, pausing in the doorway as if talking to someone. Kelly could partially make out his side of the conversation.

"Are you sure?" he said. "It's yours. I don't think I can replace it." Then he came out of the pantry looking slightly more somber. "It will take a moment to chill." He took some ice from the freezer for the wine chiller, then put the bottle in the ice and turned it a few times. In a few moments, he handed Kelly a partially chilled glass of wine filled to the brim.

Then a song came on that he'd once loved, though now it took on a different meaning, Craig Morgan's "Almost Home." Goose became distracted again singing, *"Man, I wish you'd just left me alone; I was almost home…"*

In the song's context, it was heart wrenching. Kelly felt like he was talking to her. Apparently understanding the change in mood, the dogs stopped barking and jumping for Goose's attention.

Kelly downed her wine and moved to refill the glass. She sat at the bar watching Goose and listening to music, her own mind drifting to other places and times.

Goose loomed over her, interrupting her reverie. "Did I tell you about my daughter?" he said with delight. "She was something!" He paused, and Kelly worried he might sink into that low place again. He shook his head as if to clear it, opening drawers below the bookcase and rifling through boxes of photos. Kelly followed him to help. He kept loading her up with pictures to bring to the kitchen table.

Kelly had to act surprised to see the pictures of normal times and a happy family. Still, it brought on a maudlin mood. Those days were gone, like an old movie of a World War II USO dance. For her, the idyllic life had been eroding for years before the country made that final slide, like a part of the California coast slipping into the ocean. She picked up the glass of wine and took a sip. It was warm and didn't hit the spot.

Goose saw her expression and asked if she'd like something else.

"I don't know," she said. "What are you drinking?"

"M'lady, I have a store of different top shelf Kentucky bourbons hidden. Right now, I have cracked open a bottle of the Angel's Envy rye, which cost well over a hundred dollars a bottle before the fall. Now it's priceless."

"I surprised you still have any," she said before thinking to catch herself. The expression on Goose's face was the first contrite or slightly embarrassed look she'd seen him give, and it startled her. Down deep, he was aware the life he was leading was wrong. She was sorry she'd broken the good mood.

"Goose, I'm sorry. I didn't think. I just meant that it's so rare and hard to find a stash like you have, and you *do* drink a lot, no insult intended."

He waved her off with a broad sweep of the hand, sounding more sober for a moment. "Not to worry, little lady." It was the worst John Wayne impression she'd ever heard and made her giggle. "You are right. It is hard to find, and I do drink too much. Most of the time I have enough sense to stay away from the good stuff. However, this is a special occasion and requires a special drink."

"What's the special occasion?"

He winked and shook his head. With a pronounced slur in his words, he asked, "Neat, on the rocks, or with water?"

"You have rocks?"

"But of course! When the electricity is on, the icemaker fills, and when I turn the power off, I put ice in the deep-freeze down-stairs. It runs off a battery inverter that recharges when the electricity is on."

"Very clever."

"I used to make a good living being clever." Goose stumbled off.

Kelly heard him stagger down the stairs and curse a time or two. She debated going to help him, then decided to peruse the pictures of a happy middle class family man with a wife and daughter instead. In many pictures, he wore business attire, some-times a suit and tie. He'd been pale, slightly pudgy, and would have easily blended into a crowd. It was the smile that was so incongruous. It made his face appear totally alien to the man she knew. She felt like a voyeur to his life. She was so engrossed, she didn't hear him return until he spoke.

"All that feels light years away. Those people are like strangers now."

"I'm sorry, I didn't mean to pry."

"It's okay," Goose slurred. He set a crystal glass, a fifth of Angel's Envy rye, and a bucket of ice on the table beside her then dropped into his chair. "Laura said it's okay," he added absently, refreshing his drink and turning up the music, propping his feet up on the ledge below a bank of windows overlooking the valley and creek below.

Goose was distant, perhaps seeing ghosts again, and Kelly was sorry to have broken the jovial mood but had her own deep thoughts. She poured four fingers of bourbon over ice and sipped from her glass.

Damn, that was good.

She had to be careful and take small amounts. It felt good to hold the liquor in her mouth for a minute before swallowing. She had never been able to hold her liquor well, and she hadn't had any at all in quite a while.

The music was all over the place with different genres and eras, and it fit her just fine. There was "A Guy Walks Into a Bar" by Tyler Farr, then the old standby, The Eagles' "After the Thrill is Gone." That one prompted her to take a long drink in remembrance of her marriage. Later it was more upbeat with "All My Friends" by the Revivalists and "Circles" by Post Malone. Kelly was only slightly surprised by the time Goose hummed along to a 2pac song, "Dear Mama."

She kept sifting through the photos, though not so much to pry into Goose's life. She knew all she wanted to about him for now and didn't know any of the people. It was more that so many of the places were familiar to her and reminded her of happier, easier times. It was like watching old home movies.

From time to time, Goose got up to let the dogs out or refresh her drink. Kelly didn't realize how much she'd drank until she stood to go to the bathroom and stumbled. Goose caught her. Damn, there was that electricity again in their touch. She was glad he didn't notice her sharp intake of breath. It had to be because she hadn't been with a man in a while. It couldn't be Goose. She steadied herself. Had she had two four-finger glasses of bourbon or was it three? On her way to the bathroom, she kept trying to recall. It couldn't possibly have been four. Could it?

When she returned, she had a serious look on her face. "Why is this a special occasion?" she slurred.

Goose laughed, then leaned his chair down from the tilted back position. "I'll tell you on one condition. You ask no questions, and we don't talk for a while. Just listen to the music and look over the valley."

"But it's dark and—"

Goose shook his head. "No speaking. Just nod if you agree."

Kelly nodded drunkenly; she never would have been this pliant had she not been drinking.

"In my more sober moments, I realize I may be in over my head, and I'll deny this if you ever bring it up or tell anyone." Goose hitched a heavy breath. "You've seen the man in those pictures. I wasn't trained for the life I've been living the last couple years. When it started, I didn't know much about shooting anything other than deer or rabbit hunting. I was just mad plumb through and didn't care if I died. Now I'm less mad and that's liable to get me killed."

"Do you still want to—"

"Uh uh uh… no talking. Tomorrow I'm going to go out and chase fifty hardened killers and, well… you know. Things happen."

"But—"

"No talking. Cheers." Goose turned up the music and leaned

his chair back again. "Diamond Girl" by Seals and Croft, then "Drift Away" by Dobie Gray and "Tennessee Whiskey" by Chris Stapleton. When "Don't Close Your Eyes" by Keith Whitley came on, it brought tears to his eyes again. This was a side to Goose no one alive had ever seen before tonight.

Kelly was frustrated. She had so many questions, and she wasn't used to holding back but had given her word. She relaxed and let the music wash over her. In a few minutes, she refreshed both of their drinks. Thirty minutes later, he did the same.

Things got hazy after that, with the alcohol and the music. Kelly lost track of time. It was her turn to refresh the drinks, and when she stood to get the ice, she staggered and fell into Goose's lap. He caught her and started to help her up. She felt a surge of need and put her arms around him for a passionate kiss. This was so much more electric than a casual brush of the arm, and her need couldn't be satiated. She brazenly wanted more and wasn't sorry.

Goose was shocked and surprised that this beautiful woman wanted to kiss him. She was sloshed, and he tried to push back, but she held on like a wildcat. In truth, he had little willpower to resist as drunk as he was and as lonely as he had been.

What was odd was that as out of it as he was, this wasn't his normal drunk. Usually, Laura stayed with him during those drinking sessions, talking to him and guiding him. Now Laura was gone and here he sat with a beautiful woman in his lap kissing him to the sounds of great music. Down deep, he was a man and had needs so he went with it.

Even so, Goose couldn't bear to enter the master bedroom. Elizabeth's bedroom wasn't an option either, so they stumbled to the lower level, caught up in kissing like there was no tomorrow, hands roaming each other's body, finding buttons and snaps.

He'd put a single bed in his former office by the window. He paused. It was made, with fresh sheets.

"I cleaned," Kelly said huskily as she pulled his shirt off and pushed him back into a sitting position on the bed.

Any response Goose might have had turned into dumbfounded awe as she stood before him undressing. She moved slower than their frantic previous pace, and Goose appreciated it. As he'd suspected, she was well covered in tattoos. Under the tattoos was an exquisite body, well-muscled thighs, flat tummy, and the perfect amount of curves in the hips and breasts to make a man's mouth water with anticipation. It was his sharp intake of breath that brought a smile to her face. She had seemed shy at first while undressing. Goose sat on the bed, back against the headboard, frozen in awe. Kelly knelt on the bed and straddled him, her chest to his. She held his face between her palms for a more measured and passionate kiss than they'd done upstairs.

Things became foggier after that. Another frenzy of activity helped rid Goose of the rest of his clothes. Kelly had vague, confusing thoughts of an almost angry sexual tryst at some points. She took charge and sometimes got rough. Then he did too, handling her strongly, a hand in her hair grasping roughly, another on her rump, leaving a red mark. There was passion and tenderness mixed in too, although overall, it felt more like sex with an ex-boyfriend. They both had their own demons.

It was late. The sun had already risen, striking Goose in the face. He was burning daylight. He sat up immediately, shocked to find the gorgeous woman curled next to him, stirring to wakefulness. A bolt of pain shot through his head and a wave of nausea rolled his stomach.

"I am so sorry," he said, his craggy face showing shock and embarrassment. "I must have gotten drunker than I realized. I should have never done this. It's all my fault. I hope I didn't hurt you or force you. I was drunk…"

A wave of fiery anger rushed through Kelly. Her cheeks flared red, and she slapped him across the face, hard. "This was on me," she said. "Don't take that from me and treat me like a victim! I'm tired of being flotsam in this stream of life. I can make my own decisions and mistakes without always being the helpless woman." She had so much more she wanted to say, but tears were already running, and she didn't trust herself to say more.

"Mistakes?"

Kelly saw the hurt expression on Goose's face, but it was done. She was too confused and emotional to have a rational conversation right now. He had already stood to get dressed and handed her clothes to her, turning his back.

"Take your time. I need to go get cleaned up and ready for my trip," he muttered, not making eye contact, and was out the door before she could reply.

Goose hadn't been this hung over in a long time. There was enough water in the tank for a cold shower without turning on the electricity. The cold water would help settle his mind and stomach. He wanted to linger in the shower, it was helping, but the water was running low. Then he heard knocking at the side door upstairs. He tried to ignore it, but the knocking got louder. It stopped after a moment, and the next thing he knew someone walked into the bathroom.

"What in tarnation?!" Goose grabbed a towel and stepped out of the shower too fast, causing his head to swim with dizziness and his stomach to lurch again.

Brian stood in the door of the bathroom with a toothy grin, on the edge of laughter. "Mom told me to go ask how I can help you get ready for your trip and not to take no for an answer. Sometimes she scares me more than you." When Goose glowered and began to grumble, Brian scampered away full of mirth. "I'll wait in the other room."

Goose wrapped the towel around his waist to brush his teeth and shave. He had trimmed his beard before and didn't plan to shave it all the way off, although perhaps it was time to trim more and shave his neck and cheeks. He heard the side door of the house near the barn open again with a squeak and assumed it was Brian. His head lifted with alarm at hearing Kelly's voice.

"Mr. Truman?"

Goose ignored her, hoping she would leave. Then he heard her coming toward the bathroom.

"Mr. Truman, I'm coming in. Are you decent?"

"Hell no, woman. Get out of my house!" The yell hurt his head and made his throat feel raw.

"You'd better cover up then. I'm coming in. As you know quite well, I've already been in your house and seen everything." The double entendre in her statement made his face another shade of red.

When she rounded the doorjamb into the bathroom, Goose immediately pulled the towel tight around his waist and held the wash towel over his chest, though for what reason he didn't know. Perhaps to hide his pale skin and scars. "You shouldn't be in here. It's a mess, and I'm not decent and... well, you shouldn't be here."

Kelly held a stack of clean towels. "I turned on the power the way you showed me to do some laundry. There should be hot water now."

"I already showered," he said meekly.

"I can see." She mischievously eyed him up and down for the fun of making him uncomfortable. "You'd better hurry and get dressed. The judge will be leaving to go back to LaGrange soon."

"I will, if you'll leave!" he said tersely, trying to get his surprise under control.

She turned with a giggle and tossed over her shoulder, "Then hurry up," before walking out of the bathroom. "By the way," she called in from the other room, her tone more serious, "I took a walk this morning and I ran into some people from the community. Apparently, the judge got an urgent call from LaGrange on his SAT phone last night. Something terrible happened near LaGrange. I expect you'll want to learn what that's about too, so I invited the judge here for refreshments and to meet with you before he leaves."

"You did *what*? I didn't tell you you could—what's happened in LaGrange? Dammit, woman!"

"Just say thank you, Goose," Kelly said sweetly from the other room in a tone that reminded Goose of an old movie *The Cutting Edge* in which the female lead always said, "*Toe pick*" just after tripping the male lead.

"But—"

"Goose...." she drew out from the other room, interrupting the coming rant.

"Thank you, Kelly." He sounded completely exasperated.

Laura appeared beside Goose, gazing into the mirror, both their faces looking back. *"Listen to her. She's making sense."*

Goose's eyes watered. "Oh my God, Laura, I'm so sorry! I was drunk. How can I—"

"It's okay." Laura looked a little melancholy herself.

Something didn't sound right, and Kelly peeked into the bathroom. She saw a man whose lower half was covered by a towel, his upper half pale and scarred. He was leaning forward, hands on the sink, head bowed. She couldn't tell if he was crying.

"You have clean clothes on the bed, and I left you something to eat in the kitchen," she said softly, understanding more about this complex man every day. "I'm going to bring the judge here in about fifteen minutes so you and he can talk in private. I'll leave a pitcher of lemonade on the counter before I go."

"But..." Goose started to protest, before Laura appeared

again with a stern shake of her head. Things were moving too fast. He needed another drink, but this wasn't the time. He finished in the bathroom and moved into the bedroom to a stack of clean, folded clothes on the master bed that was never used.

Two years ago, Laura would have done and said all that Kelly just had. In the last two years, he had learned to run the washing machine when he had no other choice, although he never took the time to fold anything and hadn't seen a folded stack of clothes since Laura left. So many little things brought back painful memories. That simple stack of clothes almost made him pour another drink. But he had some killing to do.

Ten minutes later, he was clean and dressed, his beard trimmed, and he had shaved his cheeks and neck. His hair was wet but combed back when he stepped into the living room. Kelly and the judge were already engaged in small talk, and Kelly had just laughed a cocktail party kind of sound at something the judge said. The scene was so incongruous to the world they lived in now. Seeing Kelly that way made Goose take a sharp intake of breath for a moment before he caught himself. That wasn't Laura, and this wasn't Kelly's home. Goose made a purposefully heavy step, and they both turned to him.

"Look who's all cleaned up," Kelly teased.

The judge stood and extended a hand. He was a tall man who'd gotten thicker over the years. He'd been the center on the high school basketball team when he and Goose attended. "Mr. Truman, it's a pleasure to see you again. You're looking much better than I expected."

"We don't have to be so formal, Jerry. You've known me for years. Everyone knows I've been a drunk for two years now. I'm an old son of a bitch, and splashing around in a cold shower won't change that."

The judge let out a long exhale and smiled wryly. "You're right. I had hoped…" He trailed off. "Anyway, we have things to talk about. I assume you're aware the governor has worked hard to get two SAT phones to each town like LaGrange. I have one and I believe he gave you one as well."

Before Goose could reply, Kelly said, "You two have business to discuss. I'll be in the barn if you need me."

After she left, the judge turned to Goose. "You're making her sleep in the barn?"

"I didn't want her to get too comfortable in the house. I'm trying to find her a place to live. This is Laura's home. And it's nice out there. Heated and cooled and has a bathroom and shower."

"I know. I came to a couple of your poker games in the old days. It's still the barn, though. You have a lot of open space here."

"But…" For the third time this morning, Goose had said *but*, out of words and feeling out of control, and it was starting to piss him off. His countenance got firmer. He wanted to change the subject. "So, tell me about this thing that happened in LaGrange. I can tell you up front, though, I don't have time to help. I've got a gang I need to get back on the trail of, and I need to ask if any of Sheriff Douglas's people have any information that might help me."

The judge sat up straighter. "We may be after the same people. Although in LaGrange, we can't give you much aid other than information and a few supplies. We have a lot of homes and people to protect, and we're stretched too thin already. We're strictly on defense for the time being. As a friend I'd rather see you do the same. You have a good place here and that gang is too much for one man. Surely the governor can send some troops or deputize more Rangers to help—"

"Tell me what you know," Goose interrupted tersely, ignoring the judge's advice.

After the judge had relayed all that Bart Ellis had shared, Goose jumped up and started pacing. "I took time off from the hunt. I was drinking and trying to find Kelly a place to stay, and people got killed because of me!"

"Goose, you're one man."

"*I am only one, but still, I am one. I cannot do everything, but still, I can do something; and because I cannot do everything, I will not refuse to do something that I can do,*" Goose quoted.

"I know the quote. It's by Edward Everett Hale. It could get you killed, though."

"Then my mission is done. I'm dead inside already," Goose said flatly.

"I don't believe that. I think there is another book in the Goose Truman series."

"Who knows? It may be about someone else. We haven't got to the end of book one yet and I've got more bad guys to kill. Don't expect me to bring any of them to your courtroom."

"It would be a waste of time and rope. You have a mission from the governor, and from God I suspect. Although I do wish you'd deputize more men to help you like the governor asked."

"We'll see." Goose sat and leaned back in his chair, blowing out a long breath, tilting his head to stare up at the ceiling. He needed a drink but needed to be on the hunt soon too. That took precedence. "Jerry, how'd we get here?" he asked philosophically.

"What do you mean, Goose? Bad government, corruption, a decay in the moral fabric and customs, followed by a world economic crisis the likes of which has never been seen. You should be aware of all this. You worked downtown. You had to see the news."

"You're partly right. I was more in my right mind back then. It was nice of you to be polite about my mental state and drunkenness since. I didn't watch the news much back then, though. We had already lost the media as the impartial watchdog of the nation, as they were meant to be. I guess I'm speaking rhetorically. It's just so hard for me to wrap my head around how the ethics for so many change so fast."

The judge's eyes lost focus for a moment as if remembering. He reached in his pocket for a travelling cigar case. "Mind if I smoke?"

"Let's move to the screened-in patio. Laura wouldn't like it in the house." The judge raised an eyebrow. "I know, I know. Despite the rumors and partial truths, I haven't gone totally 'round the bend yet, Jerry."

The judge sat down in a whicker rocker overlooking the valley to a creek and held the cigar case out to Goose. "Join me? For old times and good luck in your hunt."

He took one. "Can't really refuse when you put it like that." A smile tried to inch its way onto Goose's craggy face.

The judge pulled out a punch tool and made a circular hole in the end of the cigar. Many people preferred to clip the cigar. He preferred the symmetry and neatness of a punch tool. It fit his sense of order. He handed the tool to Goose and lit the cigar with a torch. "You sure you want to hear my opinion? We go way back. This is one of the few places I can let my hair down and rant. The folks in LaGrange need a steady image."

"Sure, Jerry. I'd sure as hell like to have someone try to make sense of all this. Besides, you don't *have* any hair." Goose chortled.

"If you're asking my opinion, I believe everything started decades before anyone knew what was going on. There are some stats about how often members of the House or Senate cross the aisle to vote for a worthwhile bill. It rarely happened in the last twenty years. We also lost the impartiality of the press, and that was huge. We needed a watchdog. Then we had all the social justice riots, infighting, and parties flexing their muscles for control with lockdowns and other draconian measures that made no sense other than as a test of their power." Jerry sat up straighter. "You're aware I was a Democrat most of my life?"

"I figured. You had a hard reputation on the bench, though. Even so, I never heard anyone say you were unfair."

"So what made you think I was a liberal?"

Goose cocked his head. "When you ask it that way, I never figured you for a liberal, just a Democrat. Many people in this state were raised Democrat because their family was or they were in a union or... well, just because."

"Because I'm black?"

"Jerry, I didn't mean it like that. We go back a long way. You never met my best friend Chris. He moved back to Mississippi before everything went bad. I dearly hope he's all right. The point is, he and I were always like two peas in a pod, a positive and a negative. Anyway, he and I shared a similar value system. It's one of the things that made us such good friends, even though he was raised a Democrat and I wasn't. With so many people around him repeating the same lies about conservatives and our leaders, he probably bought into it. I don't blame him or think that makes him weak. It's just human nature. When a president was elected that he personally identified with, that was a big thing for him at a level I couldn't truly understand. He and I talked, and I kind of get it from his point of view. The best way I can think about it is that if a person from LaGrange was elected president, that would be a big deal to us no matter if he espoused our politics or not. Even if he were a scoundrel, he would be *our* scoundrel, and we'd hope he would take care of us."

Jerry leaned back and took a draw on the cigar. "But he didn't take care of us."

"No, but that's not the fault of those who believed. We need hope and faith, both as a people and a nation."

"Turns out he was more deeply involved in the shadow regime

than any of us guessed," Jerry went on. "The measures they
implemented took more and more control of the people, their freedoms, and income. To keep their system propped up, they had to
tax people out of a reason to work. They also ran corporations off
or into the ground. They fooled us. They didn't want a prosperous
nation. They wanted a lavishly wealthy elite ruling class with the
people living like serfs under their thumb."

Goose took a draw on his cigar.

The judge paused and shook his head. "That was the beginning of the end, but even the left didn't believe it. There was a
rigged election, and they got their people in enough offices to
control the country."

"I remember."

"Do you recall when the former president got himself named
to the United Nations as Secretary-General?"

"Yeah."

"Soon after that election they removed the current president,
and the vice president took over. One of her first acts in office was
to invite the U.N. and their peacekeepers into the U.S. They
thought that because a former U.S. president was leading the
U.N., Americans would be more likely to accept the invading
troops. Up to that point there had been no appreciable revolts or
revolutions, despite all the lies, deceptions, lockdowns, freedoms
taken and even the takeover of our government. They had no
reason to think we'd finally find our backbone when they brought
in the U.N. peacekeepers. They were wrong. Things got crazy all
over the country overnight."

Goose stood, flung his cigar to the porch, and stomped it while
muffling a curse. "That's the weekend Laura went to Lexington
while Elizabeth finished that semester of college." His eyes filled
with tears, and Jerry worried if Goose would lose his sanity in
one of the bouts he'd heard of.

Goose seemed to get control and went on. "I tried to drive and couldn't get there. Roads and bridges were out, there were riots everywhere, and not a drop of fuel to be found. I had to go back home and try again by horseback. It took too long. I didn't make it in time."

Jerry put his hand on Goose's arm. "I'm sorry, I should have skipped that. I can go now."

"No, I need to hear this."

"After that weekend, the former U.S. president and newly minted U.N secretary-general declared martial law and put the U.N. in charge. We all expected a civil war. We were disappointed, and outmaneuvered. They had studied us and planned for decades. They knew what the people would do better than anyone expected. I've heard they have a secret five thousand–person sociology and psychology think tank that's been running scenarios for decades. They simply shut down power, utilities, and food supplies and withdrew to hidden bases around the country to wait."

"That's while I was killing the bastards in Lexington and saving the governor's life," said Goose.

Jerry nodded. "After a few months, they started the food and supply convoys running again, but only in peaceful areas. Any sign of violence or an uprising and the convoys stopped."

"I was pretty out of it at that time. Why did people accept it?"

"Goose, you have to understand, the currency of the left is credit. They had been conditioning people to live beyond their means and expect free things for decades. I fell into the trap of a large house as much as anyone."

"Me too," Goose said morosely.

"We all did. Then, like any glutton, we wanted more, more, more. Going back is hard. Like, how much harder it is to lose a hundred pounds than gain it? Eventually they'd be done in by their own avarice, yet not until they'd brought the country to its knees."

"I still don't get it all."

"The first shot across the bow was taking mortgages from fifteen years to thirty many years ago. Then we allowed states to so overspend their own budgets they had to raise taxes in other states to get the feds to help pay their bills. It's easy to give away food, jobs, education, and medicine when it comes out of someone else's pockets. Essentially that's what credit is, spending money you haven't earned."

"What about the U.N. and their troops?"

"When hyperinflation gripped the U.S., it started crashing economies around the world. They miscalculated that. The U.N. ended up declaring martial law in almost every country they controlled. A few countries reverted back to an oppressive monarchial rule to regain control."

"I suppose I never understood how bad hyperinflation could be."

"Think of it like this: hyperinflation is when the prices of goods and services rise more than fifty percent a month. At that rate, a loaf of bread might cost one amount in the morning and a higher one in the afternoon."

Goose let out a low whistle.

"That's the point when governments print more money to pay for spending. An increase in the money supply is one of the two causes of hyperinflation. I suppose we tried printing money or controlling inflation, but the U.S. was in such shambles by that time, I don't know for sure."

Goose stooped to pick up the smashed cigar and relight it.

"By that time, the U.N. forces were leaving in droves. I heard the secretary-general took his family and left with them. I don't think he had a choice. They would have turned on him here. Those countries wanted their troops home, and they in turn wanted to be with their families. Meanwhile at home we kept printing more money to pay soldiers and buy food. Money was becoming worthless, but they were desperate. People had already been stockpiling. Men and women emptied their 401k accounts for a truckload of groceries. Throughout history, the shortages normally start with durable goods, such as automobiles and washing machines. If hyperinflation continues, people hoard perishable goods, like bread and milk. When the daily subsistence supplies become scarce, the economy falls apart. This time the subsistence supplies were what people wanted most and early on."

"I was drunk and self-indulgent during all that," Goose muttered. Laura gave him a hug. For once, it didn't soothe him.

"People lost their life savings when the dollar became worthless. It hit the elderly the hardest. The banks had all shut down, and checks didn't buy anything. The foreign exchanges and money markets were shut down, and even if they hadn't been, we had nothing to offer them."

"Didn't people know? Couldn't they see it coming?"

"People knew. Most of what I've said was in a paper written many years ago calling out the signs to watch for. It used to be taught in schools before the education system stopped teaching facts and became a propaganda arm of the deep state. There have been many examples of similar economic failures through the years. Germany during the 1920s is the most well-known example of hyperinflation. First, the German government printed money to pay for World War I. From 1913 to the end of the war, the number of deutschmarks in circulation went from thirteen billion to sixty billion. The government also printed government bonds, which has the same effect as printing cash. Germany's sovereign debt soared from five billion to one hundred fifty-six billion marks. At first, the fiscal stimulus lowered the cost of exports and increased economic growth. By the time the war ended, German debt was around three hundred million marks. Production collapsed, leading to a shortage of goods, especially food. Because there was excess cash in circulation and few goods, the price of everyday items doubled every three days. The inflation rate rose twenty-one percent per day. Farmers and others who produced goods did well, but most people either lived in abject poverty or left the country."

"But we have nowhere to go," Goose pointed out.

"Yeah. And surely you remember Venezuela?"

"Kind of. I knew some of what happened, but it was a world away and didn't affect me, so I mostly shrugged it off."

"In Venezuela, prices rose forty percent in 2013, sixty percent in 2014, a hundred and twenty percent in 2015, four hundred and eighty percent in 2016, and sixteen hundred percent in 2017. By 2019, inflation was up four thousand percent."

"Damn! I had no idea."

"The Venezuelan government tried printing money and promoting a new cryptocurrency, the 'petro.' None of it worked. People began using eggs as currency. A carton of eggs was worth 250,000 bolivars compared to 6,740 bolivars in January 2017. Unemployment rose to twenty-one percent, similar to the U.S. rate during the Great Depression. Coincidentally, it was Chavez who orchestrated that mess and his protégé Maduro who perpetuated it. It was that group and their Venezuelan company that helped rig our presidential election with that software company they snuck into the U.S. like a Trojan horse."

Both men leaned back, drawing on their cigars. It was a lot of information to digest, but Goose needed it.

"There are other examples I won't bore you with, like Zimbabwe or America during the first civil war, and a few others."

"First civil war?"

"It's not official. We aren't printing new textbooks these days, so who really cares? Many are calling the time of social riots, police shootings, lockdowns, and conflicts with the U.N. an undeclared civil war. The more I think about it, the more I agree.

Modern wars are asymmetrical. Which means they don't always have battle lines or cannons or whatever. Yet you sure as heck have two diametrically opposed groups trying to subdue the other by any means they can. We definitely had that."

"So what now?" Goose asked, sounding younger and in need of hope.

"I don't know, Goose. Rebuild, I guess. No one knows how much technology and knowledge has been lost. We have no idea if an army is about to invade. We can only focus on each small town as it was in the Old West two hundred years ago. One thing is for damn certain, though. We won't make any progress rebuilding without law and order, and that's sorely lacking in this country right now."

"Americans are good people. Surely they'll pull together for the common good, don't you think?"

"I hope you're right. In the beginning, I was very pessimistic. I've gotten a little more positive lately."

"Positive?" Goose looked shocked. "What about any of this gives you hope? Especially considering what you just told me about the gang and what they did. I haven't even told you a tenth of what I've seen and done the last two years."

The judge gave a wry smile and shook his head. "I get it, Goose. I know I sound crazy, and considering all you've seen and what you do, I don't blame you. However, in LaGrange I'm seeing a real change in people. Before everything broke down, people lost their ethics, quit going to church, and expected the government to do for them. They just became lazy physically, morally, and spiritually. They'd become spiteful and lost their sense of personal responsibility."

Now it was Goose's turn to laugh. "Watch it, Jerry. You're sounding as negative as me."

"That's just it. Without the news and special interest organizations to stir up hate, and without the U.N. here as an invading force, people are starting to work together and try to build something. Considering how far we've fallen, people have a new appreciation for what they had."

"How does that apply to all the gangs and bad people I have to chase?"

"Every society has always had its criminals. At least now they aren't mixed in with us pretending to be the good guys. It's as if we are getting back to the days when good guys wore white hats and the bad guys wore black ones. People are starting to hate the destruction those people wreak. When people return to core values, the criminal element becomes a small percentage of society that can be managed. When people lose their morality and ethics, the criminals become such a high percentage of the population that it can't be managed without becoming a police state.

"Before the fall, ethical people had become the minority. They were an easy target to be attacked and belittled. That left the nation only two choices: either allow chaos to run free, which isn't sustainable, or hire thousands more policemen and become a police state. I think they wanted the police state all along and were using the U.N. peacekeepers in that capacity before it backfired on them."

"What makes you think they wanted a police state? They tried to *defund* police."

"They wanted *their* police. Police controlled by the party. Hitler did the same thing prior to World War II, using the youth to start sweeping social movements, defunding police, and creating party police to do his bidding."

"I guess that's ancient history now. What makes you think people are returning to core values?"

"It's hard to explain. When people have to live within their means and cannot borrow from their children's future or a neighbor's wealth via taxes and fees, they all become conservatives. The hope I see for this country is that right now, there are no loans, credit, or mortgages. They need a neighbor to be wealthy to create jobs and make goods or raise cattle so it will be near them to purchase. For the first time in a long time, we are once again revering entrepreneurship and cheering for success. People understand now that hard work as opposed to credit or handouts is the path to eating, having shelter, and the ability to trade for luxuries. If they are close at hand because of someone's success, all the better, because the access will be easier and the cost less. People are more protective of the things their work earns because they know exactly how hard they worked for it. They want to conserve and protect those things and build a store of food or wealth for days when they can't work. That attitude is turning them all into conservatives."

"So what about charity and goodness? If people are working so hard and protecting what they earn and it's so dear to them, will charity and goodness be lost in this new society?"

"I don't think so. Sure, there are bad guys like the people you chase. We even have some malingerers and miserly people in the community. I think every society is like that. However, most people know how hard they work to live, eat, and keep their families warm and under a roof. They see a person who can't work because of an injury, sickness, or some other misfortune, and you can almost see the *'but there for the grace of God go I'* in their eyes. The churches in LaGrange tell me when there is a call for help or a need, the community is responding better than ever."

"That sounds good, Jerry." Goose stood. "However, in order to keep that hope alive, I've got bad guys to kill."

"You say it so easily…" The judge sounded as if he wanted to say more.

"It's what I have left in life." After a moment of awkwardness between the two men, Goose chuckled. "Or die trying." He laughed, pretending it was a joke.

"Is that what you want?"

"Naww," Goose said in a drawn-out way, but his expression gave lie to the words.

"You have a lot to live for here if you just look around." The judge swept his arm around in a vague gesture that might have meant the house, farm, animals, or people nearby, perhaps even in the secret room in the barn.

Goose became uncomfortable and reached to shake the judge's hand, indicating the conversation was over. "I need to get saddled up. I appreciate all you've told me. It will give me something to ruminate over while I'm on the trail."

"You be safe."

"Oh, and Judge," Goose said from a few feet away, not fully turning back, "if I don't come back, I've left some papers in the house transferring ownership of this place. I'd appreciate it if you'll see that they don't get run off or taken advantage of."

"They?" The judge sounded confused. When it hit him, he added, "You have my word."

After the judge left, Goose searched his stores for a few things he would need, then wrote a message and shoved it all in a box less than half the size of a shoebox. When he was done, he walked across the street to the Le Cheval community center and sought out Kevin from the community guard. "I need a fast rider to take a message. I'll pay well in fuel or trade."

"I have some time off. I'll do it myself." Kevin spoke properly. It was apparent he didn't like Goose yet could use the work.

Goose pursed his lips. "Here is the package and address. It will take you a few hours to make it. I need it there as fast as possible. I'll be riding blind without this man's help. His name is Wade Myers. I've written directions on the package."

"Yes, sir." Some of the stiffness drained away, replaced by curiosity.

Goose turned to walk away and after a couple steps turned back to Kevin. "You like her, don't you?"

Kevin was clearly uncomfortable with the question. "I don't know. I guess. Uh, I mean, she's nice."

"Pretty too." Goose grinned, enjoying the color rising to Kevin's face before he got more serious. "It's okay to admit, son. She isn't so much older than you that it would be a bad match. Although she's seen a lot of hard times you haven't. It changes a person. Be careful."

"I can handle myself," Kevin said defiantly.

"Calm down, son. I didn't mean nothing by it. I don't reckon I've got much of a chance of coming back from this thing. She's a good woman, and I aim to leave my place to her and her son if I don't make it back. She will need a friend to help make sure Kim and the community don't try to take it from her. If that happens, I need you to be a friend first and a suitor later. If you need help, you can call on Wade or Mac McIntosh over past the other side of Le Cheval. Either of them will come running and bring friends. The judge is an old friend too. I've left a note for him if we need, and he'll support the claim."

"Kim wouldn't ever try to take nothing away from —"

Goose held up a hand. "Boy, don't go saying something you don't know. It's best to learn to listen. Particularly when you're talking to people who've seen more than you." Goose stopped talking, sensing he'd said the wrong thing again by the expression on Kevin's face. "Look, I'm sorry. I didn't mean nothin' by all that. None of us know for sure how anyone else will act. It would just make me feel better knowing Kelly had someone on her side if I don't come back. If that happens, she'll need a friend. And if your people don't act the way you think they will and things get a bit hairy, I wanted you to have some people to call on, that's all I'm saying."

Kevin nodded curtly and solemnly replied, "You have my word."

Goose stepped forward, reached to give Kevin a firm hand-shake, and looked him in the eye as an equal to build trust. "This is a man-sized bunch of work and information I'm trusting you with here. The ride to my friend is a life-or-death kind of thing, as well as looking after my place and Kelly if I'm killed and knowing some of my secrets. Don't underestimate what all that means in terms of trust."

Kevin stood straighter. "Yes, sir."

Goose nodded. "You'd best get moving, boy... err... Kevin. I need that delivered as fast as you can." He walked away, not bothering to look back.

Thirty minutes later Rocky was saddled, and Goose was ready to travel light. No packhorse, only what food and ammunition he could carry in his saddlebags. He took his favored Winchester SX-AR .308 and Springfield competition .45, as well as a few other goodies and ammo. He took a bedroll, a piece of tarp to use for ground covering or as a small lean to and a water purifier. He left the alcohol and cigars behind. This was shaping up to be a tough job. He didn't need the tobacco scent giving away his position or anything to cloud his mind and slow his reflexes.

"Kelly?" Goose called as he walked back to his barn.

"Yes?" she replied with a twinkle in her eye and a playful tone in her voice, trying to keep things light, considering where Goose was going and what happened last night.

Was she sounding seductive on purpose? He shook his head to clear his lustful thoughts. "The day before I met you, I rode to Turners Station to ask the Amish people to come by and help me put up hay. They should be here tomorrow. Can you direct their work if I tell you what to do?"

"Sure, Goose." Her playful tone was replaced by a more serious response.

"I've already given them half their pay. I stacked the rest of the trade goods I owe them in the first stall. They'll stay a few days to cut hay in my field and at the neighbor's. They'll need to stack it in my barn and the neighbor's barn on the ridge behind me." Goose walked out of the barn to point to the field and barn.

"What about the neighbor?" Kelly asked.

"They didn't live here for years before the fall. I haven't seen them since. If they ever show up, I'll talk to them. I think they'll appreciate trading some hay for the security and upkeep I've provided."

"Okay. What about the Le Cheval people?"

"They never liked me and weren't nice to the Amish people, either. Screw 'em. The Amish speak perfectly good English so don't let them fool you. If they don't like you, they'll only speak what sounds like Dutch. They'll do that if anyone from Le Cheval comes over to talk to them. I need you to run interference if anyone from the community comes over to get nosy or try to run them off."

"You can count on me."

Goose gave her a long look. "Yeah, I reckon I can," he drawled. "Don't let Kim or none of them community people try to push the Amish folks around. They're good people, and we need them a lot more than they need us. They know how to live in this kind of world, and they work a hell of a lot harder than any of our people ever thought about."

There was an awkward pause where neither of them knew what to say. Was this a handshake moment or what?

Finally, Goose patted the big black and white horse. "I'd better get going." He reached for the pommel with his left hand, putting his left foot in the stirrup. "Don't know when or if I'll get back. You know where the food is. Be sparing. Remember, no

power or lights at night or when anyone can see." He gave her a
long look that was almost tender. "If I don't come back, it's yours.
There ain't no one else to complain about it. Take care of yourself
and Brian." He kicked the horse into a fast gait.

Kelly wanted to say, "Wait what?" but was speechless, and he
galloped out of earshot. She watched Goose until he disappeared
over the last hill with an odd feeling in her stomach she couldn't
describe.

Sarah Redman had no idea where they were going. She was
beyond humiliation. She hurt all over and was sure she had
broken ribs and other injuries. She lay on the floor of an Army
truck, some of the soldiers and civilian convoy drivers around her.
At first, they'd tried to help cover her nakedness or wipe away the
blood and treat her wounds. After several were severely beaten
for it, the others sat stoically trying to look away.

Each bump or pothole jarred her body and elicited a whimper
of pain. She passed out and woke often during the trip. During
lucid moments, she felt terror at the thought she might be pregnant by one of these bastards. That fear was replaced by a morbid
sense of relief at the thought she most likely wouldn't live long
enough to find out. When she woke from time to time, she heard
bits and pieces of conversation from her fellow prisoners.

"Where are they taking us?" Rena, one of the civilian drivers,
asked.

"Shut up!" Mike Tate, one young National Guardsman,
hissed. "You'll get us all beaten. They already raped and killed
nine of us before we loaded in the trucks."

"Private Tate, you need to calm down," Sergeant Burris said
in a voice raw from years of barking commands. He'd been
regular Army for many years before joining the Guard and had a

calming influence. "We need to accept that there is no help coming. If we are going to get out of this, it's up to us. The only lead I have is that we're headed back north toward Cincinnati on back roads. This is going to get a lot worse before it gets better. Y'all spend some time getting your minds right with that. I'll be thinking of a plan. When you're ready, we'll talk more."

Sarah passed out again, confident that the sergeant had things under control as much as possible.

The convoy headed north going fast, not bothering to stop at any of their normal distribution locations to pick up profits or news. Crazy Joe contemplated putting them back on the expressway at Pendleton, but that was too close to the regular government convoy stop and people who might inform on them. This had been the gang's most daring raid yet. They needed to get back to their base in English, Kentucky, to seal the win.

They headed northeast on Highway 22 to Smithfield, then on to New Castle, Kentucky. It was a larger town and normally a bigger risk. However, the gang had raided them several times, and these days the residents knew what to expect if they did anything to displease Crazy Joe. Displaying evidence of a successful raid on a government convoy might go far in cementing his hold over the town. There was also the fact that he liked to brag and display evidence of his power.

They didn't even stop going through Smithfield. The old "Our Best" restaurant was closed but occasionally opened to serve meals on the weekends when they had enough extra food to sell. Crazy Joe had given strict instructions that they were off limits. The food was good, and he liked to sit for a normal meal sometimes at a restaurant and be served, like in the old days. His protection extended to the small town around it, although there wasn't much to steal in any event.

Crazy Joe pulled the convoy over at Henry County High School just outside of New Castle. "I want these trucks parked in a perfect line! I want the sides rolled up on each of the trucks to display the prisoners. Van Gogh, get the major on her feet and in full display. I don't care if you have to tie her to the hood of the truck. I want all who see us clearly on notice that they live in *my* territory and they pay homage to *me*! And if they don't…" Crazy Joe pointed to the trucks where the prisoners were already being prodded to the side where they would be on display for onlookers.

"Terry!" Crazy Joe yelled to the skinny lieutenant. "Take ten men and ride ahead. I want every single resident lining the streets like a 4th of July parade. I don't need to tell you how to handle malingerers, do I?

"No, boss. I'm on it," Terry said tightly, the wounds on his face red and scabbed over from the last time he'd displeased Crazy Joe. He fast walked through the column, calling out riders to join him and instructing them to split up when they hit town, shooting into homes and kicking in doors to get everyone on the street. "Tell 'em anyone not lining the streets will be shot!" he yelled.

Van Gogh sauntered over to Crazy Joe, watching Terry and the other riders leave. He was gaining confidence and starting to swagger. He now wore the missing ear as a medal or accomplishment, daring anyone to say something about it. "Boss, I got the boys tying that major up on the hood of a five-ton truck. She can lean back against the window, but she's up there like a fresh-shot buck."

"Good job, Van," Crazy Joe said absently. "Get everyone a drink and a smoke break. We'll give them about fifteen minutes to get everyone on the street then head out."

ABERRANT

As Goose exited Le Cheval heading toward the four-way stop in Pendleton, he couldn't get the image of Kelly out of his mind. The mix of emotions wasn't something he needed on the trail, yet traveling on horseback gave a man time to think.

Things had gotten out of control last night. He wasn't used to drinking with company and usually got angry, sad, then angry again when drinking. Not last night. Last night was more like social drinking he'd done in the good times. It was nice to have a pretty girl to talk to, and for the first time in a long time he wanted to sing along with the music, not wallow in it, in grief. Kelly apparently needed it too and appeared to be enjoying herself. He recalled showing her some old photos of his life before when he was a clean-shaven, white-collar, country club and ski boat kind of guy. Goose had lost track of time, but whether it was eighteen months ago or two years ago, the man in those pictures was dead. The sooner people forgot about him the better.

The aftermath of the music, singing, and revisiting old pictures became blurred in his mind. There might have been some dancing, and there definitely was kissing, and then moving to the bedroom while frantically undressing each other. He hadn't thought of it at the time, but why hadn't Laura said something? It was her home and she should have done something. Come to think of it, where was she now? The thought that she might be mad worried Goose.

He slowed as he approached the old Dollar General store and post office in Pendleton. They'd been empty and looted since the beginning. Even so, a man didn't live long these days without being cautious. Next came the two big truck stops straddling the expressway. There would be people there for sure, since the location had turned into an informal trading post since the fall. Once the convoys began stopping there to rest or drop off supplies, the convoy commander made a deal with the leader of the current denizens of the post. She promised to trade supplies if they would make the post more permanent and defensible. That deal took some thought. Supplies and safety were in short supply, but the personnel to man a place like the truck stop and the bullseye it would paint on them were both serious considerations. In subsequent trips the convoys dropped of a retiring military man and his family and another family moving from northern Kentucky to help at the post.

Goose waved to a man standing at the front of the truck stop by Highway 153. After a moment, the man waved back, recognizing Goose. Goose wasn't a waving, small talk kind of man anymore, but he also didn't want to be shot by some nervous sentry who didn't know who he was. Goose needed nothing from the small trading post and didn't want to waste the time. They rarely had much anyway if a convoy hadn't just come through. They certainly didn't have as much as Le Cheval did. However, Le Cheval was a virtually closed market, and they allowed only certain people.

Ten minutes later, he came to the four-way stop in Pendleton near a couple of gas stations and a liquor store. Decades earlier, there had been an old drive-in movie theater here too. He only paused long enough to search for a cigar or drink before remembering he'd left them behind and nudged his horse left toward New Castle. One option was as good as another until Wade got in the air to scout for him. The gang had headed away from Louisville after a raid. Larry and the guys hadn't mentioned any raids over near Shelbyville, nor had Mac on 42. The meant New Castle was his best bet.

Soon the metronome of the shod horse clip-clopping on asphalt lulled his mind into more daydreams. If anyone had been around, they would have seen his face redden at the thought of what happened between him and Kelly last night. The ferocity of the tryst surprised Goose. That wasn't his normal way. In truth, he hadn't *had* a normal way in two years, but last night was different. It wasn't mean spirited, just intense. There were things she wanted and did that made him feel like a novice. Yet her eyes pled with him to be in control and not be gentle. He didn't understand at first, but it satisfied a need they both had.

In the morning when he'd tried to apologize about taking advantage of her after too many drinks or perhaps even for a few bruises, her anger and tears surprised him. It was his home, and he controlled her destiny. Using that control for sex was wrong. He'd tried to apologize and promise it would never happen again. Her anger and outrage at his apology shocked and confused him. Ruminating on it now wasn't helping. No matter. He didn't expect to return from this mission anyway. Kelly and Brian would have his home and supplies. He couldn't think of better people to leave them to.

Perhaps she and Kevin would become a couple, although somehow Goose doubted it. There was a sadness and wisdom in her blue eyes that spoke of too many emotional scars that caused her to see life in a way Kevin didn't. She needed a man who had seen the elephant and had his own scars. On the off chance that

Goose made it back alive, he intended help her find a guy like that.

Just then, his musings were interrupted by the beeping of his phone. It took Goose a moment to remove a riding glove and retrieve the phone from a zippered pocket inside his jacket. "Hello?"

"*Goose! How are you? It's been two years! I'd have wondered if you were dead or alive if I didn't keep hearing stories about you.*"

"Wade, you ol' jarhead. I'm glad to hear from you. I didn't expect a call for another hour or two at least. That boy must have made great time."

"*Yeah, he showed up all hell bent for leather about some important mission you'd entrusted him with. He looks up to you.*"

"Me? The boy hardly even knows me, looks at me like I'm dirt most of the time. He's a rider in Le Cheval's protection detail. They don't like me, either."

"*Doesn't matter. You don't have to like someone to be in awe of them. And from what I hear, you haven't given people much to like lately.*"

"I had my reasons," Goose said, not trying to hide his sullen tone.

"*I understand. I want to talk to you about that some time. I'm so sorry. I'd have come by sooner, but my parents are in poor health and I hate to leave them at home during these days.*"

"I'm sorry to ask you now, and I understand if you'd rather not. I wasn't able to explain much in the note I sent with the SAT phone, but I really do need your help."

"*I'd have helped anyway. It just so happens you have good timing. A buddy of mine who used to work downtown for the hospital company came here bringing his brother and their wives. I think Laura used to work with him.*" Wade paused before pushing the talk button again. "*I'm sorry to bring her up, Goose. That was insensitive of me.*"

"It's okay, you didn't mean nothing by it. I need to get used to it."

"Well, what I meant to say is that with them here I can get away more. So why don't you tell me what you need?"

Goose filled him in on the high points of the gang's activities and what they'd been up to recently as well as some of the missions he'd taken on for the governor.

"That's pretty dangerous. Why is he sending you out on your own?"

"It's not so different from the Texas Rangers of old. Those guys did the job solo more often than not."

"Maybe, but for a big job they came together as a group."

"Someday there might be a bigger organization. The governor has allowed me to recruit. I just haven't got around to it yet."

"Hell, Goose. Why not? From all you're telling me, this gang's too much for one man. Why not call in some help?"

"The people I could call aren't worth a damn, and the people who are worth a damn I won't call."

"What's that supposed to mean?"

"Just that I don't know any badass Special Forces guys in the area. This is more of a police matter anyway. The only people I know are guys like you and Larry and the cowboys, and I don't want y'all mixed up in all this."

"Don't forget that I'm a Marine and I've seen things I don't even tell you about. I can hold my own."

"I know that, and that's why you more than anyone knows I can't call on you all. You just said you've got aging parents, a wife and daughter, and a farm to look after. The kind of killing I've been doing lately keeps a person awake at night. I'm already having nightmares in my life, so I can handle it. This is a way for me to do some good on my way out."

"On your way out? Goose, I will not help you with some suicidal death wish."

"It's not a death wish. I told you what this gang's doing with all the raping, killing, and burning. If I don't stop them, who will?"

"I still say you should call on Larry and the cowboys. They're all good men on a horse and with a gun. The country needs citizens to step up right now, and I'm sure they would. It's easier to sleep at night for a righteous killing in defense of another."

"Maybe so, but each death taints your soul a little, like putting rocks in your pocket. Your steps get heavier. Dammit, Wade! Cowboys is nothing more than a silly name for a bunch of guys who used to take trail rides together. They aren't killers!"

"Okay. But this country was built on people like those horsemen stepping up when they're needed. I agree, though, let's drop it for now. I can be in the air in about fifteen minutes. Tell me where to go."

"You're searching for a truck convoy surrounded with bikers. They've been raiding close to I-71. Their last raid was in Crestwood. It was a doozy. I'm not sure how many hours head start they have or how many stops they'll make along the way. I suspect they are headed back east on back roads."

"Makes sense. I've heard a rumor of bikers in New Castle, so I'll head that way first."

"Good. I'm headed the same way, but it will take me several hours to get there on horseback. Stay high and don't make yourself a target."

"Roger that. It will be at least two hours before I can get over to New Castle. I have a stop to make first."

Goose was about to ask about the stop Wade had to make that was more important than this mission, then decided not to. Wade was already doing him a huge favor. No reason to pry.

The convoy through New Castle resembled a Cold War parade in Russia. The people lined the streets as they'd been instructed, but there was a desultory, dispirited look about them. Some clapped as they'd been told, but the cheers did not reach their faces. The more Crazy Joe thought about it, the more he imagined they were defying him, and the angrier he got.

"Halt, gawd damn it!" he screamed.

The convoy came to a stop, the motorcycles wound down. Some of the men leaned forward on their handlebars, anticipating the next command. The citizens glanced around at each other nervously. Crazy Joe set the kickstand and swung a lanky leg with a pointed boot full of silver over the hog and walked toward the curb. "This is supposed to be a gawd damn parade!" he screamed. "A parade needs cheering. If you won't cheer for a simple military show of strength, you better damn well cheer that you're on that side of the curb and not this one." He pointed to Sarah, naked, bloody, battered, bruised, and bound on the hood of the truck.

The men in the convoy got the message and fired their guns in the air, cheering to get the citizens going. Soon the citizens fell in line, though many had tears in their eyes as they cheered. Crazy Joe crossed his arms over his chest for two long minutes watching in dissatisfaction, then motioned Terry to him. "I want outriders on each road leading into town. Make sure they find a suitable spot with a long view. I want to know if anyone heads this way."

"On it, boss." The skinny lieutenant hurried off to give instructions, his reddish gray ponytail bouncing.

That activity killed the cheering. Something was happening. People were nervous and scared. "Van Gogh!"

"Yeah, boss," the one-eared man said with his new, almost permanent sneer.

"Set up camp here. We are spending the night, and every damn townsperson better throw us the best party of our lives or they're going to regret it!" he yelled loud enough for all to hear. "We'll use the courthouse at the town square. There should be places to lock up the prisoners in the basement."

Van Gogh hurried off to get things moving and take over the

venerable old courthouse. A collective groan from the crowd was filled with dread of what was to come.

"Some of you may not have fully grasped the situation yet," Crazy Joe addressed them in a booming voice. "Let me spell it out. The America you once knew is dead!" He paused for effect. "In fact, it died long before the decline, but most of you were too dumb to see it. None of that matters now. What was once American is now hundreds of feudal kingdoms. While it's true that some of those kingdoms are controlled by soldiers from the old America, do not assume they are coming to save you or build the country back to what it once was. They serve a master, the same as my men do me. I control this area! I am your king, your tsar, your emperor! That means each one of you are my subjects. You live and die at my whim. Those who I decide to kill won't die easy. Some leaders control through love, others by lies. I won't waste time with either. I find fear works best!"

As he scanned the crowd, Crazy Joe observed some women sobbing openly. This pleased him and he smiled. "Today when I drove through town, I didn't see the fear and obedience that I expect! I assume that's because you don't fear me enough. Therefore, I have decided to spend the day here so we can get to know each other.

"Here's what's going to happen. You all will go home and clean yourselves and dress for a party. Every damn one of you better be back at the courthouse square dressed to the nines and bearing a gift. My men will take a roll and ask questions. Remember that my men can be very persuasive with their questions. Don't hide anyone or lie. We *will* find out, and not only will that person be killed, someone very close to them will be tortured and killed too." Crazy Joe turned toward the courthouse, then back as if he remembered something, a sadistic smile on his face. "And ladies," he paused to be sure he had their attention, "you had better look damn good when you show up to my party. I don't care if you're fourteen or sixty-four. Any one of you that doesn't look like she ain't trying her level best to impress me is going to regret the hell out of the night, *if* you live through it. I can promise you that whatever you're imagining ain't the half of it." Then Crazy Joe added what he thought was a gracious smile and laugh. "For the rest of you, you might regret it. I suspect you won't, no matter what you tell your men later. Either way, you'll be alive and will have learned a valuable lesson."

At that moment, a man charged Crazy Joe with a guttural yell and a raised hunting knife. Crazy Joe never flinched, staring the crazed father in the eye as he charged. At the last second, Van Gogh shot the man through the temple with his hide-out revolver. The scene eerily resembled the iconic photo of a Vietnamese prisoner being executed more than sixty years prior.

Crazy Joe watched the man spasm in death, his lifeblood pouring to the ground and the gray matter of his brain exposed. Above it all, he heard anguished screams from the man's wife and twin daughters being restrained by Crazy Joe's men. He walked over to face the wife. She was a looker. Her daughters were young and skinny with red hair, showing promise of growing into their mother's looks. Without warning, he slapped the woman so hard across the face she sagged in her captor's arms, her eyes going glassy. "You do understand what's required of you and your daughters at the party tonight?"

"But my husband…" she keened drunkenly, woozy from the slap.

"Your husband made a choice. Frankly, it was a selfish one. Now you have no one left to provide for you and your girls or protect you from threats lesser than me. Nevertheless, what's done is done. If you and your daughters don't show and are not suitably impressive tonight, you may find yourself in the same shape, and then who will care for your daughters?" Crazy Joe changed his stance and softened his visage, attempting to sound more reasonable. "Look, lady, everything you fear is going to happen with or without your compliance. You can run and we will catch you. You can fight it and we'll beat and maybe kill you. Or you can accept it and make the best of it. It's your choice, just like your husband made his. Remember this, though: our choices affect those we love as well." He tilted his head toward the two sobbing teenagers.

"What about my husband?" she begged through sobs.

"If you all please me, you can have his body tomorrow for a proper burial." Crazy Joe turned to walk to the courthouse. "Van Gogh!" The one-eared man ran to catch up.

"Roll his body out of the street. We'll see how tonight goes," he said in a low tone only for his trusted lieutenant. "And make sure those three are presented to me at the party and that I have a suitable room for the night."

The smaller man nodded. Everyone knew how sadistic Crazy Joe could be with women. He doubted they would all live to see morning. If they did, they'd never be the same.

Five PM rolled around. There were tables of food and booze set up in the courtyard. Men played music inside and out. Much of the party was in the courtyard, and a smaller selected group was inside the largest courtroom that now doubled as a ballroom. Beds and chairs had been hastily set up in some of the second-floor offices for Crazy Joe and his lieutenants.

Crazy Joe sauntered through the outside party. "Terry!" he yelled, waiting for the ponytailed lieutenant to hurry to his side. "I want two teams to go through all the homes in town and bring anyone you find here."

"On it."

"Van, hang a noose from the front portico of the courthouse, then make an announcement for everyone to enjoy the party and let them know if we find anyone not in attendance there will be an additional show."

The one-eared man gave an evil chuckle and nodded, running off to find some rope.

"Let's go enjoy the party," Crazy Joe said to the rest of his group.

They set up a dais for him and his leaders in the courtroom, complete with food and booze. Major Sarah Redman was bound and on her knees on the floor at the end of the dais on full display, bloody, bruised, and nude. She had a despondent air to her posture that did not reach her eyes. A spark of rage burned there that couldn't be quelled.

The room fell deathly quiet when Crazy Joe and his entourage entered. He strode purposefully to the dais, stepped up, and addressed the crowd. "This is a party. I want music! I want people dancing and having fun!"

The band struck up, and people began to dance nervously, and drinks were poured. Crazy Joe settled into a large king-like chair that had formerly been for a judge. The murmuring abated, and the room quieted as three women entered the courtroom. Actually, one woman and two teenage girls dressed like grown women. All three stared ahead as if in a trance, slightly unsteady on their feet. The girls wore garish makeup and dresses their father would have never allowed had he been alive. The term "over my dead body" flitted through Sarah's mind as a fresh wave of rage washed over her. She had long since become immune to her own pain and embarrassment, consumed by a need to live and exact revenge.

Crazy Joe stood as they approached the dais. "Have we been drinking, ladies?"

The twins giggled. The mother retained enough sobriety to respond, "Yes, and a few prescription drugs we found on the doorstep," with a look that would have been defiant had she not been swaying and glassy eyed. Seeing Crazy Joe's visage tighten in an angry scowl that was recognizable even in her state, she quickly added, "It *is* a party, isn't it?"

A hush fell over the room as Crazy Joe pondered his words. Feeling as if the town was subdued and these women would learn later what it meant to displease him, Crazy Joe decided to be magnanimous. "You are so correct. We have a place beside my throne reserved for you ladies." He reached out a hand to each of the young women to help them up on the dais.

Before the music started, a commotion from outside disturbed the party. "Gawd damn!" Crazy Joe yelled, storming out of the courtroom and out the front door, followed by most of the crowd, who fanned out into the courtyard.

Terry's men had three men bound, beaten, and kneeling before the front portico of the old courthouse. "Boss, we found —"

Crazy Joe held up his hand for silence until nothing could be heard except for a cough in the back of the crowd. "If we are going to be a kingdom of laws, then we must go about this properly. As your monarch, I can pass judgement." He grinned. "Van, bring my chair and a robe on the double. I think the party can wait a few minutes."

"Yes, sir."

Van returned with a group of men carrying a large judge's chair and robe they found in a closet to the front step of the courthouse for him to preside.

"People," Crazy Joe said once he was seated, "before we begin, let me remind you that we are under martial law and I may pass summary judgements. The laws may be harsher than what you're used to, but they are just and must be followed."

They had brought Sarah out to kneel beside Crazy Joe on a chain like some kind of pet. He never spoke to her anymore or even took much notice. She could tell most of the townspeople didn't buy Crazy Joe's load of hogwash, although a few looked confused, as if his words might have merit. She wondered how long it would be before he had them fully in his sway.

"Terry, give us the evidence of what you've found against these men," Crazy Joe demanded.

"Well, uh... it's... it's like you said, boss..." Terry was clearly uncomfortable speaking in public with so many watching. "You're in charge, and you gave the order that everyone assemble at the courthouse and—"

"And disobeying an order given during martial law has many different punishments, the ultimate being death?" Crazy Joe finished for him.

"Yes, sir. Just like that. Well, uh... I... uh... found these two hiding in one house and the old man in another."

Van whispered in Crazy Joe's ear, and he asked, "Terry, did you find anything else?"

"Yes, sir. We found guns and food and all kinds of things."

"Those are just for hunting and food to keep our families fed!" one of the men protested loudly before a vicious butt-stroke from his captor silenced him.

"Nevertheless, I find all of you in violation of what amounts to a curfew order, subversion, and hoarding. First thing, I will share all of their supplies among others in the community."

"Yes, sir."

"Secondly, each man will be hung by the neck until dead." Crazy Joe pointed to the noose hanging above him. "Get it done now, Van. I have a party to get back to."

There were shrieks in the crowd, and an elderly woman fainted. Sobs and pleas rang out. Crazy Joe grabbed a full-auto AK from the man next to him and emptied a thirty-round magazine into the air. "Enough!" he yelled. "Van! Get it done, and I mean right now! If any damn one of these bastards says a single word or doesn't watch, they get strung up too!" Crazy Joe screeched, spittle running down his chin.

No sooner had Crazy Joe finished his rant than three of Crazy Joe's henchmen hoisted the old man a few feet above the porch and slipped a noose around his neck. They dropped him off the side of the porch. His legs kicked twice. There was a coughing, gurgling sound, and he died. Crazy Joe never even looked. He stared the crowd down, looking for another victim, earning his nickname.

Next was the middle-aged man. He was a large, broad-shouldered man in his prime. Crazy Joe's men didn't risk anything with him. They gave him a butt-stroke to the head, knocking him woozy before taking him to the rope the old man had just been lowered from. He too was strung up and dropped over the side of the porch. Somehow the man ducked his chin at the right instant and the fall didn't break his neck. He was fighting the strangulation, making the crowd restless.

"Van!"

The one-eared man dove at the victim's legs, wrapped his arms around the victim's thighs like a college athlete making a textbook tackle, and yanked down as hard as he was able three or four times. A crack echoed across the courtyard, and the crowd gasped. Van glanced up to see the struggles had ended and the man's head cocked at an unnatural angle. Then the man's body fell on top of Van Gogh as the support they tied the rope to gave way.

"To hell with this," said Crazy Joe. "I have a party to get to." He took two bounding steps off the porch, pulling his Glock 21 from the drop-leg holster, stormed up to the last captive, and blew his brains out. The two men holding the captive were spattered with blood and gore yet afraid to utter a single complaint.

Crazy Joe turned to the crowd. "We have a party to get back to! Start up the music." Before entering the building, he stopped at the steps to address his men, not caring if the townspeople heard. "Make sure these people understand who's boss here. When I ride back through this town in a year, I better see a lot of babies that look like you ugly sons of bitches. If any man, woman, or child even looks sideways at what you're doing, shoot them. No questions. No warning."

"Yeah, boss."

Shortly after, Crazy Joe was back on the dais, drinking, listening to music, and smoldering on the inside. When the beast was loose inside him, it was hard to calm. He only made it through three songs before standing. The music stopped, and people turned to him.

"Keep the party going!" he bellowed. "I've got some things to do. I'll be back later." He held a hand out to the mother with her twin daughters. "Ladies."

Despite the drugs and alcohol, the girls started sobbing. "Van, take them to my room," Crazy Joe instructed, and the crowd of his chosen men roared their approval. This was the leader they wanted, ruthless and crude with a sadistic streak.

Van Gogh led the mother and her daughters to Crazy Joe's room. The men had found a nice brass bed and set it up with a lamp and radio with a power cord leading to a generator out the window and down a floor. The girls walked like zombies, eyes glassed over with drugs, tears streaming down their faces.

Crazy Joe entered the room with a gleam in his eyes and a lascivious look, closing the door behind him as he started on the buttons of his shirt.

Over the next couple of hours, the guards in the hallway heard all manner of hits, screams, and unearthly moans, like an injured animal, and through it all crying and pleading. At one point, Crazy Joe leaned out the door shirtless, hair going in all directions, eyes crazy, demanding more wine.

Late in the night, the screams subsided. Crazy Joe and the girls never returned to the party. Dawn had only just crept over the horizon when Crazy Joe stepped out of the room, dressed, hair in place, and all business with a smile at the corner of his mouth. "Van, get the men mounted up. We need to get home."

"Yes, sir," Van Gogh responded with a hint of concern on his face. It was the only trace of his old self that had shown since Crazy Joe took his ear.

Less than thirty minutes later, the gang was mounted, the trucks running, the exhaust creating a cloud of mist in the chilled morning air. When men spoke, their breath would fog. Soon the mist would burn off and the day would warm.

They gave Sarah Redman castoff clothing to wear. She stared ahead blankly in a catatonic state as she was placed into the front seat of a truck.

"She gives me the willies," Terry said as they loaded her.

"Yeah, man. Crazy Joe done went and broke her up here." T-Bone tapped his temple. Both men spoke in whispers to avoid being heard by others in the gang. They didn't worry about what Sarah might hear, convinced she had taken full leave of her senses. "Look at her eyes, man. They're crazy."

"Shit." Terry took another look at her. "Those eyes are like Crazy Joe's when he goes into a killing rage," he said with a hint of hushed alarm. "That's spooky, man."

"Doesn't matter." T-Bone lifted a case of food into the truck. "We need to get going. I want to get back to English. I got me a crib and a honey. We been gone too long."

"You're getting old," Terry taunted. When T-Bone puffed up like he wanted to fight, Terry raised his hands. "I didn't mean nothing by it, man."

T-Bone snorted and slapped the skinny man on the back hard enough to make him stumble. "Let's get the truck loaded."

. . .

Sarah watched the banter between the two men. She didn't care about the same things she used to. She no longer worried that people saw her nakedness or that she had been pawed, physically abused, and tortured. She had retreated into a part of her mind that these men couldn't reach. That part of her mind could still think, reason, and do all the things she had been trained to do. She no longer felt pain as she used to. All the petty things in life that used to matter now seemed so trivial.

One thing was certain. People deserved to focus on their lives and do all the trivial things they cared about. They deserved to be unaware of the animalistic life-or-death fights that happened all around them. They might see a burned home, a dead body, or a policeman leading someone away in handcuffs, yet they never really understood how close to a biblical struggle between good and evil happened around them every day and how woefully undermanned the powers of good were.

Sarah would bide her time. While she may die from being tortured before ever getting loose, in her new way of thinking that was simply the penance she would pay for being unprepared. However, if she did get loose, she would forever be a soldier in the army of good, fighting a religious battle against evil, trying to wipe out every last one of these scumbags.

Starting with Crazy Joe.

IMPENDING

WADE LINED up the paraglider on the gravel road leading to Larry Curry's home at the back of his farm in Simpsonville, Kentucky. The small wing and fan didn't need much space to land. Wade would have landed it right in Larry's front yard if he hadn't been concerned with the power lines. They could still cause a great deal of damage, even though no energy was coursing through them. The gravel farm road leading from the main road to Larry's home stretched for a mile, passing his barns before getting to the two-story white home sitting back where it wouldn't be seen from the road or neighboring properties.

Larry, Bruce Ellis, Roger Travis, and another man were shoeing a horse beside the barn. PD was feeding the cattle and easy to discern from a distance as he was a mountain of a man. Wade didn't see Tony Sanford, but he was normally close by. On seeing Wade fly over low and wave, the men stopped their work. Wade banked the paraglider to land closer to the barn.

While Wade shut down the fan and began unstrapping, the men walked over to greet him. To an outsider, it must have looked like some western movie, the five men walking from the barn in jeans, cowboy hats, and boots, striding across the lot with a barn in the background.

Larry enjoyed referring to his friends as cowboys. "Hey! You're not from around here!" he joked, reaching to shake Wade's hand.

The rest of the men encircled Wade, shaking hands, slapping him on the back, and asking about his parents and shared acquaintances. It was a courtesy in the south to not rush directly to the point without proper greetings and enquiring into family members and acquaintances. While most of the men were in a church group together and had homes and farms near Larry's larger one, Wade lived further away and was more of a loner, like Goose had become.

"I came to talk y'all about Goose," Wade said, getting to the point as soon as possible after the niceties.

"Come over to the barn and have a seat." Larry's face became more serious, and PD let out a long breath.

Goose was a close friend they all cared about who had mostly been lost to them when his wife and daughter had been killed. When it first happened, they'd all been so busy simply surviving there hadn't been time or fuel to visit him and risk leaving their own families. The stories that had come to them got more and more crazy over time. They assumed the stories of death and mayhem involving Goose had to be exaggerated. Then as time allowed, each of them tried to visit him at one point or another. He usually rebuffed their advances, too drunk and crazed to recognize them. Mac was the only one who ever talked to Goose sober. Even so, Mac didn't get more than a few words at a time out of Goose. He seemed determined to drink himself to death or die killing the evil men who plagued the new world, as if doing penance for not being there when his wife and daughter were murdered by some of the same.

That was until they'd run into him recently at Mac's place.

Although he wasn't the same man they used to ride the trails with, they began to see signs of the old Gus slip through from time to time at the party. It was enough to give them hope that he might make it back. Until now.

Larry reached into a cooler and offered Wade something to drink.

"I talked to Goose today," Wade said in a rush, accepting a can. "He sent a rider to my house to bring me a SAT phone, asking me to scout some bad guys for him."

The guys nodded quietly. They knew the business Goose was in and expected he would find his quarry and offer no quarter. A part of his ruthlessness went against the gentle way the world had been for most of their lives. Yet, if someone didn't do the things he did, those men would do it to innocent families in homes that had once been rural and now were in the untamed frontier of the new America.

"When we saw Goose at Mac's the other day," said Bruce, "he was a little gaunt, with bags under his eyes, but for the first time in a long time he knew who we were. He had a woman with a lot of tattoos with him, and her son. Maybe he's coming around."

"If he's doing what I think, he won't get time to come around," Wade said ominously. "He mentioned the woman. I think he likes her. He said he left a note with the judge to leave the farm to her if he doesn't return from this hunt. He asked me to be a witness to his wishes if she needs."

That made the men sit up straighter and glance at each other.

"What this mission about?" PD asked.

"He's chasing a gang that took down a government supply convoy."

Roger spat chew to the ground. "They did *what*?"

"I heard something about that at the trading post yesterday," said Larry. "I figured it had to be exaggerated."

"Apparently not," Wade continued. "From what I understand,

they collapsed some rock walls on the expressway near Crestwood, both in front and behind the convoy, and shot 'em up good
until the rest surrendered. They committed all sorts of atrocities
on the survivors, then took the trucks, supplies, and a bunch of
prisoners and headed home."

"Where's home?" the other guy, an old friend of Roger's,
asked. Wade later learned his name was Lance.

"That's where I come in. Goose asked me to find them in the
paraglider and call him on the SAT phone. He said he'll handle it
from there."

"How many men would it take to take out a government
supply convoy?" Lance wondered aloud.

"I have no idea," Wade replied. "Goose thinks it might be
thirty or forty."

"Well, he can't go fighting thirty or forty men alone!" Larry
said in shock.

The looks on the faces of the men displayed their concern.

Roger stood up. "So what will you do after you find the
gang?" he asked.

"Goose said after I call him on the SAT phone to go home."

"Reckon you could swing back this way and tell us what you
find?" Roger asked. "We'll give you some fuel for your
contraption."

"What are you thinking?" Bruce asked in alarm. "You've got a
farm and a family to look after."

"I'll talk to my wife. She won't like it, but she understands
more than you think. Mine and Tony's places are right on
Highway 53. If that gang ain't stopped, how long before they get
bigger and come for us?" The group quieted, and the normally
taciturn Roger continued. "I s'pose we could close our small farms
and move here. Larry has offered, and I know some of y'all
already have. But what happens when the gang gets stronger and
finds this place too?"

"They haven't been in this area, and we are pretty well hidden back here," Bruce offered, though more quietly this time.

"We can't just hide." Larry was warming to what Roger said. "They'll find us eventually. And what about the church? We've been feeding the poor when we can there, which lets everyone know we have food. Half the people there know about where our farms are." There was a long pause. "I have some movies about the history of the Texas Rangers and what Texas was like before the Rangers were founded. There is a lot about those times and how people lived that's not too different from how we live today. One thing I do know for certain is that a lot of people would have died, and civilization would have been a long time coming to that area without the Rangers."

"I watched those with you," said Bruce. "Texas was part of the Province of Coahuila y Tejas, belonging to the newly independent country of Mexico at the time. The Texas Rangers became world renowned simply by their duties, to protect a thinly populated frontier against hostilities, first with Plains Indian tribes and, after the Texas Revolution, Mexico. They were described as state troops, then later as a police force that covered a vast territory, many times alone against larger forces. Even so, they were never a true police force. They were one of the most colorful, efficient, and deadly band of irregular partisans on the side of law and order the world has seen. They were called into being by the needs of the frontier and by a society that did not have and could not afford a regular army. In the early years of the Rangers, a high proportion of all west Texans served from time to time. It was a civic duty."

"You sound like a narrator from a TV show," Roger teased. "But who is taking on that civic duty nowadays?"

"Goose," Wade put in. "All by himself."

"Stephen F. Austin established the Rangers in 1823," said Larry. "I guess that makes our Governor Beatty kind of like

Stephen F. Austin. By the 1830s, there were sixty to seventy families from the U.S. settled in Texas, and there was no army to
protect the citizens against attacks by native tribes and bandits.
The early Rangers were small, informal, armed groups whose
duties required them to range over the countryside and who thus
came to be known as 'rangers.' According to the TV show, Austin
wrote that he would '...*employ ten men... to act as rangers for the
common defense... the wages I will give said ten men, is fifteen dollars a
month payable in property...*'"

"I remember that part. I think they ultimately got up to sixty
men that would be known by 'uniforms' of a light duster and an
identification badge of a gold star with a ring around it made from
a Mexican peso. Robert McAlpin Williamson was the first major
of the Texas Rangers. Two years later, the Rangers grew to over
three hundred men."

"That makes Goose like that Robert McAlpin whatshisname,"
Roger quipped despite being the quiet type.

"I don't know if it would work now." Lance sighed heavily.
"People used to give a shit back then. They risked their lives for
law and order and to protect their neighbors. They knew the real
meaning of sacrifice."

"Like Goose," said Wade.

"Hell no. Not like Goose," PD interjected vehemently, getting
the men to sit up and pay attention. "He's our buddy, and I'm not
putting him down. Goose already lost everything that matters to
him. He ain't sacrificing nothing. That's why he won't come
around us or talk to us. When I went to check on him, he wasn't
as drunk as he acted. He just didn't want me there. He worries we
would do what Roger is about to suggest." They all knew Roger
was kind of a mentor to PD. "Roger has a wife, a family, and
people who depend on him. Still, I know he wants to ride out and
help Goose. It's not really for Goose, though. He's thinking of
other families the gang will attack and other farms, just like those

Rangers did two hundred years ago. I'm sure all those men weren't single with nothing to lose like Goose. Sacrifice is about making a hard decision when you have something to lose."

Larry stood up to shake Wade's hand, having reached a decision in his mind. "You need something to eat before you get back in the air?"

"No, I'm good."

"Do you know where you're headed?"

"My best guess is somewhere near New Castle."

"Do you have enough fuel to come back here like Roger asked once you find them?"

"Yeah, this thing don't take much," Wade answered curiously, not sure why they were asking.

Larry nodded. "We've got some talking to do, but I 'spect you'll be guiding us to the fight."

"Just so long as you save a horse and bring some extra hardware for me." Wade strapped into the paraglider. "I can't carry much weight in this thing."

Goose turned left on Highway 146 at the four-way stop. On horseback, it would take him a few hours to make it to New Castle. There was no help for it. He might have barely had enough fuel and good roads to have made it with his truck. But with so many roads and bridges out, it wasn't worth the risk to be without a horse. It might take longer, but nothing would stop him. Horses were more dependable these days.

It took thirty minutes to descend the winding slope to a valley after turning on Highway 146. A few years ago, it would have only taken a minute in his truck to descend a barely recognizable slope.

Thankfully, when he got to the bottom, he found the bridge intact. In the distance, Goose could barely make out a line of vehicles approaching, two horse-drawn wagons and a buggy. He relaxed the tenseness he'd been holding in his shoulders, moving his hand away from the gun holster attached to his right thigh.

In the old days, men on horseback might have been bandits or rogues. A person had to stay aware. These days most of the bad men found enough gas to fuel their raiding parties. That would probably change as stockpiled fuel went bad and became even more scarce. The horse-drawn procession came closer, and Goose also pondered that even the bandits in the Old West probably never attacked anyone from a horse-drawn wagon. He could now discern details of the two large, heavy wagons drawn by four massive Belgian horses and a black buggy drawn by a single horse that led them. They weren't close enough to discern features yet, but Goose recognized the black buggy that Amos Massey, the patriarch of the family, drove.

When Goose and Amos's group met, Goose reined his horse up. "Good afternoon, Mr. Massey," Goose greeted formally.

Amos Massey was dressed in an old-fashioned, semi-formal way that was common for an Amish elder. He wore dark shoes, pants, and a vest with a blue shirt and flat-brimmed straw hat.

Amos Massey nodded almost imperceptibly. "Mr. Truman," he replied. Then he added, "Well met."

"Yes, sir. I am glad you are well. Your family looks well."

Amos gave a slight nod, his face impassive under the gray beard. Although Goose was a trusted friend to this Amish community, many of the elders didn't engage in small talk unless you caught them at the right place and time. Before things had gone to hell, Goose used to give them rides to Wal-Mart or to pick up a piece of equipment in his truck. Sometimes they'd let down their guard and talk at length about all kinds of things. Many times, they spoke in their Pennsylvania Dutch dialect that Goose had difficulty understanding.

"I 'spect you're on your way to my place," Goose said, getting to the point.

"Yah," Amos responded succinctly. His wife Dorothy appeared anxious to speak but would not until it was proper.

"I apologize for not being at my place when you get there. I'm chasing some evil men. Have your people seen a large group of men on motorcycles?"

"We have heard of them. All the English in the town," Amos tilted his head to indicate behind him, using the Amish term for almost everyone outside their community, "are crying and wailing after sinful men went to their town. We stayed away from the town on small roads." That was a long speech for Amos.

His wife Dorothy grasped his arm tighter.

"I've heard the stories about them. They're killing, pillaging, and more," Goose said, stone faced. "They're worse than you know. It's my job to chase them. You all should be on the lookout and try to avoid them."

Again, Amos merely nodded. To their way of thinking, the English had always been sinners; only now it was more in the open and, worse, no longer hidden in the words of a politician, unscrupulous business executive, or con artist. "You have the fields marked for hay cutting?"

"Yes, sir. Mine and two extra fields owned by my neighbor that are overgrown. Same as last season. If you'll fill my barn, the rest is yours. It's a lot of work. I have a stack of trade goods for you as well."

"The boys work hard. It may take a few days or a week." Amos indicated two wagons of children, nieces and nephews, behind him. "You leave too much in trade, though. We will only take what we earn."

"Mr. Massey, I'd appreciate it if you'd take it all. There is a good chance I may not be coming home. I'd rather good people like you have it. And if I ever need something, I know I have a friend in you." Amos gave another imperceptible nod.

Goose turned to his wife and tipped his hat. "Ma'am, there is fifty pounds of sugar in the trade goods. I remember being told last time that's something you all run short of."

"Thank you, Mr. Truman," Dorothy answered properly. A wide smile told the rest of the story.

"I left a woman and her son at my place," Goose said more to Dorothy than Amos. "They are all alone. I aim to leave them my place if I don't come home. They have no friends."

Dorothy smiled in a more motherly way this time. She'd known Goose for many years and grieved at his drunken, killing ways after the loss of his wife and daughter. She prayed for him. Perhaps the Lord had intervened. "I will greet her," Dorothy promised.

"Well, I'd better get going and see what that crying and wailing is about."

"Is this horse good for you?" Amos asked before Goose could leave, earning a raised eyebrow. That was about as much small talk as you would ever get from the elder. He was trying to be friendly, discussing the horse he had taken in on trade, trained, and sold to Goose when he was still Gus, before the world went to hell.

Goose nodded. "He's about the best horse a man could have."

"Be careful in your mission," Amos said, shocking Goose.

Goose touched the brim of his hat and reined the horse back on its way, waving to the rest of the clan as he rode off.

The gang rolled into the town of English with their convoy of bikes, trucks, stolen supplies, and prisoners. As towns went, English was underwhelming, barely a town at all, comprised of a couple of dozen homes, two churches, several small businesses, and an old historic school with a second floor on one side. Crazy Joe had appropriated the second floor for his lavishly appointed suite. They set up the largest room on the main floor to be a throne room, to hear cases, complaints, and dispense his law. The basement held supplies, prisoners, and spare rooms for the men. The rest of the gang was quartered in the couple of dozen homes nearby. Some residents fled, some were killed, and others enjoyed the lavish parties and lifestyle supplied by the gang. Many had nowhere else to go.

The convoy rolled into the parking lot of the old schoolhouse, circled, and came to a stop. Crazy Joe parked his sleek black customized Fat Boy right up front. While most men customized their bikes, anyone besides Crazy Joe would have been given a lot of grief from the purists about the super-wide tires on his hog. Before the world changed, they'd once seen Crazy Joe stomp some guy's head to a bloody mess over just such a comment in a bar. When the paramedics carried him out, they couldn't be sure if the man would have serious brain injuries. Since the fall, Crazy Joe would most likely shoot an offender instead of stopping at a beating.

"Chain the major near my place in the throne room," Crazy Joe instructed. "Van, I want you and Terry to choose five or ten from the others to present to me tonight at the party. Get them cleaned up and looking good. I want to choose three to share the room with the major."

No one had to ask what party. There was always a party, even if it was merely a drinking, dope-smoking affair.

"Got it, boss."

"You know what to do with the supplies, then get the trucks out of sight, in a barn or garage here in town, just in case."

"On it, boss."

"Van, move your shit into the schoolhouse. Pick a room and kick out whoever is in it."

That comment raised some eyebrows. Crazy Joe was a notorious loner and liked his space. He'd appropriated the entire second floor for his rooms. He only allowed a few trusted members on the first floor and a few more in the basement. He didn't want people to always see his most sadistic side.

The last time the entire gang stood in this parking lot, the boss had made Van Gogh cut his own ear off. Now he was giving him a coveted spot in the main building close to Crazy Joe. Those in the gang weren't sure if that was something to be coveted or feared.

T-Bone took Sarah to the intended room with a powerful grasp on her bicep. They assumed she'd lost her mind. All she did was stare straight ahead with that glassy, faraway look, stumbling along with T-Bone's longer stride. It was the same look his old lady used to give right before she lost it and broke things. When they entered the room, T-Bone stopped at a table in the hall to take a key from a dish. Inside the room, there was a chain bolted to the wall with cuffs at one end. The room stank of blood and urine. There was a bed, dresser, and washbasin. "I'll be back with water," he said, "and something to wear that the boss will like."

Sarah turned a killing glare on T-Bone.

T-Bone threw up his hands. "Lady, you do you. I could give a shit less. I'll bring clothes, soap, and water. What you do with them is up to you." He turned to walk out the door, then stopped. "Not sure why I'm telling you this, but there is a reason they call him Crazy Joe. He may want to rape, torture, or kill you. You had better hope he wants the first because I think he likes the other two more. I 'spect you think you'd rather be dead right now, but when you're dead, it's all over. No chance to get through this to something better, something that really matters to you."

"All that matters to me is killing Crazy Joe." Those were the first words Sarah had spoken since the convoy had been taken on

I-71 near Crestwood. Her voice sounded scratchy and alien to her.

T-Bone rushed in, swinging the door shut behind him. "Missy, don't you ever go sayin' nuthin' like that out loud," he hissed. "You won't die easy. He enjoys inflicting pain like nothing you've ever seen."

Sarah gave him a silent, hard-edged stare.

T-Bone stood straighter, peering down at Sarah, and exhaled. "Mebbe you've seen some of what he can do. I'm sorry 'bout that. Ain't nobody needs to go through what you have. But you more than anybody knows you want no more of that if you can help it."

Sarah crossed her arms defiantly.

"You do you." T-Bone sighed wearily, then said in a lower voice, "Dead people don't kill nobody."

A few minutes after T-Bone left, Sarah took a slow, calming breath and steeled herself. As she slowly washed and dressed, she kept muttering to herself, "Dead people don't kill nobody."

ENMITY

Many of Larry's friends had moved a good amount of their belongings to his farm. It was larger, off the beaten path, and centrally located. Additionally, it had the large cattle herd and fields they all worked so hard to maintain. Each of the men had homes or farms of their own, but the plan was to rally here if anything catastrophic ever happened.

Despite what Larry had said, there had been little talk after Wade left. Roger was the first to speak up in his normal taciturn way. "Y'all do what you need to. I reckon I'll head that way when Wade comes back."

PD always had Roger's back, and that was two. When Lance nodded to Roger, they had three.

Larry glanced over at Bruce, who merely shrugged.

Larry turned back to the group. "I been thinking on what Roger said a while ago. I think he's right," said Larry. "If this thing don't stop, it will eventually end up at our doorstep and be a bigger problem than we can handle. I'm not sure I can shoot anybody, so I'll pray on that and hope the Lord provides some direction for me. I know I don't want to see any of our wives or families killed or worse. Maybe doing lawman work over there will stop them before they come here and keep our families safer. Also, Goose is family to me also, same as all of you."

Tony hadn't been here when Wade stopped in but was due any minute. He normally followed Larry's lead.

Bruce nodded. "Sounds like we're going." Bruce may be slow to join and would grumble in the best tradition of soldiers around the world, but he was part of the family and had the skills they needed.

While they waited for Wade to return, the men had to find ways to burn off the nervous energy. There was work to be done around the farm, but no one wanted to be far from the barn. When Tony showed up, they filled him in. Tony merely nodded. He didn't need to say much. He understood why they needed to do this, and he was part of the outfit.

"You already wear the long duster and look the part of a lawman," Larry teased.

Bruce nodded. "The duster and gold star have always been the uniform of the Texas Rangers."

The conversation soon petered out, and each man drifted off to work on minor tasks to keep themselves busy. Larry came back from the house in his duster and another one for Bruce.

Roger chuckled. "I reckon I'll need to get my old duster out."

"Well hell, I don't have one," PD grumbled.

"Then you can't be a Ranger," Roger laughed.

"I'll just be a Ranger with no duster."

Larry walked into the shop to see what Bruce was working on. He had some old copper gutter pipe and was cutting with metal shears and hammering.

"They won't be gold, but if we shine 'em up good, at least people will see what side we're on," Bruce explained. "Maybe they'll work with us or at least not shoot at us."

"Isn't the Texas Ranger star supposed to have a ring around it?" Larry asked.

"Yeah, but I couldn't quite do that easy with the shears and only a couple of hours."

"Are we allowed to wear these?"

"I don't know. Goose is, and we're going to help him. My focus is on not having the good guys shoot at us thinking we're bad guys. We'll worry about the rest later."

The horsemen got engrossed in helping with the stars, filing off the rough edges and burnishing the copper to a shine. They didn't notice when Larry's wife Connie stepped into the barn.

"What are you all doing?" she asked.

All the men looked embarrassed, as if she had caught them with their hands in the cookie jar. Connie was used to Larry being childlike sometimes and impetuous. When Larry took her aside to talk, she smiled, anticipating another funny story.

The others observed some arguing, tears, and finally hugs. When Larry and Connie came back to the group, Connie's eyes were red and puffy from tears that hadn't quite stopped.

"I don't like this," she said, "but Larry is right. Goose is family to all of us, and if this lawlessness doesn't get stopped, it will end up on our doorstep and hurt more people. I just have one selfish promise I want from each of you." Connie paused for effect. "Bring my husband home safe!"

"Yes, ma'am," they chorused.

Connie wiped her eyes. "I'll go make you boys some food to take with you."

After she left, Larry looked sheepish, and the other men took on a more somber expression, imagining similar conversations they needed to have with their families. It would go much worse for them, because if things happened as quickly as they expected, there wouldn't be time to go home and explain before they had to leave. Anyone who'd been married knew that asking for permission to do something they'd already done didn't go over well. They joked among each other that it might be better if they got shot on the mission than face their wives after.

Wade flew over New Castle, high enough that people wouldn't spot him easily. The streets were fuller of people than Wade would have expected. They crowded the courthouse square as if for a festival. There was even a makeshift stage with a band. This alone alarmed Wade enough to circle twice more and confirm what he saw.

The gang was here! The trucks were parked outside the court-house, along with a slew of Harleys, many of them modified and not the type an accountant pretending to be tough on the week-ends would ride.

Darkness was approaching in an hour or two. Wade had to hurry, making this last sweep and getting the information to Goose. He would be making the last part of his journey in the dark, depending on Larry and the horsemen to have light for him to navigate and land by. His wife would worry, but he would jot down a note to her and drop it at his home on the way to Larry's.

Wade flew back down Highway 146. Two horse-drawn wagons with men in black suits were heading east on the highway led by a black carriage. A large man on a black and white horse was heading west, the gap between the two groups widening as Wade banked to land a dozen yards in front of Goose.

While Wade unbuckled from the machine, Goose rode over to the side of the road and tied the horse to a fence post, loosening the girth, then walked back to meet Wade with a hand out to shake.

"It's nice to see you. It's been a long time," Goose said.

"Too long." Wade was a bit surprised by Goose's friendly

demeanor. "Things have changed a lot since we last met. We've changed."

Goose chose to ignore the elephant in the room. When he and Wade rode horses together, he'd been Gus, working in an office cubicle, worried about his next promotion. Even though Wade had known his childhood nickname, it was hard for him to use it because they had worked in a professional environment. The man everyone now knew only as Goose had longer hair, a gaunt, hollow look in his piercing blue eyes, and a beard. Goose ignored the invitation to open up and moved on.

"What'd you find?"

Wade exhaled and leaned against a 55 MPH sign that would rust long before it was ever needed again. "They're in New Castle," he said without preamble.

Goose glanced over at his horse. Wade put a hand on his shoulder, and Goose whipped around with killing in his eyes. The look on Wade's face sobered Goose. "I'm sorry, man. I have been in the middle of so much the last year or so I'm kind of on a hair trigger."

"It's okay, man. You've seen some terrible shit. I've been there. No one is unchanged. So what are you going to do?"

"I'll do what I've got left to do. It's all I have anymore. I've got to kill as many of those scumbags as I can before they get me. I don't know anything else."

"The governor said to kill them?" Wade asked with a mixture of awe and disbelief.

Goose looked down at his boots, showing the first sign of shame in a long time. "No. He wants me to capture them when I can and call for someone to pick them up. We both know that's not realistic. It would take hours or days for the guard to meet me. I'm usually alone facing more than a few and they're shooting at me. I can't take the risk."

"Have you captured any of them yet?"

"No."

Both men got silent. Goose reached to his cargo pocket for something to drink. It was empty. In a moment of strength and with a stern look from Kelly, Goose had left with only a single flask of moonshine.

"It'll be dark soon. I need to get in the air," said Wade. "I'll try to get back here in the morning to help guide you in and give you a lay of the land before you get there." Wade started walking back to the paraglider.

"I won't be here," Goose called after him. "If I ride all night, I can get there around two or three in the morning and surprise them."

"Goose, that's crazy!" Wade threw up his hands, causing the horse to dance sideways. At moments like this, it was easier to think of him as Goose. The man he'd once worked with in an office cubicle truly was dead.

"Crazy would be facing those men awake and alert," Goose retorted.

Less than an hour later, Wade swooped in low over his home. His father and wife had two 55-gallon barrels burning on either side of a clearing he used to take off and land. Wade dropped a note tied to a screwdriver he carried in between the two barrels. He circled once to see that they got it and flew off to the northwest for Larry's farm. Wade had grown up in the area and felt sure he could get close, even in the dark. Larry's farm and neighboring properties had a distinct set of buildings, roads, and barns he felt sure he could find at night. Even so, it wouldn't be easy. There were no streetlights, running cars, or homes with electricity to give a point of reference. Though some had candles, generators, or solar, very few ran lights at night. The world had reverted to an old-fashioned agrarian cadence, where people worked daylight to dark, then slept well, waking when the roosters crowed. Wade knew his wife would be angry when he saw her next. Or *if* he saw her again. He depended on his father, a levelheaded veteran who had seen a lot in life, to take care of his family while he did what he needed to.

Wade had spent enough time in the air and flown over Larry's farm a few times, including earlier this day. He knew the direction and approximate flying time he needed to get there. A low-grade panic began to settle in when he circled the area he expected the farm to be in for the second time, not finding the landmarks he was looking for. He could land this thing on a dime, but the odds of hitting a power line or tree limb in the dark and getting broken bones far from help was a serious concern.

As he banked the paraglider for an oblong circle that would cover another area, he spotted a fire in the distance. When he got closer, he saw a second fire and the shape of Larry's three barns and landed. The men had taken turns tending the fires on either end of the gravel lot near the barns.

"Wasn't sure we'd see you tonight," Bruce said dryly.

"For a few minutes, I didn't, either." The relief was noticeable in Wade's voice. "Where is everyone?"

"Larry couldn't reach Tony on the radio. He rode out soon after you left to check on him. He should be back in an hour or so. Roger and PD are working on Larry's truck. It ran rough then died when we started it."

They walked over to Larry's truck. When the two approached, PD stood. "We can fix it, but we're going to need to scavenge parts from another truck."

"What about Larry's neighbor?" Roger suggested.

For a group of men who went to church together, the thought of stealing from their neighbor felt like an act of betrayal as much as a crime.

"Larry said he hasn't seen him since before the world

changed," said Bruce. "He has another home in Florida, so he probably stayed down there where it's warmer when everything went to hell. Too hot for me in the summer, though."

PD said, "He has a truck in the barn we can scavenge from."

"Why not just write him a note?" suggested Lance. "If he comes back, we owe him the parts plus something."

Roger nodded. "Reckon that's about the best we can do."

"Whatever we do, we need to hurry," Wade pressed. "Goose is riding all night to fight the gang at New Castle. He won't survive it if we don't get there before he attacks."

It was past midnight when the truck was ready. Larry hadn't returned with Tony yet. Connie had come out with the food. She wasn't too worried. It was a long ride through an area where Larry knew most of the people. Sometimes he got to talking and lost track of time, however, and in this case he should be hurrying.

The men got the horses loaded and their gear ready. They would use the livestock trailer instead of the nicer living quarters trailer since they needed the extra space and had no intention of camping. Bruce knew where Larry kept his extra guns and ammo. If he wasn't back by the time they got loaded up, they would pick him up on the way.

By two a.m. they had everything loaded, the truck fueled up, and decided to head out. The five men barely fit in the quad cab truck. When the headlights came on, they spied two men in dusters coming up the gravel farm road. They got out to greet Larry and Tony.

"We were coming to look for you two," Bruce told him.

"It's a longer ride than you think. People are going to have to get used to the new times it takes to go someplace," Larry said wearily. He wasn't getting any younger.

He led the young sorrel he'd ridden to the dry lot and unsaddled it. Bruce had already loaded his older spotted horse for the trip. Tony loved his quarter horse and preferred to ride his own mount. There was just enough room in the trailer to fit it in. Larry spent a few minutes with Connie, then they all loaded into the truck. Wade and PD got in the truck's bed to make room for the two older men.

They turned out of the farm, left on Todds Point Road heading east. Their luck held as they had open roads with little damage. Many of the roads were in such bad shape they couldn't drive much faster than thirty-five miles per hour safely. This wouldn't be a good time to break down. AAA didn't exist anymore, and a number of bridges were out. Each time that happened, they had to unload the horses, find a way around through the fields and soft ground, then reload.

Several hours later, they turned left on Highway 53, before cutting over toward Eminence Pike on Drane Lane, where they had to go around three more bridges. Kentucky had a great deal of creeks and rivers covered with anything from a culvert pipe to a bridge. Unchecked time and weather would soon damage the roads and infrastructure. Few people realized how fast things fell into disrepair without regular maintenance. Even a creek that a child could step over would tear a road apart if the culvert became full of debris and multiple rainstorms over the course of a year kept rushing water over the road, tearing up asphalt.

It was after four a.m. when they reached the roadblock at Eminence. There was a car, a couple of sawhorses, and two men who looked like they'd rather be home in bed. A truck pulling a livestock trailer didn't alarm the guards much. One of them walked in front of the sawhorse with a hand up to stop the vehicle, a shotgun cradled in his arm. PD was driving and put the truck in park.

"Bruce," said Roger, "you got those stars?"

"Yeah, but they're just made up. They don't really mean anything."

"Hand 'em out. Let's pin them on. Folks need symbols these days. If nothing else, it lets them know we stand for law and order."

All the men wore dusters similar to those of the Texas Rangers except for Wade, who didn't bring one, and PD, who hadn't found one big enough to fit him. After hastily pinning the star to his duster, Larry got out and approached the lawman.

"Hold right there!" he commanded. "Step in front of the truck facing the headlights and put your hands on the hood."

"We're just—" Larry began.

"Face the truck and put your hands on the hood!" he shouted. "No one else in the truck move. My partner has you in his sights and we're a mite nervous."

Larry complied, speaking in a calming voice, "I am wearing a gun, but I'm not here for trouble."

"What's the star for?"

Larry had forgotten he'd pinned it on and glanced down, almost laughing at the crude copper star. "This is just to let you know we're the good guys."

"Is this some kind of joke?" the deputy snapped.

"No. Nothing like that. Our friend is chasing the worst of the criminals for the governor, kind of like the old Texas Rangers used to."

The deputy didn't appear convinced, staring at Larry. "Uh-huh," he muttered skeptically.

"We haven't been sworn in yet. We just wanted anyone who saw us to know what side we're on before they shoot. Goose is chasing a motorcycle gang, last seen over in New Castle."

That got the deputy's attention. "A motorcycle gang in New Castle?"

"Yeah."

"Y'all need to come with me." He moved the sawhorse and instructed the other deputy to stand guard. "Follow me to the courthouse," he told the group. "We're aware of that gang and have been worried about them. The sheriff and judge will be shocked that you all are friends with Goose Truman. No one around here really knows what side he's on. People steer clear of him. He's a dangerous man and not quite right, if you know what I mean, from what people say." Then the deputy noticed their attire. "What's with all the dusters?"

Larry shrugged sheepishly. "We normally ride horses to save fuel and avoid bad roads and needed a jacket, and well, they look the part."

The deputy looked astounded. He wasn't used to seeing a man his dad's age act like a kid. "Uh-huh," he said in a droll way before walking the few blocks to the center of town.

At the old Eminence Bank building on the main strip now being used now as a courthouse, they met the sheriff and local judge in the foyer. Most small towns in America were reverting to the feel of towns in the Old West, where a judge, mayor, and sheriff could keep order in town in a down to Earth, common sense kind of way.

"I understand you're going after Crazy Joe's gang," the judge said without preamble.

Larry looked uncomfortable. "I'd say we are more going after our friend, who is going after them. But yes, if someone doesn't go after them pretty soon, they'll come after us."

The judge let out a breath and deflated. "You got that right. We think we must be next on their list. We plan to put up a good fight, but I'm not sure we could win against their numbers, especially if they took out an armed convoy. People around here have escape plans for their families if the gangs come. They've been hiding their valuables too."

Judge Troutman was in his late sixties and had probably been a little overweight before all this started, based on his baggy suit cinched at the waist. The admission that the town may not survive an attack by the gang made him appear even older.

Sheriff Honaker was a younger man who liked to work out and wore his uniform tight. "They won't get in here, Judge," he said defiantly in what appeared to be a long-running argument. "I've got trained men and early warnings plans. We've been working with the citizens on how to shoot and defend this place. We'll cut the gang to shreds if they come here."

The judge gave a wry smile and said to Larry, "I hope the sheriff is right. He's been working hard at it, but the truth is we lost two-thirds of our townspeople in the first few months of the government failing. They moved away, to where I don't know. The remaining townspeople want to help and will try…" He shrugged.

The sheriff was clearly agitated at the judge for not addressing him directly in his reply. "So what's with those stars?" he directed at Larry to vent.

With such a friendly demeanor, Larry had a way of disarming people with his nature. "Aww heck," he said, looking slightly embarrassed, "I guess we got all caught up in going to help Goose and wanting people to know we were on the good side. We thought if we looked like lawmen, people wouldn't shoot at us without knowing who we are. The governor told Goose he should swear in deputies."

"Goose Truman?" the sheriff exclaimed, looking to the judge for support. "That bastard chased two men here and killed them right on Main Street!" He pointed to a small building that had once serviced trains more than a hundred years ago. "Told me to kiss his ass if I didn't like it and flicked the stub of a cigar at my chest. I swear, I think he was drunk too. He said he was working for the governor. I still think I should have shot him."

"And you'd have been killed," the judge said before turning

back to Larry. He'd lost some of his friendly demeanor upon learning of Larry's friendship with Goose. "I have talked to my friend Judge Berger in LaGrange. That man is working for the governor. Why, I have no idea, but from all the stories, he is no more than a drunken killer with no fear and no morals. He leaves a mess of carnage wherever he goes."

"He wasn't always like that," Larry said quietly. "He's our friend, and he's only killing the worst of the killers and rapists that small towns like this can't chase down and bring to justice."

It was clear the judge had finished with the subject of Goose Truman. "You're free to move on through. New Castle won't be in as good of shape as Eminence, though. Crazy Joe and his gang have been through there a few times and claim it as their territory. If you want my advice, don't go rolling into New Castle in the dark. You don't know what you're getting into. You should sleep here and go in when it's light. I hope you won't take offense at this, but I'd rather you do that outside our town limits. There is a spot not far outside our blockade where you and your men will be safe. If you're a friend of Goose Truman's, I have to be careful. I wish you luck, though." He finished with a rather insincere hand-shake, his entire demeanor different after learning of their friend-ship with Goose.

The party was extravagant, filled with music, gunshots, screams of passion, and screams of terror. In other words, like most of the gang's parties held every second or third day. The only thing different today was the new batch of prisoners to torture who, other than Sarah Redman, had no idea what lay in store. Crazy Joe reigned from his throne. They had professional strippers and women forced into it as a part of their captivity. The gang's lieu-tenants enjoyed torturing the captive men by forcing them to do stupid tasks, like dancing in a skirt or other demeaning things. They chained Sarah and two other women on the floor at Crazy Joe's feet. The music got louder and the stench of weed got thicker.

Soon they started snorting a white powder, and things got more chaotic. Crazy Joe took a perverse pleasure in forcing Sarah and the other two girls to snort the powder with him. Sarah tried to breathe in as little as possible without being beaten. The girls took more, and it soon clouded their minds. One girl wept uncontrollably. Crazy Joe motioned over a few women in the gang, who took her away to beat her. The women were more sadistic torturers than any of the men, except maybe Crazy Joe. Sarah shuddered watching the young girl next to her being untied and led away. Her own mind was starting to get confused from the smoke and drugs.

The other girl reacted differently. She began dancing to the music, her movements becoming more seductive, and taking her clothes off. Sarah was both sad for her and hopeful. For a fighter like Sarah, it was hard to accept that the rapes and beatings were going to happen and there was nothing they could do to stop it. She simply had to survive long enough to get revenge when the opportunity presented itself. The dancing girl may not recognize the rape for what it was in her drugged state. Perhaps they wouldn't beat her as much if she was compliant.

Soon after her capture, Sarah had learned to hide a piece of her mind and soul away from what was happening to her body. She could rise above her body and observe what was being done to her with a white-hot thirst for vengeance, yet physically, it felt like it was happening to someone else. Sarah's thirst for revenge felt like avenging a wrong done to someone else like a child or family member. In those instances, her mind became confused.

One thought kept coursing through her mind. *Dead people don't kill nobody.* That gave her the will to live.

. . .

A commotion interrupted the party, and the music stopped. Crazy Joe stood and roared, "What the hell's going on?"

Two lower-ranking gang members were arguing over who was a better shot and who had killed more men. It was the kind of stupid argument only a couple of drunks could have. Even after Crazy Joe's command, they spat insults and tried to swing at one another. Crazy Joe rocked each man with an openhanded slap to the face that echoed across the now silent room. "Take this outside! Someone bring my chair."

Once outside, he commanded they set up beer bottles on an old car thirty yards away. "Bring two of the scrawniest prisoners to me."

"Yes, sir." Terry hustled off.

When all were present, Crazy Joe explained his plan. He had a knack for some of the most devious ideas, and the crowd loved it. "Here is what we're going to do. Both of you dumbasses," he pointed to the two gang members who had been arguing, "will each shoot ten beer bottles off the hood of that old car when I give you the signal."

Both men nodded, somewhat confused, and mumbled acceptance.

Then Crazy Joe turned to the two scrawny prisoners. "When they're done shooting beer bottles, they are going to shoot an apple off of each of your heads, William Tell–style." He cackled. "Here's the kicker, though…" He turned back to his men. "Well, two kickers. For you two dumbasses, I'm going to horsewhip the loser, so you better not miss the apple."

Both men turned green and looked sick but knew better than to complain. A horsewhipping was better than having a body part cut off.

"Second kicker is this. You two prisoners are going to watch them shoot bottles. When they're done, you two are going to fight. The winner gets to choose which of my men shoots the apple from your head. Therefore, if there is a better shot among the two, you just might live through this, so you'd better fight hard."

The crowd hooted and hollered. They were afraid of Crazy Joe but loved this too. Some of the perverse, diabolical schemes he came up with served no purpose other than entertaining half of these degenerates and keeping the other half in fear of him. They lined up chairs on the porch and in the gravel lot and made wagers while someone set up ten bottles on the old rusty Dodge.

Jeff shot first. He wore an older Glock 9mm in a drop-leg holster, more for show than practicality. His hands shook, and he was already perspiring when he toed the line to shoot. He slowly pulled the trigger. The bullet pinged off the car, and the bottles never moved. Nine more shots followed. Three of them broke a bottle.

Next up was Tim. Tim was arrogant and wore a bandolier holster for his Ruger Vaquero .45. It was all for show. After emptying the revolver, all the bottles stood intact. The first shot he took after reloading knocked a bottle over. He couldn't be sure if the bottle had been nicked or the air of the big .45 long colt passing by tipped it. In either event, the bottle tipped, rolled, and broke when it hit the bumper of the car. Four shots later that was the only bottle Tim had broken.

The crowd roared and bets were paid. Crazy Joe's dark mood improved. Something about the way Sarah Redman was chained at his feet reminded him of an old *Star Wars* poster with Princess Leia chained but defiant at the feet of Jabba the Hut. "You two!" he yelled at the prisoners, loud enough to silence the onlookers. "There ain't no rules 'cept this. If you don't fight, you'll be shot. You fight 'till one man can't stand and the other can. That's how we decide who won. Now fight!"

Both men paused, surprised at how quickly this had been

thrust on them. A short time ago, one of the men worked in the mall as a retail manager and still lived with his mom. The other worked in accounting, hoping to find a girlfriend. It was an awkward and silly fight, with slaps and scratches, both men trying to kick the other while keeping his face far enough back to avoid a punch. The crowd jeered, cheered, and yelled insults. As the two men became desperate, the fight got more serious. More than once they became so exhausted they couldn't continue. Each time, they were given water and incentive to fight harder, in the form of punches, light cuts with a knife, and promises to cut deeper next time.

Soon the men were going at it hammer and tong. The former retail manager started screaming and scratching. The accountant found some inner strength and rocked him with three hard punches to the face. That broke the scrawny man's nose, sending a torrent of blood down his face. He fell to his hands, and the accountant lifted a knee to his face, rocking him on his back. To his credit, the man didn't stay down. He got up and grabbed a nearby limb from a woodcutting pile and swung it at the accountant's head. The blow didn't land fully, being partially blocked by the skinny man's right arm, which went numb after the blow. Both men fell to the ground in a roiling tussle, the accountant on top. The retail manager grabbed a hunk of the accountant's hair and pulled it with all he had. A hunk of skin and hair as large as a fist came out, leaving a bloody patch. The accountant emitted a primal scream, more guttural than people would have expected from the small man. He grabbed the other man's head with his left hand, feeling only beginning to come back to his right, and started slamming the man's head into the gravel until his eyes rolled up in his head.

Crazy Joe motioned for Terry to pull the accountant off. "We have a winner," he announced. The crowd cheered. It was a better fight than they expected. "Is the other one dead?"

"Naw, he'll live," one man announced and threw water on his face.

"Good." Crazy Joe turned to the accountant. "Now who do you choose as your shooter?"

Through bruised lips, he could only mumble, "The other guy, not the one who thinks he's a cowboy." The sound of defiance in his voice caused Crazy Joe to raise an eyebrow.

Crazy Joe looked at the loser, who was now awake and on his feet but needed help standing. "Tie him to a tree."

The bloodied loser of the brawl only made a feeble attempt at resistance. Laughing, Crazy Joe walked up and placed an apple on the man's head. "If you move and the apple falls, I'll use a grape and after that a pebble." Tears ran from the loser's face, mixing with the blood. To his credit, he kept still.

At Crazy Joe's direction, Tim nervously eased up and took the long Ruger Vaquero .45 from the holster across his chest. The men up front laughed seeing the sweat on his brow and his hand shaking. Crazy Joe motioned for Terry to be ready with his whip. He had instructions to whip Tim for missing or failing to fire and keep whipping until he shot the apple in half.

Tim looked over as Terry readied his whip and hurriedly stepped forward, straightening his arm and pulling the trigger. The loser's face exploded in a mess of bone fragments, brain matter, and gore, some of it splattering Tim's face ten feet away. His body slumped against the ropes, the apple bouncing to the ground, whole. Tim's face was a tableau of shock. In this gang, no one was immune to death. So far, he'd managed to stay on the periphery of the most violent acts of their criminal enterprise. He hadn't experienced this level of gore nor killed anyone as far as he knew.

Tim's back exploded in a lightning bolt of shock and agony, followed by the sonic crack of the whip. He whirled around to see Terry drawing back for another stroke. Tim was confused and disoriented with no idea how to make it stop. His shirt was torn, his back bleeding. He gazed up at Crazy Joe pointing at the apple with a lazy finger and a wry grin, as the whip cracked across his back again, tearing more clothing and opening his skin, causing the blood to flow more freely. Tim fired, missing the apple again, the .45 long colt tearing a furrow in the ground. The whip bit again, driving Tim to his knees. Tim saw Terry coil the whip again, and in a fit of anger he got to his knees, scrambled to the apple, and fired point blank, turning it into applesauce.

Crazy Joe stood and clapped, allaying fears that Tim had broken some kind of rule. The crowd again erupted in cheers, jeers, and catcalls. When the clapping faded, Crazy Joe pointed to Jeff with his Glock 9mm.

Shocking everyone, Charles, the accountant, strode up to Crazy Joe and reached for the apple. "If I'm going to die, I'll do it standing on my own two feet. I don't need to be tied." Clearly the little man had found an inner well of courage, and it impressed Crazy Joe. "Let's get on with this."

Apple in hand, Charles strode directly to another tree a few feet from the one the loser's body sagged from, his head a pulpy mess.

Jeff looked questioningly at Crazy Joe, who shrugged and nodded. Without preamble, Jeff walked three steps forward to shoot the apple from Charles's head at only three feet. Charles fell to one knee in relief, exposing some of his toughness as false bravado.

There was a pregnant pause, then Crazy Joe stood and clapped. "Now let's take this back inside." When the crowd started filtering inside, he pointed to the kneeling accountant. "I want you to party with me. We need to talk about your future."

ADAPT

GOOSE'S PLAN TO catch the gang in New Castle got derailed almost before it started. He'd barely gone a mile when the big black and white horse began to flounder, limping in an awkward three-legged gait. The rhythmic one, two… three, four clopping of the horse's metal shoes on pavement had changed to one, two… four. Rocky had lost a shoe.

For ten or fifteen beats, Goose considered going on. Rocky could carry him without a shoe. The horse would run himself to death or permanently lame himself for his master and friend, yet Goose didn't have the heart to ask. He cursed a blue streak and turned off the road to tie up to a fence post and search for the shoe. He kept a couple of tools in his bag but had neglected to pack a spare shoe. When he dismounted, Rocky nuzzled him as if in apology. The soft feel of his snout interspersed with a few prickly whiskers always made Goose smile. He reached into the pommel bag for horse treats. He almost heard Laura's voice in his ear saying, *"Everything happens for a reason,"* as she always did. He couldn't tell if it was really her, his addled mind, or just the wind. She wasn't coming to him as often lately. This delay meant his arrival in New Castle would be delayed by a few hours, giving him time for a drink.

It took an hour to find the shoe. It was bent, and he had to straighten it with a hammer against the guardrail. He needed to straighten a few nails as well since he didn't have enough fresh ones in the bag. By the time he finished, it was after two in the morning. He rolled into his blanket for a short thirty-minute nap. It would be close to dawn before he made it to New Castle.

The ride to New Castle took longer than Goose planned. It had been light for about an hour when he got close to town. He spied an abandoned building to the left with a faded sign atop that read "Henry County Food Market." It had probably been abandoned years before the fall. The windows were broken, the door missing, and it was full of debris. The shelves were pushed to the side, and there was a cold fire circle in the middle under the blowing leaves. Goose led Rocky inside, picked him, and changed from his cowboy boots to an old worn pair of jungle boots for the next phase of his mission. If possible, he would scout first, then set up a variety of shoot and fallback positions with different weapons and ammo dispersed so he could shoot and move with as much speed as possible. He hadn't brought the ghillie suit because he wanted to focus on speed. He covered his face with a shemagh and sharpened his knife. He left the .308 and other weapons here until he got the lay of the land. The scout needed to be done quickly and quietly. As always, he had the Springfield .45 competition model at his hip and a Walther CCP in a chest rig. For this mission, a small 9mm rifle with a 14" barrel, laser, ACOG, and Silencerco suppressor would suffice. The goal was not to be seen until he was ready and, if possible, take a few of the perimeter sentries out.

It was time to hunt.

Goose left through the back of the store, going across fields and yards to approach Center Street from behind at Dutton Alley. Dutton only had a couple of homes facing it, then opened up behind an abandoned building facing the courthouse.

The scene in the street perplexed Goose. He didn't see any trucks or bikes. A few dozen people milled about the courthouse lawn as if dressed for a night out dancing, not a day of toil, many of them crying. Soon a group of older men came out of the courthouse with a stretcher board supporting a cloth-covered body. A woman and her daughter followed them, both clearly crying and distraught, walking stiffly as if in physical pain.

While it may be some weird funeral rite here in town, these people were clearly not a threat, and the gang wasn't here. Goose walked from his place in hiding to the picnic table where they laid the body for the mourners. Most drew back in fear. None of them were armed. The mother and daughter were shell-shocked and never moved.

"I'm hunting a bunch of men on motorcycles," Goose said, choosing to ignore the body. Death was a common occurrence these days.

"You just missed 'em," said an elderly man, inclining his head to the body. He was eighty if he was a day. He wore blue work pants, a white shirt buttoned all the way up, and a fedora-style hat.

Goose took a lungful of air to avoid cursing. He'd missed them again, and his horse was played out. And they had trucks. "Damn."

"What do you want them for?" the old man asked.

"To kill them. Kill them all."

The old man nodded sagely, then the shell-shocked mom spoke. "I know where they're going."

While she had trouble speaking and couldn't look Goose in the eye, he was able to piece together the location of the gang's hideout in an old schoolhouse in English, Kentucky. There was nothing more Goose could do for the people here other than avenge their dead. This gang left a trail of bodies crying out for vengeance.

When Goose started to recross Campbellsburg Road running in front of the courthouse, the old man called out, "You going after them all by yourself?"

"Yep. My horse is darn near played out, but the longer I wait, the more of this they do." Goose pointed to the body of a young girl. "He will just have to do the best he can. I'll rest him when I can."

The old man stepped closer to speak. "If you're going after this rabble, I can help. I'd rather not too many know, though."

Goose raised an eyebrow. "Go on."

"I have a '78 Chevy truck locked away in an old garage, covered with dust. Everyone thinks it's junk. It runs, though, and I have enough gas to fill it halfway. I've been saving it for a getaway if I need. Helping you kill some of those scumbags seems a better use of it right now."

"What about my horse?"

The old man smiled and pointed over Goose's shoulder to a used car lot with a red two-horse Corn Pro trailer.

Goose grinned. "Go get your truck."

Despite being aware that the Amish were coming, Kelly was still shocked to see the procession of buggy and two heavy wagons parked at the gate to Goose's property. She instructed Brian to stay in the house and hustled out to unlock the gate. "I'm so sorry. I would have opened the gate sooner if I had known when you were coming today. Goose said to always keep it locked."

The stern older man in the buggy ignored her words and

snapped the horses forward when the gates were open. The two large wagons followed closely behind.

Before Kelly could close the gate and follow the procession, Kevin came galloping up. "What's going on?" he asked in alarm. "Who are they?"

"It's okay. They're the Amish people Goose traded with to cut hay and do some repairs on the farm. I just didn't know they'd be here this morning." Kelly walked down the lane, followed by Kevin.

At the barn, Kelly and Kevin were met by the older couple from the lead buggy and a younger, smiling man with broad shoulders and sandy brown hair.

"Welcome..." Kelly began before the older man frowned and turned to walk to the barn.

Kevin leaned in and whispered, "I don't think the elders normally talk to women outside of their families. Perhaps I could talk to him for you."

"No," Kelly said sternly, some of her old fire returning. "I can handle this."

"My name is Dorothy," the older lady from the buggy said as a way of greeting. "Is this your man?" She inclined her head to Kevin.

"No!" Kelly yelled more sharply than she intended, earning a frown from Kevin and a big smile from the younger Amish man. Things were not going the way she wanted, and she was getting frustrated. "Goose asked me to greet you all and help point you to the work, but he just walked away." Kelly pointed to the older man unhitching the team from the buggy and directing others to unload tents and farming equipment. Brian had come out of the house and was watching them and talking to some of the younger Amish children.

"May we sit down?" Dorothy asked, moving to a two-seated glider next to the barn.

"I'm glad you're here. I hope Goose is all right. I was supposed to help make sure you had food and water, a place to sleep, and point you to the work that needs done."

"We met Mr. Truman along the route," said Dorothy. "He was fine and continuing on his work."

"Oh thank God," Kelly said with more emotion than she meant to show.

Dorothy smiled knowingly, and Kevin and the younger Amish man looked on.

"What is the work you were supposed to tell us about?" Dorothy prodded sweetly.

"The fence is down in several places after trees and limbs have fallen. There are boards and saws behind the barn. There are, of course, our fields here that need to be cut and the hay stored in the barn, but Goose has also asked that the neighbor's fields be cut as well." Kelly stood to step forward and point to the neighboring fields and barn on the ridge a mile away. "Their hay is to be stored in that barn, except for whatever you want to take."

Dorothy smiled to herself at Kelly's use of the word *our* to describe these fields. "Is that all?"

"Goose did say if you had time, he would like to dig another well, but that could wait for another time. All of the trade goods he saved for you are in the first stall." Kelly sat down again.

Dorothy looked to the younger Amish man. Although no words were exchanged, he nodded and walked off to help the older man set up tents.

Noting that Brian was playing and running with the younger Amish kids by now, Kelly smiled.

～

The horsemen didn't get started at daybreak as was their plan. An hour before dawn, the town of Eminence came under attack.

All the men considered at one point or another if this should be their fight. However, if they meant to take this lawman business seriously, it had to start now. They checked their weapons, donned their dusters and copper stars, and moved up to the blockade. Only one officer manned the blockade. The rest had gone to help fight the killers and spoilers.

"What's going on?" Larry asked.

The man couldn't have been much over eighteen. His hands shook, voice quavering as he spoke. "It's a gang from Louisville. The crips or bloods or something. They've spread throughout the town and are killing and looting."

"Calm down, son. We're here to help." Larry glanced back and shrugged to his companions. The kid was scared to death and had been left alone on the blockade, confused and unsure, thinking they were under attack by a Louisville gang. They'd had reports of those gangs ranging further out each week, doing fast raids to kill, take all the supplies and a few prisoners, then disappearing like ghosts into the night. However, it probably wasn't the crips or bloods. The kid had watched too much TV.

"Yes, sir. What will you do?" the kid asked.

"Let's mount up," Larry said to the horsemen. "The horses aren't trained for this much gunfire, but this is the only way. We'll go in fast, right down Main Street, then split into two groups left and right. Don't slow or stop so they can get a bead on you. Shoot to kill and move on. We can break this raid."

"Damn right!" PD said.

"We'll see them in Hell! Or send them there!" Wade shouted.

The horsemen grinned, the shared joke relaxing them. Once on a camping trip, Larry had woken all the men talking in his sleep to a bad guy he meant to kill, bellowing, *"I'll see you in Hell!"* That would become the rallying cry of the horsemen.

Moments later, they were mounted riding seven abreast. Five

wore dusters, and all had the burnished copper stars glinting in the early morning sun just peeking over the horizon.

"When we get to Main Street," Larry directed, "Tony, you and Bruce head right on Sulphur Avenue. Remember, go fast. Don't stop and make yourself a target. We're only trying to break the attack and put them on the run. Go down a block or two, then turn left until you hit Broadway. We'll all meet at the Farmers Bank on Main Street."

Not one to waste words, Tony gave a brief nod. He looked like the Marlboro man from the old advertisements. He and Bruce moved out at a canter.

PD said, "I'll take Elm Street to the left." For a large man, he was a gifted and nimble athlete who rode with confidence.

Wade nodded. "I got your back."

Both men rode black horses. The group was already getting notice from people gathered at the Methodist Church near the Dairy Queen.

"We'll go down a ways, then turn right to come up behind Farmers Bank from behind." Larry paused at the bank. "Roger, can you and Lance move up then circle around to your right, coming back here in fifteen to twenty minutes?"

"On it." Roger and Lance spurred their horses forward in a gallop.

The town was awash in chaotic sounds, gunshots, and screams. As Larry approached the bank, he spied men from the gang crossing streets to his left and right. A few blocks away at the roadblock by the graveyard, he spotted at least seven or eight cars and trucks. There was no way the young men guarding that blockade survived the raid.

In the grassy area in front of the bank lay a dead body, Sheriff Honaker standing beside it talking into a walkie talkie, directing traffic.

"My men are moving through the city on horseback," Larry called out, not bothering to wait for the sheriff to recognize him.

The sheriff drew in a breath to give an angry retort, then sighed with a long exhale. "Thank you."

Larry gazed at the body and shook his head. It was Judge Troutman, the top right side of his head missing in what appeared to be a shotgun blast with buckshot. "I'm real sorry about that."

"This damned world!" the sheriff spat.

"This damned world needs hard men like Goose Truman manning the walls and being meaner than the bad guys." Larry hadn't appreciated the sheriff and judge's derision of Goose and escorting the horsemen through the city.

The sheriff squinted. "This isn't the time."

"This is exactly the time!" Larry thundered. "My men are riding through your city trying to break this gang. If you have any way to communicate to your men, get the word out right now that we're the good guys!"

To his credit, the sheriff only paused for a second before putting the walkie talkie to his mouth. "We got men on horseback. They're with us. Watch your fire. Let's flush the killers out of the city. We'll sweep through for the wounded later." Then to Larry he said, "We only have a few working walkie talkies left."

"You did what you could." Larry spurred his horse behind the bank to East Broadway Street to sweep that area himself.

Before long, most of the gang was on the run. Five of the cars at the blockade sped off back toward Louisville loaded with spoils and two women captives. Roger spat, watching them leave rubber streaks as they sped away. However long those women lived would seem like an eternity, and they had no one to ride to their rescue. It made him sick to his stomach.

It took hours to sweep the rest of the town and the outlying homes. Each man in the group became increasingly frustrated over the lost time. Goose was riding into a death trap, and they were delayed chasing petty gangsters. Each time they thought the task complete, they'd find another killer barricaded in a home or committing atrocities against a family. A brief firefight would ensue and the gangster would be hauled out dead. These people were learning.

It was past mid-day when the last of the horsemen came straggling back to the bank, weary and sagging. They'd been lucky. No one got hurt seriously, despite Tony's horse getting burned by a bullet, dumping him to the ground and leaving him limping, and Wade's ear dripping blood. He'd carry the notch of the bullet that spared his life from here on.

"Anything you men need, the town is open to you," the sheriff said enthusiastically. He and the town had changed today.

"What we need is to get those hours back and get on the road. Remember, we've got a friend riding into a death trap without us. He needs our help."

"Oh," the sheriff said, realization hitting him, along with guilt for delaying the horsemen. "Goose Truman."

The party got wild after the shooting exhibition. The loud rock music had a jarring, blaring sound that assaulted the ears. Outside in the lot, a stray dog licked at the blood pool oozing from what remained of the retail manager's head. His mom wouldn't recognize him now. Charles sat in a prominent spot beside Crazy Joe, drunk as a skunk and crowing at the top of his lungs. Crazy Joe sent women, booze, and drugs his way. He had a soft spot in his heart for a guy who'd faced the worst, been torn down to nothing, and came back stronger, meaner, and a little crazy like himself. Along with his normal ruffians, Van Gogh, who'd been through similar trials, would groom Charles the accountant for what was expected.

Sarah Redman lay on the floor, chained to Crazy Joe's throne like Princess Leia, eyes distant and vacant, belying the hatred in her heart. During a lull in the revelry, Crazy Joe stood like an oversized cat, stretching. "Shut up! I got something to say."

"Yeah!" Charles slurred at the top of his lungs.

"Terry," Crazy Joe prompted his lieutenant, who then slapped Charles on the back of his head hard enough to knock him forward in his seat. Then he addressed the rest of the gang. "What very few of you are aware of is that when we took that convoy, we found a surprise that will help push up our plans. My plans! We are going to expand our territory and control a much larger area than any of you could have dreamed. We will finally have our own empire!"

The crowd paused for a few seconds in awe, then erupted into yelling, cheering, and chanting their leader's name. Crazy Joe let it wash over him for a few moments before raising his hands for silence. "Drink hard tonight! Screw all the women you can! Because tomorrow we go out recruiting! Be careful of the recruits you choose. I'll hold each of you accountable for any screwups you bring in. Next week, I plan to take Carrollton and move my throne there. I will choose some of you to hold smaller towns in this area under your own control, reporting to me, of course."

"Yahoo!" Charles yelled drunkenly, struggling to rise without falling. Terry slapped him on the back of the head again, knocking him back to his seat, earning lots of hoots from the others.

"But not him yet." Crazy Joe snickered. "For the rest of you, this is a chance to rise and take more power by recruiting the right people under you. I'll expect every one of you to lead raids at all points of the compass from Carrollton to control the supplies and let people understand who is in charge."

"Hell yeah, boss!" Van Gogh yelled. Terry and the others

joined in. They would own this country. The government would have to pay dearly just to use the expressway.

"Tomorrow we will leave a small crew here to guard the spoils. I'll take half of you with me to go look over Carrollton. Meanwhile, I expect you to find some good recruits."

"Hell yeah!" Terry hollered.

"Who knows? In a few months, we may take a bigger town like Madison, Indiana. Eventually, I want to control Cincinnati and Louisville. But first things first. Party hard. Tomorrow we split up and hit the road."

Crazy Joe's words sobered Sarah like an avalanche. Any opportunity for government forces to hit the gang would be much harder once they recruited more members and split up. Until now, she had been hoping in vain for helicopters or a line of Humvees to come over that hill, guns blazing. She had no concern for her own safety. She no longer experienced pain, nor did she care if she lived or died. She only wanted Crazy Joe dead and to put a bullet in as many of his cohorts as possible.

In their revelry, no one noticed the tears running down her face. Although he enjoyed having her on display—she was beautiful and a trophy of war in terms of the highest-ranking person they had captured—he had tired of using her. Crazy Joe liked his women to be terrified of him. Their screams drove him to more passion and more violence. Sarah stared right through him with dead, vacant eyes. His slaps and blows no longer elicited cries or defense. She simply lay there taking it, staring through him.

By the wee hours of the morning, the party had died down, and the main hall was deserted except for a few passed-out partiers. Taking pity on Sarah, T-Bone showed up to unshackle her from the throne and take her to her room and another set of chains. Sarah briefly considered sparing T-Bone if she ever got her hands on a gun, then quickly dismissed the thought. He was one of them, and she had sentenced them all to death in her mind.

Lying on the foul, narrow cot staring at the ceiling, Sarah heard Crazy Joe tormenting the two girls he'd taken upstairs. In a deep, dark space in her heart, she remembered being tormented once, back when she cared. The memory caused her to grind her teeth so hard she chipped one.

One of the girls Crazy Joe was tormenting had been a driver in Sarah's convoy, the other a young local girl. Sarah's guilt at allowing Crazy Joe to capture her convoy stabbed her heart like a knife with each scream of torment from the girls.

Soon there was only one girl screaming. The woman from her convoy that had been a friend to Sarah had gone silent. Everyone knew what that meant when Crazy Joe was in one of his moods. With a flicker of her old humanity, Sarah turned her head to a dark corner by the cot and silently wept.

LOOMING

IT WAS mid-day by the time Goose and Sam, the old man with the truck, got on the road hauling Rocky in the red two-horse trailer appropriated from a used car lot that would probably never reopen.

"We can head over to the expressway. It might be faster. I don't think the gang will want to go that route and advertise where they're taking all those trucks and loot." Goose stared straight ahead as if he could will the distance between him and the gang to shorten.

"Works for me," said Sam, starting the truck. "Then we'll head right on Port Royal Road once we pass the old golf course."

"Okay." Goose's body hurt all over. He needed a drink something fierce and had a burning desire to kill these scumbags. If anything, the death and carnage he witnessed in New Castle only intensified that desire. To make matters worse, Laura hadn't been talking to him much lately. It probably didn't matter. If the good Lord allowed him to go to the same place as her, he would talk to her soon enough. He wasn't naïve and did not expect to survive this mission. His goal was to hurt the gang so badly that someone else would finish them.

Then, as if in response to his thoughts, Laura appeared beside him in the truck, sitting on the bench seat between him and the old man, her right hand caressing his forearm, making the hairs tingle. She leaned her cheek on his shoulder. *"Don't be so eager to leave this world, honey. They need you. I'm okay."*

Sam caught Goose looking at him out of the corner of his eye. Goose stared directly at him and right through him at the same time. His eyes had turned red, and tears streamed down his face. Everyone had heard tales of the crazy, drunken killer that was Goose Truman. Sam was witnessing the crazy part firsthand, and it brought up old memories of his time in Vietnam. He'd been a seventeen-year-old door gunner in a helicopter in the air cav. No matter what they admitted afterward, every damn one of them had cried many times over there and thousands of times since coming home. He knew what it was to live with demons or, perhaps in Goose's case, angels. Sam turned back to focus on the road to leave Goose to his thoughts.

"But there's nothing here for me," he said through tears and a deep sound of anguish. "They all hate me. Everywhere I go, I bring death. This is a miserable way to live."

Sam knew the conversation wasn't for him. He tried to shut it out. Old thoughts and memories came back. He too had tears streaming down his face.

"I think Kelly cares for you. I think she could even fall in love with you," Laura whispered faintly.

"Nooo!" Goose yelled so loud that Sam jerked the wheel, causing the trailer to wiggle behind them. Goose's exclamation wasn't in an angry voice, but a higher-pitched voice of shock.

"It's okay," Laura soothed. *"Don't do anything you don't want to but know that I approve. I think she is good for you. We will have our time again."*

"It won't matter. This is a one-way trip for me," Goose said with a flat tone that showed his mind was made up.

Sam raised an eyebrow, feeling like an eavesdropper.

"Don't be so sure. The Lord works in mysterious ways. But don't be so eager to die for this, Gus. This country is sick and full of wounds, but she isn't dead. She can live if hard men like you can lance the boils and clean out the pus. Many of the citizens won't understand your work at first, though."

Before Goose could reply, she vanished.

That was the hardest part. When she left, he felt empty and sick inside. He turned to Sam to ask him to stop the truck, but they were already sitting idle on the side of the road. Goose hadn't noticed, but they'd been there for twenty minutes now.

He pulled up on the lever and jerked the door open, rushed outside, and puked. With his hands on his knees, he vomited until he got dry heaves, wiping his mouth on the arm of his jacket. When it was over, Goose was thankful; the puking had covered the sounds of his sobs. He stepped back to the horse trailer to check on Rocky and take a leak, peeing on the trailer tire.

When he was done, he leaned in the passenger window and asked Sam, "Why'd we stop?"

"This is the junction of Port Royal Road and Vance Road. I figure the gang went on ahead to the river and took 389 to English. The road is wider and better for all those military trucks. They're hours ahead, anyway. I figure you'll want to sneak up on 'em and scout a bit. Vance Road will be better for that."

"You're right. I've cooled down a bit. I'll scout around and hit them in the wee hours of the morning."

"When they're mostly sleeping."

"Yeah, I don't expect I'll make it through this thing, but I'm not going in trying to die, either."

Sam merely raised an eyebrow.

"Oh. Yeah, I guess you heard the 'one-way trip' remark."

Sam nodded.

"I was talking to Laura, my wife…" At the perplexed expression in Sam's eyes, he said, "Never mind."

"It's all right. I was in 'Nam," Sam offered.

"She was here! Right fucking here! I'm not crazy!" Goose shouted, regretting it the moment the words were out, then walking away a few steps. Not before seeing the look of sympathy on Sam's face, though.

"I'll take you on a little further to where Vance Road and 389 come together. That will leave plenty of woods between you and English. If it was me, I'd cut through the woods on the right side of the road a few hundred yards and parallel the train track going into English. They're not likely to guard that as well."

"Much obliged."

Larry and the horsemen hit New Castle about the same time Sam dropped Goose on Vance Road. By the time they reached New Castle, the truck was overheating, steam pouring out of the grille.

"I was worried about that radiator hose. It had dry rot, but it's not like we can just run out to NAPA these days."

Larry pulled the truck over in front of the courthouse. "We're going to be here for a while. Even if we find another hose fast, the engine's going to need time to cool down."

"There are a lot of people gathered up there." Bruce pointed four or five blocks up Main Street.

"What's up there?" Larry asked.

"The funeral home," Wade said ominously.

Larry's face changed. "Let's go. We'll hang back on the edges to be respectful. We need to get a lay of the land. The truck needs to cool down anyway, and I'm sure not going to go poking around people's homes and cars while they're at a funeral."

As the horsemen approached Prewitt's Funeral Home, several

in the crowd took notice. Larry expected to be challenged and was surprised when they weren't. Many of the people obviously noticed the copper stars on their dusters. It took some getting used to. They felt like imposters wearing the copper star, but it smoothed the waters. People were starved for someone to bring order to this chaotic new world and avenge the wrongs.

Most of the men saw someone they knew in the crowd. Each time, there was a silent nod between the horseman and townsperson. No one wanted to interrupt the ceremony. There would be time to talk later. The horsemen were eager to get back on the trail, but this couldn't be helped.

It took an hour for the ceremony to finish, and people began filing by the two caskets. Some of those who had recognized the horsemen made their way to the back to greet the men in dusters and copper stars and catch up on news.

Larry explained the mission and the help they needed, and several townsmen ran off in different directions to find the supplies to fix the truck. The mood among the horsemen brightened considerably. Within thirty minutes, the truck and trailer became the center of activity. While the repairs were being made, they unloaded the horses to let them stretch and get some feed and water. A mechanic from New Castle had taken charge of the repairs, cussing the biker gang steadily under his breath while he did.

"We're gonna need some water," he said to the crowd, and a few people scurried off. "I don't know if I can get this running. At best, I can patch it up for a one-way trip."

"It may be a one-way trip even if the truck runs," Roger noted.

As it always did when one was in a hurry, all manner of little things went wrong. One was finding the right length replacement screws; another time it was a part that wouldn't fit. A couple of hours later, everything was in place. The mechanic got in the truck and turned the key. The starter turned, and the engine grunted, and nothing else. He tried three more times.

"Fuck!" He banged his palm on the steering wheel. The horsemen and townspeople looked on with apprehension. Almost every person in the town had been wronged by the gang. Now, as if in answer to prayer, men in dusters with bright copper stars on their chests came to bring justice, only to be thwarted by fate. For the horsemen, it was more than justice they were after. Their friend was already after the gang, perhaps already bringing the fight to them, facing overwhelming numbers, thinking all he cared about in life was gone.

A feeling of helplessness settled over the group. So close, yet so far. Then the voice of an old man intruded on their thoughts. "I'm about out of gas, but if we can scrounge some up, I can take two of you. Or two at a time if we find enough gas."

Larry closed on the old man. "Do you have a truck and trailer?"

"I've got my truck, and your friend and I kind of appropriated a two-horse trailer from the used car lot there."

"Don't reckon they'll be opening back up any time soon," Lance said.

"Probably won't ever see him again. When things started going bad, he packed up to go stay with his daughter and her family in Tennessee. Said he'd be back when things got better," one of the townspeople offered.

Larry took charge. "Let's find a hose and syphon what fuel we can from my truck to yours. Tony and me can go in the first trip and scout around while waiting for the rest of you. It's going to take all night. I hope Goose holds off on his attack."

"We'll scrounge around for more fuel while you're gone," said another.

It was after suppertime when Larry and Tony headed out of

town. The mechanic had promised to get Larry's truck fixed but warned it might take a few days.

The rest of the horsemen settled in to wait. That was the hardest part. Yet at the same time, a new feeling began to settle over them. The day before when they'd left Larry's farm wearing dusters and copper stars, they'd felt like imposters. They were simply men riding to help their friend and using the excuse of being a Ranger to avoid too many questions with good people they met along the way. Now, as they surveyed the town and the expression of hope in so many faces, an awareness about how much people needed the guidance of law and protection of order dawned. Most of these people didn't have the skills to fill this role. The horsemen did and were desperately needed.

T-Bone had missed his pocket, accidently dropping the key to Sarah's chains when he left her room. She suspected he had some decency deep down inside and dropping the key was no accident.

At first, she did nothing, expecting a trap. Later, as the party wound down, Sarah edged over to the key, first pulling it close with her foot, then picking it up with her free hand. She waited, listening for someone to come and beat her or worse for picking up the key. No one came. She muffled the lock under her grungy scrap of blanket and slowly turned the key. It came open. She could barely contain her excitement.

Then someone came!

Sarah quickly reattached the chains and lock, hiding the key in her mouth.

Crazy Joe opened the door, obviously drunk and on drugs, a spaced-out girl on each arm. He stared down at Sarah. "Tomorrow you and I are going to get to know each other better. I haven't decided what I'm going to do with you. You're not as pretty as when I took you. You're no fun to beat because you don't cry anymore and you always look like you're plotting to kill someone," he slurred. Then almost to himself, he said, "Can't give her to any of my men. She'd slit his throat in his sleep. Ain't really worth the food she eats anymore." He stepped out and closed the door.

It took almost an hour for Sarah to slow her breathing and pulse rate. She hated the control this man had taken over her life and body. Even more, she hated the control he had over her mind and emotions. She was a strong woman and fought against it, yet each time he spoke, she wanted to run and hide or curl in a ball and cry. Sarah was repulsed by what he'd done to her and how he made her feel. She wanted revenge a hundred times over.

Dead people don't kill nobody.

The cast-off comment by T-Bone was a mantra that helped calm her mind and give her purpose.

The minutes and hours slowly passed. Somewhere an old-fashioned clock ticked loudly. Earlier, there had been the sounds from several parts of the building of men rutting and women screaming. Some in pain, others in pleasure. Later the sounds changed to men talking over a late-night smoke, peeing off the porch, laughing about the day's exploits, and planning tomorrow's mayhem. Not long after that, the noises died down to snores echoing all throughout the building and some men talking in their sleep.

Sarah took a chance. Although she covered the lock with the blanket, the sound of it opening was as loud as a sonic boom to her. In reality, it was a muffled click that couldn't be heard more than a few feet away. She carefully disconnected from the chains and cast about for something to wear other than the red silk teddy they had forced upon her. There was nothing. She gently eased open the door a crack and peered down the hall. All was quiet. She was able to tiptoe to the front door without being caught.

That was when her luck turned sour. Two men sat in rockers on the porch, long guns across their laps, smoking. There had to be another door. Of all things, a woman in a red silk teddy walking through the room wouldn't concern the men if they woke. The higher-ranking men had rooms. Many of the lower ones who hadn't appropriated a house in English slept on pallets in the main room. Several feet away from the back door, through the glass of the door, an ember of a cigarette glowed hot when a guard took a drag. She was trapped.

She needed to think. She stood for a moment in indecision. Then fate handed her the slimmest of lifelines. On a pallet close by lay a gang member not much larger than her. He was naked from the waist down, wearing only a torn and bloody shirt, his leg draped over the woman he had taken earlier. They were both snoring. Sarah's attention was on the man's pants and gun in a bandoleer holster beside him. With as little sound as possible, she scooped them up and tiptoed back to her room.

The pants were dirty and disgusting yet better than nothing. The old-fashioned olive-green army fatigues fit tight on her butt, and she had to roll the cuffs up. She had once been well proportioned with curves she wanted to tone. Now, she was becoming leaner by the day. She tucked in the red silk teddy to wear as a shirt. She would find something better soon.

Again, she listened to the sounds of the building. It was quiet. She needed to get out soon, but how? The only choice she had would be to shoot one of the guards and run. She dared not take the time to find the keys to a bike and figure out which bike the keys went with, not to mention she hadn't ridden in years.

She checked the weapon. It was a long-barreled Taurus Judge. Her dad had had one, more as a novelty than anything else. However, it could make an enormous hole in someone with the right ammunition. She opened the cylinder on the revolver to check the loads, finding two .410 shotgun shells and three .45 long colts. The .410s appeared to be buckshot from the writing on the shell. It was difficult to tell in what little moonlight came through the window. The .45 long colt was a more old-fashioned shell that was fat and lethal. It would go into a man like a golf ball and come out with a hole the size of a baseball. That thought brought an evil grin to Sarah's face, imagining using it on Crazy Joe.

Those thoughts brought a new dilemma. She had the power and access to kill Crazy Joe right now and put an end to this. She held out no false hopes that she would live long after the deed, but her life didn't matter anymore. Her tormenter would be dead. Another thought much deeper down urged her to slip out the back door, shoot the guard, and run like hell.

The deep down part of her lost. Her need to avenge herself and so many others won out. Her life didn't matter.

As she reached for the door, shots rang out.

Her mind was in turmoil. The building was in an uproar. She heard shouts as they grabbed their guns, the wooden floors a drumbeat of running feet. Sarah couldn't know it, but the guards were dead. Orange flames leapt up when someone tossed a Molotov cocktail amongst the Harleys. Fuel tanks exploded. They would inevitably catch other bikes on fire. Similarly, the supply building with extra fuel and ammunition had also been fire bombed.

While she was trying to gather her thoughts, a round exploded through the plaster of her room, imbedding itself in the wall by the cot.

Sarah hit the floor.

NASCENCE

GOOSE HAD TAKEN the old man's advice, changing into his jungle boots and sneaking in through the woods by the railroad track. Earlier when he made his first scout, he almost shit himself when a pistol round imbedded itself in a tree above his head. Unbeknownst to him, he'd crept up downrange of the shooting competition that afternoon. When the first man's shot missed the apple, no one except Goose knew or cared where it went after that. Luckily Rocky was tied a mile back in the woods.

Throughout the afternoon, he scouted for weaknesses. By nightfall, he had the setup figured out. Many of the gang were dispersed in surrounding homes, definitely making things more difficult. They parked most of the bikes together, and excess fuel, supplies, and ammunition were stored in a guarded outbuilding. That was an opportunity he didn't intend to pass up. Guards were posted and alert in several locations. That was to be expected.

Darkness fell, and most of the gang moved indoors to party. Goose trekked back to Rocky to get a couple hours' rest. He would attack in the wee hours of the morning when they were least alert.

And when he could do the most damage.

Larry and Tony waved goodbye to Sam. He'd told them what he'd shared with Goose about going in via the railroad track. The two men scouted into the woods a fair amount to find some landmarks, then came back to wait for the next two horsemen. They hadn't heard a shot from the town, so they had time. Either that or it was already over.

Not wanting to risk being seen by any roving patrols that might come out this far, they found a spot in the woods and dismounted to wait.

About an hour and a half later, the old Chevy truck came over the rise again, sounding much too loud in the night air. It was Roger and Lance.

The two men offered to scout closer to the town and see what they were up against. Roger took the railroad route, and Lance rode warily alongside Highway 389.

At one thirty in the morning, Bruce and PD arrived with the third trip. While they were unloading, Sam told Larry, "The townspeople are all behind you. I haven't seen this kind of community spirit in months. They've been kicked, knocked down, raped, and killed, and still they're doing all they can to help. None of that means spit if y'all go out and get yourselves killed. Matter of fact, it will make things worse."

"Reckon so." Larry spat tobacco juice on the gravel edge of the road. It was a nasty habit he'd given up in his youth but somehow found his way back to lately. There were working tobacco farmers in the area and barns full of cured burley tobacco. It wasn't great, but it was available and gave a better jolt than coffee.

"Anyway, I'll return as fast as I can with your man. It'll be close to three a.m. when I get back."

Larry grasped the aging Vietnam vet on the shoulder and gave his heartfelt thanks. He hadn't meant to be brusque. He had a lot on his mind that seemed more appropriate for a youngster than a seasoned man with more than his fair share of gray. Concern for Goose topped it all. It was like he had a death wish. Larry knew the good man inside Goose was still there if only he could find his way back from the dark place in his mind he'd retreated to after his wife and daughter died. Then Larry had the rest of the cowboys to think about. Should he have counseled restraint when they wanted to rush into the fight? They weren't trained for this. It was unlikely they would make it through unscathed. They could all die, leaving sobbing widows behind.

To add to all that, now Larry felt responsible for the people of New Castle as well. He hadn't meant to give them hope, but it happened. He couldn't let them down. Yet neither did he want to get his friends killed in a misplaced sense of duty. Also, he was plain scared. He'd never been in the Army or any law enforcement. The only shooting he'd done was at deer, coyotes, and rabbits. He wasn't sure he could do this and didn't want to let his friends down. He wondered how the other guys were dealing with these thoughts but dared not ask them at this point. Aside from Bruce, who'd been in the Army, Wade was the only one with serious combat experience in the desert wars. That made Wade the natural leader for this mission. The few times Larry tried to ask about Wade's experience, he skillfully changed the subject or deferred. Yet when he needed advice, Wade would inexplicably be right there with just a few words to help, then just as quickly melt into the background.

Wade had his own demons to deal with. Larry would respect his privacy but try to keep him close. Just then, Larry's musings were interrupted by Lance's return. Roger had come back a few minutes earlier, and they'd chosen to wait for his report until Lance returned. They were far enough from English that they could have had a fire and speak openly, yet something about the mission made them wary enough to not risk either. They spoke in hushed tones.

"I got within about a mile of the town along the railroad track," Roger started. "Couldn't see much and didn't want to go closer and spook someone. I don't think Goose has made his move yet, though."

"How can you tell?" Larry asked anxiously.

"Even though it's dark, the town didn't appear shot up or anything. Also, if they'd been attacked recently, I think there would be a lot more guards out, and roving patrols. He's in there, though, that's for sure. We're going to have to be careful of a friendly fire incident. He isn't aware we're coming."

"How can you be certain he's in there?" asked Tony.

Roger chuckled. "'Cause I liked to pissed myself running into his horse and camp out there."

"What?"

"I was trying and get closer on foot to see what was what. I was leading Smokey through a thicket searching for a place to tie him when right at my shoulder I heard a '*he he he*' in a husky voice. I stepped back so fast my bum knee gave out and I landed on my butt. When I got up, that big black and white horse of his was nosing me for a treat. I tried to call for Goose quietly so my voice wouldn't carry, but he didn't answer."

"I guess that's good," said Bruce. "We know he's here and hasn't attacked yet. If we could just coordinate with him, this would go better."

"He's got a satellite phone," Lance chipped in. "Wade told me Goose gave him one too, to keep in contact while scouting. I doubt he'll have it on if he's crawling up close to them, though."

"We'll try it when Wade gets here."

There wasn't much else they could do while waiting for Sam to bring Wade and his horse with the last trip. It seemed like an eternity before the old Chevy truck hauling the red Corn Pro horse trailer once again came easing down the road. It only took minutes to get Wade's horse and gear unloaded. Sam was strangely reticent when he said his goodbyes and got the truck turned around and headed home. Larry didn't blame him. The shooting would start soon.

At Larry's request, Wade tried the satellite phone several times to no avail. They gathered to make a game plan when gunfire erupted toward English. The methodical boom of a heavy round stood out. They exchanged knowing glances; Goose favored a .308.

"Guess we've lost our chance to be sly." Larry's exasperation was evident in his voice. "Lance, what's it like going up the road?"

"I wouldn't advise a gallop. They've got men and a blockade closer to town. The road shoulders are shadowed. I'd split in two single-file lines on either side until we get close enough to take out the guards."

Larry's mind recoiled at the idea of sneaking up and killing the guards. Yet he knew it was the only way. "How long will it take?" he asked to give himself time to think.

"All of forty-five minutes. Maybe an hour."

"Damn!" Larry reacted in surprise. "That far?"

They couldn't see Lance shrug in the dark. "We might do it faster. We are far enough back on purpose so they couldn't hear the truck. We've got to sneak up three or four miles on the shoulder. Anything faster might get someone killed."

"Okay. Let's get to it. Roger, you, Lance, and PD take the right side of the road. Bruce, Tony, and Wade are on the left with me. Let's try to stay even with each other."

There was a chorus of agreement among the horsemen, then they moved off to check their saddles, weapons, and ammunition.

Larry eased over to Wade. "You mind staying close to me for

bit? I ain't done this before and don't want to get anyone killed out of stupidity."

"I got your back," Wade said in a way that made Larry feel more confident.

Goose shifted to his first shooting position. He'd been lucky in taking out three of the guards by stealth. Two years ago, he couldn't have done it. That was a lifetime ago. He didn't keep a body count, but if the good Lord held him accountable for the lives he'd taken, he would have a lot of explaining to do. There wasn't any guilt associated with the killings themselves; the men he killed were degenerates who would rape and kill until they were put down like rabid dogs. What bothered him was what Laura would think. She believed in law and order and abhorred the baser side of human nature. Goose supposed that was why she never came to him when he was killing. Even that fueled his rage. Most times, he was drunk. It was hard now to recollect why he'd decided to do this sober.

The first guard Goose approached had been at the back of the old schoolhouse. He left his long gun at the hide and walked up casually to bum a smoke, all the while holding the stiletto fighting knife in the shadow by his thigh. When the man let down his guard to reach for a cigarette, Goose struck. Quick as a cat he closed the last two feet, putting a hand over the man's face and driving him back against a tree, simultaneously plunging the stiletto knife between two ribs with all his strength. One reason Goose couldn't have done this two years ago was experience. It was not like the movies. Despite how sharp the knife was, it took strength and will to drive a knife through muscle, bone, and flesh that deep. Any hesitation at the diffi-culty or savagery of the kill would have allowed the man to fight back. Once the knife was hilt-deep in the man's chest, the fight ended. He died fast, and the wound didn't bleed much. Goose dragged the body to a dark shadow by a bush and continued his hunt.

The other two men were easy to kill. They weren't overly alert or well trained. They kind of made rounds. Goose only had to watch them saunter past a shadow, move to it, and wait for their return. The maneuver was tried and true. Leap out behind the man with a hand over his mouth while drawing the stiletto across his throat. Goose had learned over a year ago how hard he had to press down on the throat while slicing to cut deep enough to kill fast. Those cuts were bloody and spurted.

After three kills, he decided he was pressing his luck and moved back to cover. He scouted and supplied three shoot locations. After that, he would wade in amongst them, killing and looking for Crazy Joe. Let the devil take the hindmost.

Back at the hide, he watched the buildings and guards. If they didn't search for the men he'd killed soon, he would sneak back to try and take a few more.

However, he wasn't that lucky. The activity around the schoolhouse increased dramatically. Something was wrong, and they were searching. They found his second kill first. He'd cut deeper than necessary on that one, leaving only a little bone and skin to keep the head attached. It flopped against the man's back. Goose let out a chuckle watching two of the hardened criminals lean forward and puke. Soon another man yelled from behind the building, and Goose decided it was time to for the next phase.

He shouldered his bag and moved as close as he dared, tossing two Molotov cocktails at the mass of motorcycles outside the old schoolhouse, and two at the storage building he'd seen them moving supplies and ammunition to most of the day. With that, the entire scene erupted into a frenzy of commotion, yelling, and fire.

Let bedlam reign!

This was his world, where he ruled and dished out death with an evil grin.

Once back at his hide, he unlimbered the SX-AR heavy he'd always preferred. He was under a bush in the tree line, the .308 on a bipod. With the gang's bonfires and the fires Goose had set, there was more than enough light to use the scope. He was prepared to do as much damage as possible with a dozen magazines, both ten and thirty round, loaded with .308 Maker rounds from Georgia. They were a small company owned by a friend from the old days. The ammunition wasn't easy to get but was the hardest hitting, most accurate ammunition out there. He would need it in this fight.

He opened up with the big gun, taking out the guards on the porch first. Then he sent a full magazine of .308 rounds after the roving guards trying to mount a defense or put out the fires. In all, he figured there were five more down before he turned his sights on the old schoolhouse. All he could do there was put rounds through windows and doors, hoping to do damage, hit a lamp, or kill some bad men. Although there was a chance he would hit a prisoner, Goose couldn't worry about it. They were likely dead anyway if he didn't kill the men on a rampage of stealing, raping, and killing. He emptied the thirty-round magazine into the house and changed hides. He was already taking some unfocused return fire.

The next shooter's nest faced directly at the front door of the old schoolhouse. Goose didn't have to wait long before men began spilling out, looking for a fight. He downed three before they got wise. They may not have all been kill shots, but a .308 maker round would make even a leg wound likely to bleed out before they got medical care.

This position was only good for a dozen rounds before he started taking return fire. He had one more site to move to. He'd be lucky to get two more from that location before he had to wade in. His hope that Crazy Joe himself would come out and lead the defense hadn't panned out. He'd taken out a dozen scumbags, which was a couple dozen short of what was needed. It would get harder from here.

Kelly was getting used to shocks by now, so when an old Chevy truck pulled up to the gate, she handled it in stride. She now had a gun holster on her hip, and Kevin had been coming over frequently to keep an eye on things and talk to the Amish workers. Brian had actually gone to the fields to learn some of the farm work and try to help. The Amish people were very demanding of their own children and their work, but the adults largely ignored Brian, which made him try even harder to keep up.

An old man in a Vietnam ball cap had stepped out of the truck, and Kevin was walking up the lane with a wary look on his face, still fifty yards behind her.

From the other side of the gate, Kelly asked, "Can I help you?"

"I'm a new friend of Goose's. I ferried him and a few of his friends to a fight they're getting into over in English, Kentucky. They told me about you."

"Friends? He didn't tell me anything about friends." Kelly unlocked the gate. Kevin had just approached and was listening in.

"I'll be honest, ma'am. This fight is too big for Goose, and he needs someone to talk him down. I've seen men struggle with their inner demons, and I've gone through a bit of it myself. He seems to be in a crisis mode right now, and if he doesn't die in this fight, he just might start to mend. He'll need some help, though. His friends are going to try and help him in the fight. If they do pull his ass out of the fire there, it might help if someone could

calm him or back him down some. I'm going back that way soon.
I just thought…"

Kelly paused, then looked at Kevin, whose face showed a
sadness at her reaction to Goose and knowing what she would do
next. "I'll get my things together. When do you want to leave?"

"As soon as you're ready."

"We only have a few gallons of regular gasoline, but you're
welcome to it." This time it wasn't lost on Kelly that she had said
we. "Kevin, I hate to impose, but would you mind so much to stay
here and keep an eye on the place and Brian while I'm gone? I'll
explain to him what's going on before I leave."

Kevin's face was crestfallen, but he was a gentleman and very
fond of Kelly, and truth be told, he was beginning to understand
and respect Goose. "Sure. I'll sleep in the barn. I *know* Goose
wouldn't want me in his house," he teased, attempting to lighten
the mood.

Sarah was hyperventilating. The first shots brought back memories of her convoy being attacked. From there, her mind leapt
forward to the moment she lost the illusion that the world was
primarily good and how she'd been insulated from the animalistic
reality just outside her awareness. There was a cruel, barbarous
place in men's souls lurking beneath a thin veil of civility. She was
now part of that savage world. With this new awareness, a part of
her understood she could never go back. She would either end
this existence as predator or prey.

She breathed in and out, deep and slow, to calm herself as she
lay on the floor beside her cot. Outside her room, pandemonium
reigned. Flames leaping high above the windows, random explosions interspersing the constant din of yells, cries, and shots. Only
a few shots had come into her room. That was enough to keep her

down. Even as she calmed, she began to plan. A few minutes earlier, she'd been in a quandary whether to fight or flee. This attack on the lair of the gang tipped the scales. She would fight.

She had pants and a gun. That was all she needed. She had to be patient. She would only get one chance at Crazy Joe. She couldn't risk being found out too soon.

Crazy Joe was furious. How *dare* someone attack him? In *his* home!

"Terry, take a few men and shove cars in front of the schoolhouse. Look for manual shifts so you can put them in neutral."

"Sure, boss!" he yelled above the crackle of flames.

"T-Bone, take some of the prisoners. I want them to pull as many of the bikes out of the fire as they can. Shoot any that hesitate. And Van, I want three five-man teams here on the double. Scrounge up trucks for them. I don't care where you get them. They're going to hunt these bastards and call in to us when they find them."

Van didn't say a word. With a smirky military salute, he was on his way.

"Van!" Crazy Joe called, stopping the one-eared man in his tracks.

"Boss?"

"Take that little runt Charles with you. See what he can do."

"Yes, sir." Van's salute was more formal this time.

"Terry!"

"Yeah, boss?" Terry said from so close behind him Crazy Joe jumped.

"When you're done getting those cars in place, I want you to gather every man Van and T-Bone don't need. I want sandbags and barricades around this building, and I want them to scavenge anything possible from the supply building. After you do that, make sure we have enough transportation to follow this bastard anywhere he goes."

Crazy Joe resembled the devil himself, standing in silver-tipped cowboy boots amongst the flames and chaos, hair going all directions, an evil gleam in his eyes, and guns strapped to both hips.

TRIBULATION

LARRY and the cowboys were in a bind. They were close enough to engage quickly if they only knew where Goose was. The good news was that the sun was coming up, casting the whole scene in a soft, misty light.

As they snuck up to the roadblock, they found two dead men. No live ones. Larry dismounted the men. Wade nodded imperceptibly and signaled to Roger and the men on the other side of the road to do the same. The scene was like a war zone of explosions, fires, and guns going off. Luckily, no one had noticed the horsemen yet to send fire in their direction.

"We need to do something, Wade," said Larry, "but I don't know where Goose is. We can't run in and get him shot or get shot by him."

"I agree. Let's get as close as we can while not showing ourselves. When we figure out what's what, we can go in guns blazing. I'll tell the other guys."

They tied the horses in the woods, hoping to keep them out of sight and use the trees to provide a little more ballistic protection. When they got closer, Larry glanced up at the sky. It was growing lighter by the moment. The outlaws were getting organized and building a defense. They needed to act soon. The small town was a flurry of activity. One thing caught Larry's eye; a gangster with a ponytail was getting cars shoved grille to trunk around the building. As they watched, he detailed other men to take up fighting positions behind the cars.

"Reckon we're going to have to put a stop to that," Larry said as much to himself as Wade.

"It'll be a tough nut to crack, no two ways about it. Least they've only got one side of the building fortified for now."

"It would be suicide to charge that."

"Maybe for one man, but we can do it with squad tactics. It's what we came here to do. Might as well get started."

"Wade, you're going to have to lead. I know nothing about squad tactics. I'll follow you."

Wade paused as if he would object, perhaps battling his inner demons, then made a decision and nodded. "Just this once." Then Wade turned to get the other men's attention. He had seconds to brief them before—

"Damn!" Larry rarely cursed. The firing reached a fevered intensity. Goose was hitting the men behind the cars from the flank. He was rolling them up and mowing them down. It must have been three to five bodies that he dropped; it was hard to tell in all the smoke and fire. One thing Larry would never forget was the mist of blood behind the cars as the big rounds struck home. One man was hit in the chest, his body arched back, and the blood cloud hovered above him for a few seconds. A second man took a .308 round above his left eye, shearing away the left side of his head. The right eye stared at Larry accusingly.

Goose had them on the run. Several were dead, and the others fled. Larry drew in breath to call out for Goose, but he was already gone, sprinting toward the back of the old schoolhouse.

Unexpectedly, rifle shots erupted so close to Larry he almost peed himself. Two feet away Wade was shooting at a group of five killers sprinting around the old schoolhouse on a collision course with Goose. "Take 'em out!" Wade shouted. "The ones by the back corner!"

Every one of the horsemen was a top-notch marksman, having grown up with weapons and spending many years hunting or target shooting. The five men following a little man with a patch on the side of his head never had a chance. Two would-be killers danced like Pinocchio on strings guided by a palsied man to a deadly song of lead. Others simply melted to the ground like water, poured into sand. The one-eared man got away.

Goose had been lucky. They had burned him a couple times with near misses, leaving a crease or hole in his gear as he rolled up the firing line from the flank. So far, he didn't have any holes big enough to spout fluids and was still in the fight. He wouldn't have bet money on that ten minutes ago.

Seconds before he crashed through the old wooden door of the schoolhouse, he heard another crescendo of firing, expecting to be hit any second. The gang may not know how many were attacking yet, but Goose did. He was the only target.

The last thing he saw before disappearing into the school-house was two gang members drop to the ground with holes in them. It was a mystery, and Goose didn't have time for mysteries. He was in their nerve center. For the moment, he went unnoticed in the confusion, although that wouldn't last. He needed to find Crazy Joe fast.

Goose slung the SX-AR and drew the competition .45, moving forward in a tactical advance. Twice he surprised a gangster with a greeting of lead as he cleared rooms, finishing them with a quick double tap, his mag changes well-practiced and smooth. The whole place was like an anthill that had been kicked. In seconds, the bodies would alert them to a killer in their midst.

The third door Goose tried had a padlock on the outside that wasn't locked. It wouldn't stop anyone from going in, but it would be hard to get out.

"Hey! Someone shot Andy! Hell, Reggie's dead too!" The shout came from down the hall.

Goose needed to get out of sight fast. Lifting the padlock, he slipped into the dark room, pushing the door closed, trying to muffle the click of the door handle. He leaned forward to listen for the men down the hall when the feel of cold metal pressing against the back of his head reminded him he hadn't cleared the room.

"Who are you?" The words were snarled at him in a woman's voice, low, and sounding more like an accusation than a question.

Goose was in a quandary; he could pretend to be one of the gang or come clean. It took only seconds to decide he was tired of all the bullshit and never expected to leave here alive anyway. Besides, he had just lifted a padlock from the outside of her door.

Hands up, he turned slowly to see his captor, trying not alarm her. Goose adopted a haughty piratical mien. "I'm Goose Truman, and I came here to kill every last one of these bastards."

"Ha!" she barked, low enough to keep the sound from traveling. "I've heard of Goose Truman. He may be a drunken, child-killing son of a bitch, but he is too much of a stone-cold killer to be caught flat footed in a slave's room."

At least she had lowered the gun.

"I never killed babies. I've killed men and even some evil women. I've killed about everything that walks or crawls over the last couple years. Right now I'm here to kill Crazy Joe for what he's done to countless women and children."

"You won't do much killing hiding behind my skirts in here. Besides, he's mine."

Goose raised an eyebrow that probably couldn't be seen in the dim light. He took a closer look. The first thing he noticed was that she was pretty. There was a hardness to her eyes and face, though, that may never leave. The negligee top she wore, and ample bosom, made him think of things he shouldn't and felt like a huge betrayal of what Goose was sure she'd been through. Her red silk top was tucked into dirty cargo pants, too long in the leg and tight around the butt, cinched with a rope. She had no shoes but had managed to arm herself with an easily recognizable Taurus Judge. Goose reflexively touched his head, thinking what it would have done had she pulled the trigger a few seconds ago.

"Whoever gets him, gets him," he countered.

She raised the gun again when there was a shout from down the hall. "Denny! Take two men and check every room."

"Time to go," Goose said. "You coming?"

She barely hesitated a second. "I'm in, so long as we don't leave this place 'till he's dead. I'm Sarah, by the way."

Goose barely nodded before opening the door. He made eye contact with three men to his left, just as they saw him. Three rapid shots from the .45 gave the unlikely duo the seconds they needed. The first man took a shot through the throat, tangling the other two as he fell. The second man took a round in the shoulder. The third was lining up to return fire when a deafening roar at Goose's ear made him duck. The attacker wasn't dead, but he was out of the fight with a load of .410 buckshot to the face and chest. Someday he'd have to talk to that woman about firing a gun so close to his ears.

For now, they had to run. The attackers came from the left; they ran to the right. Sarah grabbed at his shirt as she trailed after him, yelling, but he couldn't hear a thing. Then it became obvious. This hallway ended at stairs going up. There wasn't even a window. With no choices left, they went up. Two-thirds of the way up, Sarah was hit. The first shot took her leg out from under her. She would have toppled all the way down had Goose not caught her. He couldn't tell how much damage had been done. Seconds later, she was hit twice more, a scalp wound bleeding profusely and a crease along her ribs, near the armpit.

As Goose dragged her over the top stair, out of the line of fire, he was hit in the back with a sledgehammer that stole his breath and threw him forward on the floor. The last thing he saw before his universe went black was blood spatter on Sarah's face and a lot of blood staining the floor under him.

Crazy Joe stood on the porch behind hastily constructed barricades, directing more men to the cars. He saw Terry struggle to his feet as the lone survivor of the flanking attack on that line. No less than five or six men could have done that much damage, taking his people by surprise.

Then the chilling shout came: "They're in the building!"

"Damn!" he swore, spitting as he pivoted to enter the building. "What's going on in here?" he bellowed.

T-Bone stepped in with another load of salvaged supplies. "Drop that. You're with me. Send one of the other men to watch your prisoners."

T-Bone dropped the supplies in a corner and pulled his gun.

One of the lower-ranking men rushed to Crazy Joe. "We got 'em trapped upstairs! They killed three men before we trapped them."

"Then why the hell haven't you gone up to get them?!" Crazy Joe screamed.

"We tried! They've got big guns. Any man that sets foot on those stairs gets shot."

"T-Bone."

"Huh...oh yeah, boss." He'd glanced into the empty room

where Sarah had been and got a sinking feeling. At least Crazy Joe hadn't noticed.

At that second, the crescendo of fire increased dramatically outside. They heard someone cry out, "It's the law!"

Crazy Joe grabbed T-Bone. "You're in charge here. When I come back, I expect you'll have this taken care of. Kill the girl too." He pointed to the empty room, proving he had been paying attention.

The sun had risen, casting its full glare on a scene of fading mist, smoke, and fires in a town so small it consisted only of a few buildings and an old two-story brick schoolhouse. None of that caught his attention. What mesmerized Crazy Joe was a surreal scene of what looked like old-fashioned Texas Rangers, complete with dusters and stars glinting in the morning light as they moved up the street from cover to cover, firing on his men. They were holding their own, but it was a losing battle. Although his people had numbers, the horsemen moved in an inexorable deadly manner that unnerved the gang enough that their shots weren't well aimed as they tried to execute a tactical retreat.

Crazy Joe wasn't worried. He envisioned himself a general or pirate who not only commanded a ship but a squadron. He held no illusions about the quality of his men, which was why he went for numbers. Those numbers were about to pay off. All he had to do was wait.

Van lost one team. He didn't know who killed them, but they were down. That left two more. The devious little man was moving them into position hidden from view of the attackers beside a trailer and an old mechanic shop. From the porch, Crazy Joe broke into a grin seeing Van Gogh and knowing the Rangers didn't. The horsemen had no idea what was about to roll up on them.

They downed two more of his men as they crossed the railroad track, angling toward Crazy Joe and the heart of his operations.

Larry was calm on the outside and screaming on the inside. Few of the horsemen had much combat experience, but they rode and hunted together for years and worked well as a team. Tony, Wade, and PD were to Larry's right and working well. Especially Wade and PD, who were working shoot-and-move tactics, one man covering while the other moved in a leapfrog motion to perfection. On Larry's left, Roger, Bruce, and Lance advanced in a wider skirmish line. While Larry looked on, Lance fell to one knee, dropping his gun and trying to staunch a gaping wound in his neck geysering blood. The scream in Larry's head drowned out his thoughts.

A dozen seconds later, the sound came back louder than ever. Two groups of five men had come out of nowhere. The professional workmanlike demeanor of the horsemen evaporated. To their credit, they responded as well as possible. Bruce knelt at Lance's side, adding pressure to the neck wound. "Hang in there, man!"

Tony and PD were pinned down behind a truck on Larry's right near the old schoolhouse parking lot. They were taking fire from two different directions.

"Where's Wade?" Larry yelled. PD raised a hand palm up in confusion before pointing toward English.

Larry knelt in a ditch behind a telephone pole feverishly working the lever on his Henry Big Boy .45 long colt. It didn't have the range of the other weapons but hit hard and shared rounds with his revolver. Roger had taken up a position a few feet from Bruce and Lance behind a concrete yard decoration in front of a double-wide trailer. He was putting rounds downrange from the older AR-15 as fast as he could aim, fire, and swap mags.

They desperately needed to get Lance patched up. Every second lowered his chances. The lifesaving pressure of Bruce's hand was the only thing keeping him alive.

Then Bruce got hit.

He took one to the leg near his knee and another in his back that broke a rib and barely missed the lung. He stiffened in pain, falling to the ground, his eyes locked on Lance's. With the last of his strength, Lance reached over to put a hand on Bruce's shoulder with unspoken words in his eyes: *"Thanks, you tried."* Before Bruce lost consciousness, he grasped Lance's shoulder as his eyes went blank.

Larry didn't have time to dwell on it. Roger was now taking the brunt of the fire. He couldn't last long. The gang smelled blood in the water and started advancing. Larry tried to help but was pinned down.

Help arrived from an unexpected quarter. Wade had circled and hit the bad guys like an avalanche from behind, his Marine training allowing him to block out the desert war memories as he took out the killers in the methodical fashion of a professional soldier. Five were down in seconds. Roger took out another with a shot through the eye, then clicked on empty, the bolt locked back. A shot from the schoolhouse hit Wade, laying him out, squirming in pain.

In a rage, Larry walked in on the last guy, working the loop lever as fast as possible. A deep part of his mind recoiled at his desire to kill. Yet even after the killer went down, Larry kept working the lever and pouring lead into the man's body.

The intensity of the battle lessened, a pause while both sides regrouped. PD and Tony were firing on the schoolhouse to keep their heads down and taking return fire. Both sides had attacked and counterattacked. Both had failed to gain the upper hand.

Roger moved to a more secure place between the trailer and an old truck. Amazingly, Wade got to his feet and joined him. The round he took hit his lucky Kevlar. It had saved him so many times in the desert that he snuck it home. Larry came next. PD and Tony were now at the far corner of the trailer, firing at the schoolhouse as they each took a turn running behind the trailer to join their fellow horsemen.

When PD skidded to the spot behind the truck, followed by Tony, all the men were together except for Lance and Bruce, who lay together in a bloody patch of yard a few feet in front of them.

The moment of silence was broken when Wade pointed to the left of the schoolhouse. "They're coming again, maybe twelve or thirteen of 'em."

The groan among the men reminded Larry of the noise an old tree makes when its roots finally lose purchase and it falls. Such a simple sound yet filled with such foreboding.

"I'm sorry, guys. Looks like this is it." Larry sounded sad and tired.

Sarah never lost consciousness. While her wounds hurt like hell and were bleeding, they didn't feel life threatening. The mean man beside her was unconscious and bleeding out. While the gang regrouped to consider their losses and next move, she bound his wounds the best she could, using torn-up old clothes lying discarded in the room. She tied the dressing as tight as possible to add pressure.

"I don't know who you are," she mumbled, "but the enemy of my enemy is my friend. If you can hear me, I think I'm going to need your help. Dead people don't kill nobody."

She'd done all she could for now. She heard Crazy Joe and T-Bone downstairs haranguing the men to charge the stairs all at once. Luckily, the narrow stairway in the old building would funnel her attackers. She checked her weapon, reloading it from the bandolier holster, alternating .410 buckshot with .45 long colt.

The charge came. Sarah stood and let out a primal scream, releasing all her anger and frustration with that first load of buckshot followed immediately by the .45 long colt. The buckshot tangled the first man into the others, slowing the charge. The .45 struck a man at the bottom of the stairs center mass, spraying his companions with blood and bone. Sarah emptied the last three rounds from the Judge down the stairs, scattering the men.

"Shit. Fuck. Damn," came from the darkness below on either side of the stairs outside Sarah's view.

Sarah knelt to reload. "Shit," she muttered. "Three more rounds."

"Take mine," rasped a voice so close it startled her. He was barely conscious and trying to reach for the .45 at his hip. Sarah didn't have time for this and didn't much care about people's feelings anymore. She pushed his hand aside and took the gun, shoving it in her waistband as he passed out again. The bad guys massed for another attack.

This time they were smarter, coming single file and fast, each man holding a chair or something wood or metal as they charged. Oblivious to her own safety, Sarah stood and poured lead down the stairs as fast as she could pull the trigger. Three shots in, she dropped the Judge and changed to the .45. When the slide locked back, the stairs were empty again. Sarah knelt to find another magazine in the wounded man's belt when a stomping sound echoed up the stairs. She became frantic.

Success! Her hand closed on the magazine.

A booted foot caught her in the ribcage, lifting her in the air, her body crashing against the wall. T-Bone stood above her, gun trained on her face.

"T-Bone, you've been decent to me," Sarah said. She wasn't about to beg after all she'd been through. "This ain't like you."

"Little missy, you don't even know me. All his friends are either dead or pinned down and dying. They've lost, and whether

I'm good or bad don't matter. You're a liability. Nothing person-al." He eased back the hammer.

"Terry, you sure you can do this?"

The lanky, ponytailed man was covered in blood and swaying on his feet. "I got this," he snapped in a rare show of agitation directed at Crazy Joe. "They shot me! They killed my men."

"All right. You got half the men. Van, you get the rest. Don't get cute. Spread apart several yards and go right at 'em as fast as you can. I'll be right behind you. We'll kill 'em all and make sure we're never caught flatfooted again."

"Yeah! Hell yeah. Let's kill the fuckers!"

The men assembled to make the charge.

Van and Terry nodded over the noise to show Crazy Joe they understood.

Van tapped six men. "You're with me. Go stand over there. Check your weapons and make sure you have spare ammo." He looked at Terry. "This is your group. We'll follow your lead. You give the word and we'll run like hell." As an afterthought, and with an undertone of a threat, he added, "Don't leave us out there by ourselves."

Crazy Joe took notice that the weak, one-eared man had grown up. He had been harder on Van Gogh than any of them, and the little man ended up being stronger than the rest. There was a lesson there he'd use in the future. Hell, he couldn't even remember the little man's name before he cut his ear off.

The two groups ran off screaming like an Irish clan going into battle. Crazy Joe ambled behind them, a huge smile on his face, expecting to see the bullet-riddled bodies of the attackers. He wanted to know who they were and where they came from.

• • •

Larry had less than twenty rounds left for the Henry Big Boy. He'd have to make his shots count. "I'm sorry, fellers, I—"

"We don't have time for that shit," Roger interrupted tersely. "I'd do it again, maybe just different." He laughed. "This would have come to us if we didn't go to it. Maybe we've knocked them back enough for someone else to knock them out."

"I'm with Roger," PD said. "I figure for each one of the sons of bitches I kill, that's one more than doesn't end up in our neck of the woods. We got friends back home that will take care of our farms and families. If this gang had hit my place at full strength, I wouldn't be able to stop 'em alone. I hate to think what would have happened to my wife if they'd done that. Maybe this way we can at least kill some leaders or make it take them a year to get back up to strength before they come our way. When we don't come back, our people will know something's wrong and beef up security."

Wade opened his mouth to speak but was interrupted by a dozen screaming, charging men. He calmly shifted positions and shot one of the men in the group to his left. As a trained Marine, Wade knew that, while they couldn't win this fight, he could damn well make sure a bunch of them slid into Hell on the blood of their comrades.

The feeling that something was wrong interrupted Crazy Joe's grin. His men were winning the fight. The attackers would be dead in seconds. Then it hit him.

Engines!

An old Chevy truck pulling a red two-horse trailer crested the rise beyond the railroad tracks, followed by an old Bronco and a family car. This couldn't be good.

Crazy Joe soon found out it wasn't.

After crossing the tracks, the Chevy turned left and stopped, while the Bronco and car turned right. Men and women piled out of the vehicles, and about eight people even spilled out of the horse trailer. They didn't all have guns. Some were even carrying pitchforks for god sakes.

Crazy Joe hightailed it back to the schoolhouse, flinging shots at the new attackers over his shoulder as he ran. In seconds, his charge against the horsemen had turned from a sure win to a crushing defeat. He was alone in the schoolhouse, having sent all the remaining men to the final charge.

Caught in the crossfire, his men didn't have a snowball's chance in Hell. The women with pitchforks and garden tools were the worst, screaming like banshees, using farm tools on his wounded men. Crazy Joe panicked, trying to hit them with long shots with his pistol. A couple fell but didn't appear fatally injured.

Then he heard a loud blast from upstairs, reminding him he may still have an enemy in his home.

T-Bone's face carried a glint of smug satisfaction. He liked winning and killing more than Sarah had guessed.

"Fuck you!" Sarah snarled. She was ready to die but wouldn't go down begging.

A gun erupted, echoing louder in the enclosed room.

T-Bone's head exploded in a mist of blood, bone, and brains. His body stood for a couple of seconds as if refusing to acknowledge his death. Then it spasmed and his gun went off, the bullet grazing Sarah's arm before burying itself in the floor.

Sarah whirled around. Goose had risen to one knee, holding the .308 combat rifle. A visage of killing rage clouded his face. "Will you be okay?" he asked, more perfunctorily than supportive, while peering down the stairs.

"Yeah," she thought she said. Her ears were still ringing, and it was hard to be sure.

Goose rose unsteadily, moving down the stairs, leaking blood with every step while Sarah tied another bandage around her ribs.

Crazy Joe watched the big, haunted man come down the stairs with a face full of death, like the grim reaper himself. He'd never met Goose Truman, but they'd all heard stories. His men said that was who was attacking, but he hadn't believed them, especially when other men joined the attack. According to the rumors, Goose always worked alone. However, the man coming for him could be none other than Goose Truman himself.

Crazy Joe worked the pistol fast, making plaster fly and disturbing the aim of Goose's return fire. One bullet grazed Goose's scalp, and another caught him in the right shoulder, causing him to drop his rifle as he closed on Crazy Joe. Goose drew the wicked-looking stiletto and stumbled forward. He was hurt bad and losing blood but still had enough energy to get to his foe.

Crazy Joe clicked on an empty chamber and threw the gun at Goose, giving him time to draw his own knife. The flashy Bowie knife was more for show than use, but it could kill just as well as its more workmanlike cousins.

The fight didn't last long. Crazy Joe was weak from a life of drugs and alcohol; Goose was gravely injured and losing blood. Goose stumbled to the floor. Crazy Joe stumbled as well but ended up on top, digging his thumb into the bullet wound in Goose's shoulder, causing him to cry out and drop the stiletto. Crazy Joe tried to plunge the bowie knife into Goose's chest, but the haunted man held him off. It couldn't last. His strength was fading fast.

A sharp pain in his shoulder and ribs interrupted Crazy Joe's victory, then his brain acknowledged the two pistols shots that had created the pain. As he fell to the floor bleeding, rolling on his side he saw his attacker. "Sarah..." he gasped, blood forming on his lips.

"I didn't shoot you in the head because I wanted you to see who it's coming from. I'm going shoot you in the face. I want the image of your ruined head to be the memory I keep of you!" she said with a venom that made even Goose shiver.

Crazy Joe tried to speak, only able to get out, "Major..." He finally recognized the woman he'd abused and dismissed as a soldier and foe he should have been more wary of all along. He coughed up more blood, struggling to catch his breath.

"And know this, you son of a bitch. I'll piss on your corpse when I'm done."

With no more words, Sarah lined up the big 1911 she'd taken from T-Bone's corpse, glared, and fired three shots into Crazy Joe's face.

Less than a minute later, Wade was the first one through the door of the schoolhouse, kicking it in. He was shocked to see Goose was bloody but alive, and there was a woman who would be beautiful if she didn't look so mean, pants down to her knees, squatting over a corpse. A stream of urine diluted the blood where his head had been.

"What the hell are you looking at!" she spat.

RESURGENCE

GOOSE MADE it to his feet with Wade's help. Sarah had cinched up her pants and tucked in the negligee top, not offering a word of apology or explanation, chin held high. When they stepped out on the porch, he was greeted with a sight that made his eyes water.

To his left were the townspeople from New Castle, some of them familiar to him. Mostly he recognized Sam, the old Vietnam vet. To his right were his old friends the horsemen, standing there looking silly and wonderful all at once in their cowboy hats, dusters, and copper stars glinting in the morning sun.

Then if those Rangers with their bronze stars weren't enough, a beautiful blond woman with tattoos stepped out from the men and ran to Goose, the old Bersa Thunder 9 that Goose had lent her clutched in her right hand.

Kelly hugged him tightly, causing Goose to wince in pain and almost fall before she steadied him, helped by Sam and the cowboys. Goose opened his mouth to tease. Then closed it to chastise. He did neither. The tears in his eyes rolled down freely. The emotions he felt for Kelly and the conflict of guilt were too complex to deal with right now. And these were real men. Salt of the Earth—type men and the best kind of friends a man could have. Perhaps good would win out over evil in this land with men like these. There would be a light at the end of the tunnel for the nation if good men would band together all over the country.

Then it hit him. He hadn't died in his last mission. That thought made him unexpectedly happy. A day ago, he'd been happy to die killing the gang. Oddly enough, he gazed at Kelly, not wanting her to leave him and his farm and not knowing what that meant for Laura and Elizabeth. He didn't want them to leave, either. He felt a stab of disloyalty to Laura. No sooner had the thought came than he felt her arm on his shoulder and smelled her perfume, her lips brushing his ear when she whispered, *"It's okay, I want you to live, and she's good for you."*

Goose's eyes were red and glistening with water when Larry walked up. The men circled him as if to protect him from onlookers. None of them said a word. They might not understand what the tears were about, but their friend was broken inside and trying to mend, and as his friends, they would support him.

It only took a minute for Goose to get his emotions under control. "I didn't want y'all to do this. It changes a man."

Larry, normally the jovial teaser, got serious. "Yes, it does." There was more meaning in those three words than Goose could unpack right now. He nodded curtly.

After a pause, Roger said, "This would have come to us if we didn't go to it. Look at these townspeople. A week ago, they were getting raped and pillaged. Now they're fighters. All they needed was an example and a reminder that we live by laws. The horsemen are a symbol of those laws and retribution against those that trespass. This is vitally important." Roger dropped his head. "We lost Lance… he was my best friend, and I still say it was worth it. Thankfully, the townspeople have a veterinary doctor who says he can patch up Bruce."

"What do we do with all this?" Sam waved his arm toward the buildings and killing fields.

"If you're asking me, I say leave the bodies for carrion and take all the supplies you can salvage for your town," said Goose. "They endured a lot and risked a lot. They deserve it."

"Let's at least pile the bodies in the schoolhouse and burn it before we go," Larry insisted. "We're better than they are. I'll say a prayer over them."

"We're not all better than they are," Goose retorted, and Sarah made a barking sound that was as close to a laugh as her bitter visage could form.

"You're a better man than you think, Goose Truman," said Larry.

Any reply Goose might have made was cut off by the nods of agreement on the faces of the horsemen. Even Sam, who hadn't known Goose before yesterday, bobbed his head.

Ever the practical one, Roger said, "Let's get whatever supplies loaded and the bodies in the schoolhouse. I want to get home."

"We might have to stay a day in New Castle," Wade cautioned. "My SAT phone's been chirping all day. I called the number back, and it was someone from the governor's office. They were worried and searching for Goose, trying all the numbers they'd given him. I told them what happened and they put the governor himself on the line."

"What'd he say?" several chorused.

The old governor was well liked in these parts for fighting against corruption before the country fell. When it did, and so many other politicians and internet moguls fled to well-appointed compounds, the governor remained to be the leader the people elected him to be.

"He's on his way to New Castle and wants to swear us in as Rangers himself. He said we can use the horsemen title. He's planning to open a Ranger post there and set up a court for the people we catch. He's also going to station a few troops at the town to help with security."

"Woohoo!"

The eruption of cheers from the townspeople was deafening.

"I'm in. I want to be a Ranger," Sarah said firmly, giving them all pause.

"Horsemen," Larry corrected. The excitement was contagious. "Let's get a move on. We have a lot to do. Wade, do you think we have time to go get our wives? I know they'd be mad at missing the governor and a celebration like we're bound to have."

"Maybe so if these outlaws have enough fuel left in that tanker they stole. We need to hurry, though."

"Let's get on it, then." Larry was once again becoming his enthusiastic former self.

Sam sidled up to Goose. "Is there anything I can do for you while the doc is patching you up? You saved this whole town."

Goose started to bark a quick no and say they had saved themselves, but Laura stopped him and spoke through his voice. "Kelly, do you think Brian would like to join us in the celebration?"

Kelly couldn't describe the warmth she felt inside at hearing Goose use the word *us* when referring to them.

Excited, everyone started making plans when two quick gunshots interrupted them, driving several to hit the ground, taking cover.

"Now wait just a goddammed minute!" Sarah roared. "You never acknowledged what I said. I'm in, and I don't want no shit about being a woman or nothing. I got criminals left to hunt, and I'm in!"

"I'd say she's in," Roger stated in his normal gravelly deadpan. "After you get some of that blood washed off, ma'am. It's hard to see who you are under it," he teased. "Can't have a lawman, or law-woman, looking like a serial killer."

The others laughed and welcomed her.

Goose broke the well-wishing with an admonition. "Take it from me, sometimes killing for responsibility becomes killing for pleasure and the killer is always the last to know."

"That's *your* conscience, big man." Sarah snorted in derision. "I lost mine more than a week ago. I'll enjoy killing any rapist, pillager, or murderer I catch. Don't expect this to be the last time you see me spattered in blood."

"Bloody Sarah," PD whispered, earning a defiant stare from the newly minted horseman, or horsewoman.

The End

AUTHOR'S NOTE

Thank you for reading *Goose Truman*!

If you enjoyed one of my books, I'd be very appreciative if you'd take a moment to write a short review and post it on Amazon. A few words are all it takes.

Amazon uses a complex formula to determine what books are recommended to readers or show up when readers search for a book. How many books sell are only one small part of the formula. The quantity of reviews are also an important factor.

I appreciate each one of you for your time and interest in this story and your choice to read *Goose Truman*. My hope is that we can find common ground on a vision of what could be and you'll feel entertained and see the people and places in your mind as I do.

As with many people who write, I have dozens of stories in my head fighting to get out and be put on paper. Quite frankly, I gravitate to Dystopian and Post-Apocalyptic stories because I feel they are timely, and like most of you, I walk through life with the constant hum of "what if" deep in my brain.

Also, don't forget...I choose to write for you all. I like that people enjoy these stories and share my vision. I like the interaction on social media and when we meet at public events. I am trying to get out at conventions more often and meet people.

Please feel free to reach out to me on Facebook or Wimkin at Don Carey or on my website, www.DACarey.com. There is a blue sign-up button on my webpage for my newsletter that I send out sparingly. It will have information about upcoming books and events. With each newsletter, I'll try to give some things away as well, so get your friends to sign up.

I can be e-mailed at DACarey@DACarey.com.

Again, thank you... As people who read and enjoy these stories, there can be no higher compliment than the time you spend taking this journey with me.

ABOUT THE AUTHOR

Don A. Carey is an Army veteran that comes from a long line of Army veterans on both sides of the family. After moving around a lot and finally settling in Kentucky as a kid, he grew up with a step-family of Kentucky do-it-yourself country people who made the discussion of history and "Foxfire" skills a regular part of dinner conversation, giving a perspective that not everyone has. He enjoys sharing family stories with his readers and followers. Most of the locations in his books are real, and he's been there personally.

Don has a day job for a large company in technology leadership and still manages to make time to hunt, ride horses, hike, and camp. One of the highlights of the year for Don is an annual trip into the woods of Tennessee (Big South Fork – Charit Creek) on horseback for several other men carrying only what can be fit in the saddlebags. Feel free to follow him on social media (Don Carey on Facebook and Wimki) for a closer look at the annual trip to Charit Creek and more.

ACKNOWLEDGMENTS

For my family, friends, and workmates, I thank you so much for the times you have sat around a campfire, dinner table, or the workplace and listened to me spin a yarn. Your patience and positive support is why this story came into being. Special thanks to Felicia A. Sullivan, who gave me encouragement and direction when I really needed it. She is the difference between a great story in my mind and one on paper. Finally, many other authors in this genre have been so gracious and nice that I want to thank them. My only concern is that I'll miss someone. Steven C. Bird and Chris Pike were both kind enough to offer feedback and support early on that meant more to me than they know. L.L. Akers is a great author and has graciously given of her time and knowledge, just as Boyd Craven and Jeff Motes have. Franklin Horton is great guy, as is Doug Hogan. I also can't forget to mention Annie Berdel and Dee Cooper as well, who have both gone above and beyond to help and advise. These are some truly great authors and I encourage to you check out their books if you haven't already. You'll enjoy many nights curled up in the world they'll create in your minds.

ALSO BY DON A. CAREY

The Horsemen

Goose Truman – Book 1

Bloody Sarah (Working title – Coming late 2021)

The Arks Chronicles

Arks of America – Arks Chronicles - Book 1

Charit Creek – Arks Chronicles - Book 2

Ten Kingdoms – Eastern Chaos – Arks Chronicles - Book 3

Ten Kingdoms – The Badlands – Arks Chronicles - Book 4